FALSE GOLD

Also by Veronica Heley from Severn House

The Ellie Quicke mysteries

MURDER AT THE ALTAR
MURDER BY SUICIDE
MURDER OF INNOCENCE
MURDER BY ACCIDENT
MURDER IN THE GARDEN
MURDER BY COMMITTEE
MURDER BY BICYCLE
MURDER OF IDENTITY
MURDER IN THE PARK
MURDER IN HOUSE
MURDER BY MISTAKE
MURDER MY NEIGHBOUR
MURDER IN MIND
MURDER WITH MERCY
MURDER IN TIME
MURDER BY SUSPICION
MURDER IN STYLE
MURDER FOR NOTHING
MURDER BY SUGGESTION
MURDER FOR GOOD
MURDER-IN-LAW
MURDER FOR PROFIT

The Bea Abbot Agency mysteries

FALSE CHARITY
FALSE PICTURE
FALSE STEP
FALSE PRETENCES
FALSE MONEY
FALSE REPORT
FALSE ALARM
FALSE DIAMOND
FALSE IMPRESSION
FALSE WALL
FALSE FIRE
FALSE PRIDE
FALSE ACCOUNT
FALSE CONCLUSION
FALSE FACE
FALSE NAME
FALSE WITNESS

FALSE GOLD

Veronica Heley

SEVERN HOUSE

First world edition published in Great Britain and the USA in 2025
by Severn House, an imprint of Canongate Books Ltd,
14 High Street, Edinburgh EH1 1TE.

Paperback edition first published in Great Britain and the USA in 2025
by Severn House, an imprint of Canongate Books Ltd.

severnhouse.com

Cover and jacket design by Jem Butcher Design

British Library Cataloguing-in-Publication Data
A CIP catalogue record for this title is available from the British Library.

ISBN-13: 978-1-4483-1557-4 (cased)
ISBN-13: 978-1-4483-1811-7 (paper)
ISBN-13: 978-1-4483-1558-1 (e-book)

All Severn House titles are printed on acid-free paper.

FSC www.fsc.org MIX Paper | Supporting responsible forestry FSC® C013604

Typeset by Palimpsest Book Production Ltd.,
Falkirk, Stirlingshire, Scotland.
Printed and bound in Great Britain by
CPI Group (UK) Ltd, Croydon CR0 4YY

The manufacturer's authorised representative in the EU for product safety is
Authorised Rep Compliance Ltd, 71 Lower Baggot Street, Dublin D02 P593
Ireland (arccompliance.com)

Praise for the Abbot Agency mysteries

"Sure to please fans who enjoy clever heroines, complex plots, gentle humor, and danger"
Booklist on *False Witness*

"Entertaining . . . featuring a feisty, quick-thinking heroine"
Booklist on *False Face*

"[A] competent, reliable heroine"
Kirkus Reviews on *False Name*

"Suspenseful twists . . . a delight for fans of British mysteries"
Booklist on *False Conclusion*

"Heley expertly melds menace with humor. Fans of darker cozies won't be disappointed"
Publishers Weekly on *False Conclusion*

"Gentle humor, an intrepid heroine, and an unusual plot with quirky twists"
Booklist on *False Account*

"A good choice for fans of the British cozy, especially those with an Agatha Christie feel, combining gentle humor, an intrepid heroine, and an unusual plot with quirky twists"
Booklist on *False Account*

About the author

Veronica Heley is actively involved in her local church and community affairs. She lives in Ealing, West London.

Veronica is the creator of the ever-popular Ellie Quicke mysteries, as well as the Abbot Agency series. *False Gold* is the eighteenth Abbot Agency novel.

www.veronicaheley.com

ONE

Bea Abbot worked so hard running a domestic agency in London that a long weekend in the country sounded like a good idea. Her hosts lived in the Home Counties, close enough to London that she could get back to the office if all hell broke loose at the agency. What's more, her highly successful, portrait painter husband Piers was due to return from one of his trips abroad. And maybe, just maybe, he'd find time to join her at Marston Hall and make a start on his long-promised portrait of her. Well, she could always hope.

Friday morning

Bea turned left and braked sharply. A 'Closed' sign on a barrier blocked the road ahead.

Beyond the barrier a permanent sign erected on the grass verge informed her that one lane led to Marston Hall, while the other went to the farm shop and café.

Had she got the day wrong?

Bea checked her smartphone. Marston Hall was advertised as being open to the public from Thursday to Sunday throughout the season. And today was Friday, right?

A couple of cars drove up behind her. The drivers spotted the closed notices, threw up their arms in annoyance, reversed and departed the way they'd come.

Bea decided the notices did not apply to her as she'd been invited to stay at the Hall by the lord of the manor himself, so she drove round the barrier on to the grass verge and back again to the road, picking up speed as she went.

She'd paid several visits to the Hall over the past few months, and on each occasion the place had been thronged with tourists and their vehicles. And now? The park looked pretty enough to feature in a countryside calendar but there wasn't another car or human being in sight.

Skirting a stand of mature trees which were beginning to turn from dark green to the russet of autumn, she came in sight of the Hall in all its black and white splendour. Windows twinkled, paintwork shone, but still there was no sign of human existence and the front door was closed to visitors.

She followed the drive round the end of the house and into another world.

Marston Hall might have retained its Tudor frontage, but there'd been a dwelling on this site from time immemorial and over the years a wing had been thrown out here, the kitchen quarters had been remodelled, and so on.

A spacious, cobbled yard separated the back of the Hall from some substantial outbuildings. First, she came to an imposing gateway leading to the stables, which were currently in the hands of builders. However, there were no workmen in evidence that day, nor any of their usual clutter of vans, lorries and other means of transport.

Also – Bea took her foot off the accelerator – there was an empty space against the stable wall which was usually occupied by the mobile home belonging to the lord of the manor's invaluable personal assistant.

Surely Rosemary hadn't walked off the job? Rosemary had cut her baby teeth on complicated contracts and enjoyed creating order out of chaos. She'd been a perfect fit for working at the Hall, hadn't she?

Bea drove on at a slower pace.

Next on the left came the enormous old Tithe Barn, built in the Middle Ages to store the harvest from the estate. A pair of large wooden doors gaped open, but again there was no sign of workmen.

When Julian had unexpectedly inherited Marston Hall from Sir Florian Marston-Lang, the grandfather he'd never known existed, he'd found the house and estate in such a poor way that he'd shut everything down until roofers, electricians and plumbers had made the building habitable once more. It was true that in the main house there were many grand rooms which the family might have used, but heating was a problem and the plumbing left a great deal to be desired. Rooms filled with antiques and carpets woven for the house were not family friendly for a small boy who liked to spread his food around, and in any case, those rooms couldn't be used by the family on the days when the house was open to the public.

One end of the Tithe Barn had long ago been designated for use as an estate office, and it was into this that Julian and his family had settled until properly heated, well-lit and appropriately plumbed quarters could be contrived for them in the stable block.

In the estate office, cramped as it was, the family could leave their belongings out, workmen could drop in for a quick consultation, a landline telephone and computer equipment were on tap, there was a small kitchen, little Philip could get out into the paddock at the back for playtime, and upstairs there were two bedrooms with a shared modern bathroom.

Whenever Bea had been here before, the yard had been busy with kitchen staff and workmen. Today there was no sign of human beings or of their cars.

Where was everyone? Even if the workmen had gone on strike, the family's cars should be here.

Bea parked outside the closed door of the estate office, increasingly worried that something was amiss.

A crow cawed from the roof, and flapped away.

Bea said aloud, 'One for sorrow, two for joy.' And then added, 'No, that's magpies.'

She sat in her car and let silence fall around her. This was like the *Mary Celeste*. All human life had been removed from the scene. And where was Bruno? Julian's Alsatian was always on guard here.

There was a sighing sound and a police car drove in behind her and parked. It was an electric car. Disconcerting when it sneaked up on you like that.

Another car appeared, tooted a welcome, swept around Bea and parked outside the door to the estate office. An Alsatian, sitting in the back, barked a greeting.

Bea breathed a sigh of relief. Julian, her host, and Bruno. Thank goodness. She'd been beginning to think the place had been bewitched.

She got out of the car to be embraced by a tall young man with fair hair that tried to curl, and rimless glasses. He said, 'Sorry not to be here to welcome you.'

'Dear Julian,' she said. 'What on earth's going on?' And, to the dog, who was trying to attract her attention she added, 'Yes, Bruno. I'm pleased to see you, too.'

'You may well ask what's going on,' said Sir Julian Marston-Lang. 'I wish I knew. I won't be long, but I have to find some information for the police. Polly's running the nursery in the village, but she'll be back soon. Come on in and make yourself at home.'

Julian fished out his keys, unlocked the door to the estate office and ushered them inside, where he chucked off a pair of muddied boots. The light was winking on the landline phone but he ignored it.

The all-purpose living room looked much the same as when Bea had seen it on previous occasions, with a mix of furniture rescued from the attic and the storeroom.

Two police officers – one male and one female – had followed them in. And with them came an atmosphere . . . of unease? Or of fear?

Julian threw his keys on to a low table, saying to Bea, 'You must be tired after the journey. Make yourself a cuppa or whatever. Polly left a light lunch for you in the fridge. I must deal with Bruno before anything . . .'

He clicked his fingers at the dog, who went straight to the back door and was let out on to the meadow behind the barn. Julian filled two bowls on the doorstep with fresh water and food, gave the dog permission to eat and drink, and then introduced Bea to the police officers.

'Apologies for keeping you waiting. This is Mrs Abbot, the guest I was expecting. She won't know anything about this morning's problem.'

Neither of the two officers relaxed. The woman turned on Bea. 'Didn't you see the sign saying the house was closed?'

Bea opened her mouth to apologize, but Julian got there first. 'She's a guest, right? She was expected.'

He sounded dogged, almost angry. There was something going on here which Bea didn't understand. She decided it would be tactful to make domestic noises. 'I'll put the kettle on, shall I? May I enquire what's happening?'

Julian bent over a laptop on a desk in the window. 'We found the body of a man on the derelict amusement park site.'

'Body? Dead, as in natural causes?'

'Head stoved in. Tyre lever left on site.'

The male officer shot a glance at Julian which didn't look friendly. He said, 'The man was identified by your estate manager.'

'I regret, I cannot agree with him. I'm pretty sure the dead man was not Pete.' Julian set his teeth and applied himself to his computer.

Bea thought it unlikely that Julian would make a mistake in such a matter. He'd been trained as an accountant and blessed with more than the usual amount of common sense, which had stood him in good stead when he had to take over the almost bankrupt estate.

Julian said, 'Sorry about this, Bea. Toby, one of the daytime security guards, arrived at eight this morning to take over from the night guard. Only, part of the fence around the amusement park had been broken down and Pete, who was on night duty, was nowhere to be seen. Toby tried to raise him on his phone, and failed. The staff for the restaurant and farm shop began to arrive. Everyone assumed that the fence being broken down meant we'd suffered some more of the petty vandalism we'd been experiencing over the past few months.' Julian looked at the police officers. 'You are aware of the earlier incidents, aren't you?' It was almost an accusation.

The police officers looked uncomfortable. 'Yeah. Sure.'

Bea put the kettle on to boil and looked for the biscuit tin.

Julian explained to her. 'A while back, a group of youths thought it would be a lark to pinch some drinks from the farm shop. They were thrown out, no problem. But they came back at night several times to overturn bins, upend signs, and toss the outside furniture about. Trivial stuff but annoying. The police said they had their eye on some local characters who might have been involved, but unless they caught them at it, they couldn't do anything.

'So I took on some security. The guards operate out of a caravan parked by the entrance to the amusement park. Two men cover the daytime and early evening, Pete and another man take turns covering the night hours, and we have a fifth man who takes over for days off, dentist's appointments, and so on. When

Toby arrived this morning, he assessed the situation and reported the problem to Ian Charpentier, my general manager. Ian rang the police and then me. That was about half eight.'

Bea said, 'Charpentier? That's your new general manager? Not been here long?'

'Ian Charpentier. Major, retired.' Julian's mouth compressed.

Was he not perfectly satisfied with his new general manager? Mm. Right. Not to be discussed in front of the police? No.

The female police officer walked to the back window talking, low-voiced, on her phone.

Julian said, 'Polly had just left for the nursery with the boy, so I took Bruno and drove down to the site. The police had told Ian to shut off access to the amusement park to avoid tampering with evidence. He took the decision to close both roads, the one into the Hall and the other which leads to the farm shop, café and then on to the amusement park. Only sensible. He's very efficient.

'When I arrived, he showed me where the fence had been broken down. It was clear that something powerful with big wheels, such as a tractor, had been driven into that section of fence and brought it down. It had rained in the night, and the site was a soggy mess. We could both see that the tractor – or whatever it was – had driven into the heart of the site, churning up the earth here and there, and that later on it had left the same way it had come.

'Pete was still missing. I was worried that if there'd been an attempt to vandalize the property last night, Pete would have intervened and perhaps been injured and left on site.'

He turned the laptop round so that the police officers could see. 'Photos. These are the men in the security team. Toby is on the left in the back row, Pete on the right and in the middle is Jock, the Scot. The other two in front are both black, as you can see. I don't think the corpse is any of these. Now, shall I email you a copy of this file?'

'Can't do no harm,' said the male police officer. He read out the email address, slowly, so that Julian could send a copy of the file to headquarters.

Meanwhile, the female police officer finished her phone call. She said, 'They've got Pete's details from the registration number on his car and someone is on their way to break the news to his wife.'

Julian pushed up his glasses and pinched the top of his nose. 'It can't be Pete who's lying there.'

The female officer sighed. 'You've had a shock, Mr Marston . . .'

Bea gave the woman a sharp look. Did she not know Julian's name or how he should be addressed? Was she wilfully ignorant, or being rude? Her expression was bland, but knowing. Ah, she'd deliberately got his name wrong?

Julian didn't set her right. He was preoccupied. Concentrating on some line of thought . . . Or in shock?

Bea decided to intervene on his behalf. Offering the female police officer a mug of tea, she said in a low, confidential tone of voice, 'You'd better get it right for your records. Our host's surname is Marston-Lang – that's hyphenated. And he's Sir Julian.'

The woman coloured up. Guilt and anger. She'd known his name, all right.

Bea handed another mug of tea to her companion, saying, 'Two sugars, right?'

The female officer took a gulp of tea and set the mug aside. She wasn't going to admit her error. She said, 'It's easy to ignore what you don't want to see. No doubt you were fond of this Pete, and it's true that, due to the injuries to his head, he is almost unrecognizable. I understand your desire for caution, but you see, Pete's ID was on the lanyard around the dead man's neck and your general manager has identified him in spite of the terrible injuries he suffered. But don't worry, we'll get a conclusive identification from his wife.

'It's obvious what happened. He disturbed the yobs who got in last night, there was a tussle and he got the worst of it. We'll get them for it, don't you fear.'

She didn't mean that, either. She was enjoying this for some reason. But why on earth should she wish to humiliate Julian?

Julian stared at her and through her. He made as if to speak, but she held up her hand, listening to someone speaking on her phone again. She nodded, and replied saying, 'Understood. It seems Mr Marston's suffering from shock at finding his security guard dead. He'll need time to recover. I'll ask him to come down to the station tomorrow to make a statement about how he came to find the body, shall I?'

And then, to Julian she said, 'Now don't you fret none about the farm shop and café being closed down. There's no need for that. The body's being removed as we speak, and everything except the amusement park will be allowed to reopen this afternoon. Mr Charpentier is seeing to all that. So we'll see you tomorrow down at the station, right?'

She was enjoying this. She'd misused Julian's name twice, and he hadn't done anything about it. Her sidekick was amused about it, too.

The woman led the way to the door. Bea imagined her saying she looked forward to stringing all the aristocrats up from the nearest lamppost.

Julian stared at the floor till Bea took his arm, pushed him into a big chair, and handed him a mug of tea.

She said, 'Never mind them. I believe you. Tell me what you saw.'

Julian took one deep breath and then another. He said, 'I am not going mad. It's difficult to know for sure, but I'm not convinced it was Pete lying there. It was another man of about the same build, also wearing heavy work clothes. It wasn't Jock the Scot. No, I don't think it was Jock. He's got a touch of ginger in his hair . . . what there is of it. And Toby was the one who reported the problem. The other two guards are black so obviously it wasn't them, either.'

Bea said, 'Who found the body?'

'I did. Ian said I should wait for the police before going on to the site, but I kept thinking that Pete might be lying there, injured and needing help. It's a big site. In the old days there was a treetop walk, some swings and roundabouts and a miniature railway. They've all fallen into disarray through neglect. I'd stored anything that might possibly be used again off-site, but some of the metal struts that held up the treetop walk are still there, partially collapsed . . . a danger to shipping. Hence the site being fenced off.

'I got a hard hat from the caravan and asked Bruno to lead me to Pete. He knows Pete, of course. Ian advised me to wait but I insisted and he came along with my farm shop manager.

Bruno nosed to and fro, from the point at which the fencing had been brought down. Then he led the way past what used to be the miniature train depot, to the start of the treetop walk, which is now no more than a tangle of fallen metal struts, rotted wood and frayed rope. And there, partially hidden by some ivy, we found the body of a man.

'Not a stripling. A man of maybe forty years of age, carrying some weight. He was wearing heavy-duty work clothes, which were sodden. I can't remember when it stopped raining or when it started, but no doubt the police can work that out. That should give the rough time of death. I took some pictures on my mobile while Ian rang the police to tell them where to find us. They were annoyed that I'd gone ahead but I'm glad I did. If Pete had been lying there, injured . . . it doesn't bear thinking about. Only, it wasn't him.'

'But the police believe it was? And Mr Charpentier, too?'

'They all expected to find Pete. His lanyard was around the man's neck.' He pushed up his glasses and rubbed his eyes. 'So now I'm asking myself, could I have made a mistake? I keep picturing him. His left hand was outstretched, as if reaching for something. Am I going mad?'

Bea was practical. 'Let's see the photos you took on your mobile.'

Julian got out his phone, and found the pictures. He grimaced. 'Do you really want to look?' But he handed the smartphone over.

Not nice, no. The man's head was misshapen and decorated with mud and blood. He was lying on his side, with his left hand stretched out before him. He looked as if he'd been trampled into the ground.

Julian said, 'I suppose I must be mistaken.'

Bea rubbed a smear of mud off the smartphone. 'Lots of mud on and around the body, but the ID on the lanyard looks relatively clean.'

'Poor man. And his wife! He'd moved down from London because she wanted a quiet life. She's not young, they tried and tried for a baby and finally she got pregnant. They were so looking forward to the birth. I feel responsible for what's happened. I told Ian that we should fly flags at half-mast, make some kind of gesture of respect. Instead, he gave orders to reopen the farm shop and the café. He said life will go on as usual.'

Bea said, 'You'll see the widow's all right? You'll be covered by insurance?'

He wasn't listening. 'I suppose it must be Pete. He's missing, and who else could it be? Pete was over the moon at finding a job down here. In their previous place, there'd been problems with his dog, who . . .'

He drew in his breath. 'Hold it right there! Give me back my phone.' He studied the picture of the dead man again. He said, 'Two things. Pete had a gold stud in his left ear. You can see it in his ID photo on the laptop. This body doesn't. And, where's his dog? A security guard needs a dog and Pete's was a collie and devoted to him. So where's Beauty? Alive or dead, she'd have stayed by his body, but there was no sign of her. What's going on here?'

TWO

Friday, late morning

Bea didn't know what to think. There was a buzzing noise in the air. Irritating. Had a fly got in?

She took the smartphone from Julian, and made herself concentrate on the left ear of the corpse. The dead man had large ears with fleshy lobes. No earring. It was impossible to tell if his ears had been pierced or not. And, if it were Pete, he might have decided not to wear his earring yesterday.

She said, trying to sound confident, 'Well, if this is not Pete, then his wife will say so. The police will have to believe her.'

Julian said, 'Yes, you're right. Of course.'

'But you'll point out the problem?'

'And get them to look out for Beauty. She must have gone off somewhere with Pete . . . only, where is he?'

The buzzing grew louder, accompanied by a sort of rough drumming. What on earth? Bruno began to bark.

Julian put his hand to his forehead. 'Marcus! My cousin Mona's new boyfriend. I'd forgotten. He said he'd like to drop in sometime this week. How like him to come by helicopter! I'm not sure what he actually wants from . . .'

The rest of his words were blotted out as the helicopter noisily hovered overhead and then flew over the Hall. Julian reached for and pulled on some shoes. 'He'll land on the lawn at the front of the house and expect a silver service lunch. Look, I'll go to meet him and explain. Perhaps he'll take off again, and lunch somewhere else. With luck.'

On his way to the door, he hesitated. 'There's messages on the phone and . . . oh, I do miss Rosemary. I have someone who comes up from the village to deal with this and that, but she's not turned up for work today. Bea, can you look after yourself till Polly's back? She'll be here any minute, but I must attend to Marcus and then ring the police!'

Bea flapped her hands at him. 'Off you go. I'll deal with the messages on the phone.'

'You're an angel!' He called Bruno to heel and departed in a small whirlwind of business and distress, phone to ear, saying, 'Police, please . . .'

Bea thought, The Lord be with you. And the Lord go before you. And be with that poor man, lying there in the mud, under the wrong name.

She sank into a chair and tried to make sense of what was happening.

It was clear, wasn't it? Petty vandalism had escalated to an invasion of the park, the security guard had intervened, a man had died and the invaders had retreated . . . taking Pete and his dog with them?

At least, that was a workable supposition.

She found a pad of paper and drew the phone towards her. Now, who had been leaving messages? The first message was from . . . who? She began to make notes of the voicemail until she was interrupted by an incoming call.

A woman – Julian's substitute secretary? – was complaining that she'd been turned away from the gate and was going back home. Bea agreed with Julian in wishing the incredibly efficient Rosemary hadn't taken herself off at such a difficult time.

Back to the messages. No; another incoming call. This time it was from the housekeeper, Mrs Maggs. That redoubtable woman had been prevented from entering the grounds but was made of sterner stuff than the temporary secretary. She left a message saying she was going to confront the police and would get to the Hall as soon as they saw sense and let her in, as she had nothing to do with any shenanigans that might have taken place in the park, had she?

Bea would take a bet that Mrs Maggs would be in before lunchtime. She didn't envy anyone who got between Mrs Maggs and her kingdom. Let's face it, the housekeeper felt she owned the place in a way that Julian – who'd only recently inherited the Hall – did not. Mrs Maggs saw all its defects and loved it fiercely, whereas Julian found his inheritance a burden and only occasionally felt he belonged.

Back to the messages. One part of Bea's mind made notes.

The other part focused on Marcus, arriving by helicopter. Showing off? Trying to overawe Julian? That would take a bit of doing.

Bea had no great opinion of Marcus and, like Julian, she wondered exactly what he was after. He was a silver fox with a well-stocked portfolio, who'd been spending time in recent months with Julian's sexy cousin, Mona. Was Marcus really captivated by her charms, or was it her county connections that he fancied? Julian wasn't much of a social animal and hadn't cultivated his neighbours, but Mona had been born and raised here and knew everyone of any importance.

It was easy to see what Mona saw in Marcus. She'd been married and divorced in her twenties, had never done a day's work in her life and now, perhaps, hoped to share Marcus's lifestyle? She and her younger sister had had to leave the Hall when Julian found the roof leaking and the electrics too lively to trust. He'd let them have a pleasant house in the village which formed part of his inheritance till they could decide on their future, but Mona had long since moved into Marcus's flat in London.

Bea made more notes. There were several messages from panic-stricken staff and suppliers worried about the Hall being shut to visitors. They'd have got the word the road was open again by now, wouldn't they? The last one was very short. From Polly, saying she'd been held up but would ring again when she knew how soon she'd get back.

There were voices outside. Julian's?

'Yes, do come in, Mona. Marcus. I'm sorry you find us in such a state.'

A deeper voice. 'Are we not going into the Hall?'

'Sorry, no. It's open to the public today. Or should be.' Julian ushered Marcus and Mona into the estate office. 'You remember my old friend, Mrs Abbot? She's here for the weekend. Polly should be back with young Philip any minute now. I'm not sure that we can produce a decent lunch for you, what with everything that's been happening. Perhaps you'd like to have something in the village pub?'

'A cup of coffee and a sandwich would do me for now.' Marcus was wearing expensive mufti, with a cashmere sweater slung over his shoulders. Mona walked one step behind, also wearing costly clothing – plus a socking great diamond on her ring finger.

So she'd snagged her billionaire at last? She didn't look ecstatic, though, did she?

Bea put on her brightest smile. 'How nice to see you again, Marcus. And you, Mona? You're looking well.' And to Julian she added, 'I've checked the phone messages. Mostly from members of staff, worrying about being refused access. But there is one from Polly, saying she'd been held up. I assume because the road's been closed?'

Julian got out his phone. 'Excuse me, everyone. I'm a little worried about her. This pregnancy is taking its toll. I must just check.' He went to the back window to get his wife on the phone. He went rigid, listening. Finally, he switched off, saying, 'She says Ian Charpentier – that's my manager here – is re-opening the roads but everyone's very shocked about the death, and she's staying on to help calm the mothers in the nursery. Pete's wife is one of them, and is much distressed.'

Mona said to Marcus, 'We should leave?'

Marcus shook his head. 'Nothing to do with us. Charpentier? I ran across him some time ago, managing another place. Somewhere in Kent. A good man. Knows his business. He'll see to everything for you.'

He threw himself down into a chair, making himself at home. He flicked a finger at Mona to sit nearby. Which she did, looking slightly put out but accustomed to doing whatever Marcus wanted. She so disposed her arms that her hand with the ring on was uppermost.

Julian clocked it. 'My dear Mona. Are congratulations in order? When did this happen?'

Mona produced what she probably thought was a shy smile. It was, Bea thought, more like a full-blown invite to throw yourself on her.

Marcus was pleased with himself and her. 'The other night. She's kept me waiting long enough.' He didn't mean that, either. He knew his worth and had calculated the odds of a marriage being to his advantage or not. He said, 'Well, Julian. We need to have a chat about this and that but tell me first, what's all the fuss and bother about here?'

Julian gave Marcus an old-fashioned look, but followed his lead. 'It looks as if a couple of local layabouts borrowed a tractor and decided to do some damage here. I'm not sure why they didn't attack the Hall, the farm shop or the café. They targeted the amusement park of all places. Shockingly, a man died.'

There was tension in the atmosphere. Marcus's nose seemed to sharpen. Yes, he was definitely interested in the break-in. Why?

Mona half laughed. 'The ancient curse strikes again.'

Julian was not amused. 'Don't tell me there's an ancient curse hanging over the Hall, as well as the legend of buried treasure!'

Bea thought, What ancient curse? I hadn't heard of one, and to judge by Julian's reaction, he hadn't, either. Of course, he'd grown up knowing nothing of Marston Hall and its history. He's had to catch up, fast. And on the whole had done so. But, an ancient curse, on top of the buried treasure story?

Mona lifted one shoulder, releasing a gust of expensive perfume. 'Oh, it's nothing really, you know. Every so often we get people wanting to dig here and there. Some of those going around the house will start tapping the panelling to see if there's a secret compartment somewhere.'

Julian said, 'Well, the workmen did discover that hidden priest hole and we're including it in the tour of the house nowadays. But there wasn't any treasure in it. Just some old papers which we're going through slowly.'

'Old papers?' Marcus repeated the words. 'Giving a clue as to where the gold is buried?' He acted amused, but Bea thought he was intrigued.

Julian shrugged. 'Nothing to help us there. You know, I really can't make out why anyone would target the amusement park. The place is derelict. Nothing but heaps of old iron, rotten timbers, broken booths. The intruders drove a tractor or something with big wheels through a section of the fence some way along from the official gate. I suppose they chose that spot because it was out of sight of the security guards' caravan.'

Marcus said, 'What on earth did they expect to find?'

'Yes, it's a mystery. If they're local they must have known there was a security guard and that he had a dog. Did they plan to wait till Pete was away on his rounds before they entered the site? How much time did they think they'd have before he noticed them? And then what happened? A confrontation? I don't get it. Why didn't the vandals just leave when Pete challenged them? If there were too many of them for him to cope with, why didn't he call for reinforcements? And now a man is dead and his family are left to grieve. And for what?'

Marcus cooled his expression of interest. 'Presumably the vandals will be caught and arrested. It will have been some lads playing at treasure hunting. The local police must know who could have stolen a tractor for this jaunt of theirs. So, things went too far and your man died? I understand your distress, even though I don't suppose you ever spoke to the man.'

'But I did,' said Julian. 'Of course I did. When we interviewed the guards, Pete brought his dog with him. They were a team. As I have a dog of my own, I introduced him to Pete and his dog. I didn't want any misunderstanding about whose dog was allowed here and not there. The two dogs got on fine. Pete was an experienced dog-handler and I was glad to have him. And now . . . I don't know whether he's alive or dead.'

Mona ran her fingers back through her hair. 'But didn't you say he's dead?'

'He may be,' said Julian. 'Or he may not. In my book, he's missing and so is his dog.'

Mona stretched, indicating she thought she'd been out of the limelight long enough. 'Julian, why we came . . . we need to ask a favour. I was born and brought up here. This was my home until you came along. I want to be married and have my wedding reception here. That's all right by you, isn't it?'

Had Julian seen that coming? 'Dear Mona, I don't know what to say. I'd like to help you. I quite understand if you'd like to be married here, but I'm not sure how we could make it work. For a start, we don't have a licence to marry people at the Hall. Polly and I did spend some time working out if we could make the Hall available for weddings, but to tell the truth, it's way beyond our budget at the moment.'

Mona bridled. 'But I'm your cousin. You can't refuse me.'

'Let me talk to Polly about it. You understand that we'd have to give notice that the Hall would be closed for a couple of days. I'm not sure how much notice we have to give. Some months, I think. I'll look it up. Perhaps we could shut off the Long Gallery for the day, and you could have your reception there? How much do you want to spend?'

Mona was incensed. 'You don't expect me to foot the bill, do you? This is family!'

Julian kept his face straight. 'Your family has made a good many attempts to kill me since I inherited the Hall. What should I charge you? Five thousand pounds for every attempt?'

Marcus smoothed out a smile. 'You have indeed led a charmed life.'

'Like a cat, I've lost rather too many lives since the family discovered my existence.'

Marcus patted Mona's hand as a signal to be silent. 'Well, well. Julian, perhaps I understand your problem better than you think. I've heard you've been having a rough time here. You were clever enough to recover the money which your uncle tried to steal, but what with death duties and all the changes you're making here, you're still heading for bankruptcy.

'You've borrowed quite a bit, haven't you? You've dealt with basic repairs to the Hall, which is admirable, but now you're spending another fortune on fitting solar panels on the Tithe Barn roof, converting the top floor in the big house, and turning the stables into living accommodation, not to mention bringing in a film crew and all!'

'Yes, that's true, but—'

Marcus was not to be stopped. 'I hear you're doing a lot of repairs in the village, too? It must be a nightmare, wondering how to pay everything back. Not to mention that you've got in your neighbours' bad books, refusing invitations to this and that, and not taking the advice of those best qualified to advise you.'

Mona nodded like a mandarin doll. 'Everyone's talking about it.'

Julian nodded, briefly, his eyes on Marcus. 'True, it's going to take a while to sort things out.'

Marcus leaned forward in his chair. 'That's just it. Without sufficient money behind you, and making mistakes as you do, the future looks grim.'

Julian nodded again. 'I don't ride to hounds, I don't vote for our local MP and I don't play cricket. It's true, Polly and I don't fit in.'

Marcus sighed. 'You know, I've been wondering if there was any way I could help you. I was thinking about offering to get the miniature trains back on track in the amusement park. I've always wanted to play with trains. It's a weakness of mine, from childhood. And you must be losing thousands every month by leaving the amusement park derelict.'

Julian concentrated. 'You're making me an offer to lease the amusement park?'

'At first, yes. That's the idea I was toying with. But now, hearing what a difficult position you're in, and seeing that we'll soon be cousins, I'm wondering about making you an offer for the lot. The Hall and surrounding estate. Lock, stock and barrel. Bringing Mona back to her roots.'

Mona hadn't been expecting this. She threw her arms wide to embrace him. 'Oh, oh, oh! I can't believe it. Would you do that for me? I never thought, I never dreamed, to be back here where I belong! The parties we could throw! The weekends! Everyone would want to be invited! It's . . . Oh! Marcus, I love you beyond anything!'

Julian said, 'Dear Mona, it's not on. I can't sell.'

Marcus disentangled himself from Mona, to resume negotiations. 'Of course you would feel like that, at first. You've a strong sense of duty, but you must admit that the Hall is a challenge too far. The debts! The building permits! The staff problems! The coolness of your neighbours! Polly is overworked, and so are you. This way you don't have to feel that you've failed, but that you're returning the Hall to its forebears. You could settle your debts and walk away, go back to your old life, without a care in the world.'

Julian sighed. 'Ah, what a wonderful thought. To return to a world in which there is only a mortgage to worry about. Yes, there are some days when I wish I could return to my old life, but I've inherited the place and feel I must do my best by it.'

Marcus's mouth tightened into a shark's smile. 'I have sprung this on you too quickly. Naturally you must consider all the options and take advice from those who understand your problems. All I ask is that you don't dismiss my offer out of hand. We'll talk again, soon.'

Mona was excited. 'I can't believe it! To be able to live here again! And of course we will have a big wedding here. I've been told of a wonderful wedding planner. I'll get her down here straight away and . . .'

Marcus put his arm around her. 'Calm down, my love. Give the man a chance to get his breath back.'

Julian rose to his feet as a signal for his guests to leave. Marcus was first out, talking on his phone and towing Mona along beside him.

The room seemed very quiet now they'd gone. Julian stared into space for a count of five. Then he got up to let Bruno in from the meadow, saying, 'Well, Bea. What do you think of that?'

'He doesn't know you very well, does he? And I'd back you on the money stakes, any day of the week. I'm sure you've got everything under control. If you've borrowed, then you'll have done so on easy terms and know how to repay. I'd also take a bet you know to a pound where Marcus has got money—'

'To a penny. A couple of his investments look a trifle dodgy to me. It occurs to me . . . it would be something he's done before. I'm wondering if he's got a buyer for this place. Once I sold to him, he could resell at a profit. Mona's pleased to think he's doing it for her, but I doubt it. What I'm wondering is how he's managed to acquire so much information about what I'm doing.'

Bruno woofed out a welcome. A car was being driven up and parked outside. There was some shouting. Was that Mrs Maggs's voice? Oh yes, undoubtedly. She was complaining that someone had parked where they shouldn't.

Bea realized it was she who was probably at fault, and got to her feet just as Mrs Maggs, five foot two of offended energy, appeared in the doorway. 'Who's parked in my space?'

Bruno woofed again and wagged his tail at her.

Bea apologized. 'Was it me? I'm so sorry, Mrs Maggs. I didn't realize.'

'Oh, it's you, Mrs Abbot. Well, seeing as you couldn't know, that's all right. Sir Julian did say you'd be down this weekend and he'd be putting you up here, and it's good to see you. What a day, though! That poor man, Pete! And how his wife will cope and the baby due, heaven only knows.

'Can you believe, half the staff have decided not to turn up to work the rest of the day, and the others are milling around like bees trying to swarm and not knowing in which direction to fly! Kylie's helping Lady Polly sort out the nursery but they'll be having hysterics about the murder I don't doubt, and hysteria I will not have. It's bad for the digestion.'

Julian put his arm around Mrs Maggs's shoulders, and gave her a hug. 'It's all right. It's all right.'

Clearly, it wasn't all right. Mrs Maggs was on the verge of tears. But she hit her eyes with her fists and said, 'That's all very well, but it's shaken my team of girls up something chronic.'

'Yes,' said Julian, still holding her. 'Me, too.'

She sniffed, richly. 'You'll sort it, then?'

'I'll do my best.'

'That's all right, then. And you'd better tell that Captain Carpenter to be careful how he orders people about. I know you say he's only doing his job but there's ways of saying things and he's a typical off-comer, thinking he always knows best when he doesn't.'

Julian smiled down at her. 'It's Major Charpentier, as you very well know, Mrs Maggs. And I'm an off-comer, too, remember?'

Mrs Maggs was emphatic. 'No, you're not. You're one of us. And what I'm doing standing here when there's work to be done, I do not know.' She trundled off, eyes snapping, energy returning, to put her part of the world to rights.

Just then someone brayed out a laugh and stepped into the room, rubbing his hands. Blue eyes, fair of hair and skin, above average height. This description could have fitted both him and Julian, but there were marked differences. Julian's eyes were an intense darker blue, and he usually wore grey. His hair had a tendency to curl, he hadn't an ounce of fat on him and he had a certain presence of which he was totally unaware.

The newcomer was also above average in height but his hair was almost butter in colour, slicked back and smooth. His neck and torso were beginning to thicken. He wore expensive clothing in shades of light brown and dark green which reminded Bea of army fatigues. He had an air of forced jollity. Was this Major Ian Charpentier?

'Reporting for duty, Sir Julian! All systems go and all that.

The barriers have been removed from the roads and staff are returning to their duties. Some of them thought to take the day off, but I soon put them right about that.'

Julian exclaimed something, but the newcomer took no notice. 'There was hysteria at the nursery. Pete's wife is very distressed I understand, but Lady Polly's dealing with it. What a way she has with her, to be sure. And your young heir is proving quite the little charmer.'

Julian said, 'I told the police that—'

'Yes, yes. They said. You've had a bad shock. It's understandable that you couldn't recognize the man, what with the blood and all. There's no doubt what happened. Pete let a group of vandals into the site, had an argument with them and lost. He sold his soul to the devil and the devil claimed his own, right?'

Julian said, 'If that is so, the devil made a couple of mistakes; he killed the wrong man. Also, Pete's dog is missing.'

'Ah, ran off when his master was attacked, did he? He'll turn up when he gets hungry, no doubt. Now we have to leave it to the police to do their job. Rest easy, they're looking for the tractor used to break into the amusement park and once they've found that, they'll get the villains, yes? Some yobs down from London for a spot of treasure hunting, no doubt.'

He turned on Bea, all smiles. 'And this is the famous Mrs Abbot that you told me about? You run a little agency for domestic staff, don't you? Splendid! Let me introduce myself. I'm Major Charpentier, retired from the army but still hard at work, eh? What a sad day for your visit, Mrs A, but I'm sure you're very welcome.'

He didn't mean it. He turned away, letting her know that he considered her a woman of no importance.

Bea's hackles rose. She tried to laugh at herself, saying that his dismissal of her was understandable. To his mind, she was a woman of a certain age, who was past child-bearing and who had no influence in his world. She tried to make excuses for his conduct but it did rankle. She was not accustomed to being ignored.

Julian said, 'Thank you, Ian.' And to Bea, he added, 'My dear, I must make the rounds, see what's happening—'

'No need, no need,' replied Ian, 'I have everything in hand.

You don't keep a dog and bark yourself!' He grinned and revealed slightly over-large teeth.

What big teeth you've got, Grandma!

Julian said, quietly, but firmly, 'Thank you, Ian. I'm sure you've done wonders, but I need to get out and see for myself. Bea, do you think you could run down and check how Polly's doing? You know she needs to rest in the afternoons and the boy is so active . . .'

'A pleasure,' said Bea, aware of a hollow stomach and a need for a cuppa. 'But you mentioned Polly left us some lunch? You must be hungry, too.'

'What a good idea! Mine's Earl Grey and hold the mustard,' said Ian, all happy clappy and big smile.

He expected her to do the little woman act and serve him lunch? Bea thought, Over my dead body! She did not want to feed him. But how to get out of doing so?

THREE

Friday lunchtime

Bea decided to go into a dithery act. 'Oh, oh! I'm afraid I don't know whether . . . Earl Grey? Oh dear. Wouldn't it be better if you asked Mrs Maggs to . . .?'

'Har, har!' Hearty laughter. 'No, no. I don't want my head bitten off. She's not the calmest of ladies under stress is our Mrs Maggs. I'll see what they can muster down at the pub, get the latest news, speak to the press, assure them the police are hot on the trail of the malefactors. The pub is the beating heart of the parish, and so on, eh?'

He waited a couple of seconds for Julian to ask him to stay – which he didn't – and made his way out. Bruno saw him off with, it seemed to Bea, some satisfaction.

Julian held out his hand to Bea. She took it and held on to it.

He said, 'All right?'

She nodded. 'And you?'

Julian said, 'Don't you dare tell me I've had a bad shock and don't know what I'm doing.'

'I won't. You wouldn't. How come you took on that Hooray Henry?'

'Best of a bad bunch. Had terrific references. He was fine at first. Taught me a lot. But I'm beginning to think he wants to elbow me out of a job. The truth is that I do need a general manager but he's probably not it. I gave him a contract for six months renewable. He's been here for two and I'm counting the days. Neither Polly nor Bruno have taken to him, either. Nor young Philip.'

A 'woof!' from Bruno, a bang on the door, and Mrs Maggs shouldered her way in, carrying a tray containing a mountain of sandwiches and a couple of flasks. 'I know Lady Polly will have left you some cold meats and salad for lunch, but you need carbohydrates when you've had a shock. Home-made bread, ham, cheese, eggs and tomatoes for colour. My old mother used to say the best thing for shock was Horlicks or Ovaltine, but you'll have to make do with tea and coffee today.'

She banged the tray down on the low table. 'Don't forget to save some for Lady Polly. Dealing with hysterical women is hungry work and she'll need all her strength for what's to come.'

She beamed at them both and vanished. A soft, thundering noise rose to a shriek as Marcus's helicopter flew over the house and chuntered off into the distance.

Bruno's head appeared above the tabletop, sniffing for food. Julian waved him away and offered the plate to Bea. 'Mrs Maggs is usually right. I always listen to her.'

Bea took a sandwich and investigated the flasks. Coffee with milk in one and black in the other. Her sandwich was good, and she was hungry.

Julian munched on a double sandwich and reached for a coffee. 'Bea, can you cope by yourself? Get yourself settled in and then rescue Polly. I want to go back and check what's happening at the amusement park. I should be able to find out where that tractor came from as there's only so many entrances in and out of the park. If they went out the same way they came in, then we should be able to get an idea of where they came from.'

Bea took her bag upstairs to the back bedroom, which overlooked a vista of fields, and unpacked. The bed had been freshly made and everything was sparkling clean.

She exchanged her jacket for a sweater in her favourite willow green and renewed her lipstick. Downstairs, she packed up the rest of the sandwiches and a flask of coffee, returned to her car and drove back the way she'd come. Past the Tithe Barn where, yes, Julian had had solar panels put on the sloping roof facing away from the Hall. The initial expense had been great but the new system would provide the Hall and all its buildings with electricity for years to come. That had definitely been worth doing.

She passed the empty space where Rosemary's motorhome had stood. Crushed weeds showed the motorhome had not been gone for long. Bea wondered what Rosemary was doing. Had she taken a long-overdue holiday, climbing some uncharted peak of a mountain, or was she rowing across the Atlantic single-handed? Bea wouldn't have put it past her.

Thinking over Marcus's and Mona's recent visit, she came to the conclusion that Julian was right, and that Marcus had indeed seemed very well informed about what was happening at the Hall. How come?

For instance, Marcus had referred to work Julian was having done on the top floor of the Hall. Would that be for live-in staff?

With young Philip, or Pip as his family liked to call him, growing apace, and pregnant for the second time, Polly had refused to consider living on the top floor of a mansion, hence the work to reconfigure the stables into living accommodation for the family.

All the projects Marcus had mentioned were very sensible, provided you had enough capital to set about them. Presumably Julian knew what he was doing. Yes, of course he did.

But Marcus had referred to a film crew? Really, a film crew? Bea didn't understand that.

She reached the village only to find that, as usual, the main street was packed with cars, mostly of tourists who would visit for a couple of hours and then leave. She was lucky enough to see a car leaving a space right outside the village hall and slipped into it under the nose of a brand-new Mercedes whose driver was not best pleased at being pipped to the post.

Bea felt guilty about that. But not much.

She checked her watch. What time did the nursery finish? Was it mornings only or did it run all day?

A billboard outside the village hall advertised Oldies Tea Club, maths and English coaching, exercise classes, a ladies' choir and a church coffee morning. Evenings were taken over by dance classes, karate lessons and the uniformed organizations.

What happened on Sunday? Ah, there was a Sunday service every week at the church next door, alternating mornings and afternoons. Presumably this parish was twinned with another, allowing one minister to cover both.

Bea stood back to consider the village hall, which looked to be well looked after. Clearly, it was well used and well run.

She stepped into the foyer and was attacked by a solid wall of sound. Double doors let her into a large hall furnished with stackable chairs, a piano and a carpet of children's toys. It looked to her as if war had broken out between toddlers and carers. The children were winning.

A tape recorder had been turned on and the volume was up to howling pitch. A young woman Bea recognized as Kylie – Mrs Maggs's buxom niece – was trying to calm a group of small girls who were chasing one another around, screaming at the top of their voices. A small boy bawled his head off here, while two others fought to the death in the opposite corner.

A woman whom Bea didn't know was trying to catch a youngster who was laughingly running around with her skirt around her knees. A third was picking up a child who'd fallen and hurt itself.

Crash! Over went an easel and a pot of paint to the wails of a small child of indeterminate sex. There was no sign of Polly but the fair-haired toddler concentrating – to the exclusion of all else – on crawling off on some mission of his own, must be her son Philip.

Bea was shocked into immobility for a count of five.

Where oh where was Polly? How far along was her pregnancy? Seven months? Eight?

Bea went into action. She switched off the tape recorder, righted the easel, avoiding the spilt paint. She picked up the child who was trying to lose her skirt and handed her over to the nearest adult. She grasped one bully boy fighter by his jersey and pulled him off the loser, then took a deep breath before projecting the word 'Quiet!' into the next county.

Everyone stopped what they were doing and stared at Bea . . . who waited for Kylie to recover control of the situation.

Kylie had helped feed young Pip when Polly's milk dried up and was one of the most competent young mothers Bea had ever met, but today she was at the end of her tether. She said, 'Oh, Mrs Abbot! Is that really you? Such a dreadful thing. We're all terribly upset.'

'Yaah!' One of the pugilists tried to kick Bea, who knew a trick or two and managed to sidestep his foot. His opponent stuck a finger up his nose while he considered how soon they might resume their fight.

'Everyone! Quiet, please!' said Bea, wondering if she'd be prosecuted for bullying the children. But wherever she looked, adults and children turned to look up at her with identical expressions of trust. They might not like authority, but they understood that life was not comfortable without it.

'Thank you!' This was said profoundly by Kylie. In a voice which was rapidly returning from wobble to alto, she added, 'Now, children. Let's all sit down on the mats – no pushing there! And no pinching! Let's all settle down and have our end of morning sing-song.' And to Bea she explained, 'We're short-handed. Polly's in the room at the end on the left.'

With order in the process of being restored, Bea collected Pip – who immediately became fascinated by the gold chain round her neck – and followed directions. She found herself in a much smaller room, carpeted and curtained, furnished with comfortable chairs. Polly was kneeling and holding the hand of an even more pregnant woman who was lying full length on the floor.

Polly was her usual calm self. Not a big woman, she had competence written all over her. She had shiny dark hair in a long bob, remarkable violet eyes and would have been beautiful if she'd ever thought that that mattered.

The woman on the floor was olive-skinned and shiny with perspiration. Good-looking. And desperate. She looked to be at full term and about to give birth any minute.

'Breathe with it. Hi, Bea,' said Polly, looking up to give Bea a quick smile. 'Is Pip all right?'

'Sure,' said Bea, hoping he wasn't going to put the chain around her neck into his mouth . . . but yes, there it went. Oh. Well, never mind.

'Puff, puff! Aaargh!' said the woman, convulsing. Her grip on Polly's hand was so tight that it whitened the skin.

'And then . . . relax!' said Polly. 'Very good, Tyra. Excellent. Now I know you're not due for another three weeks, so perhaps we should ring for an ambulance. They can slow things down in hospital.'

'No, no! Not till Pete comes. He promised he'll hold my hand from the moment it . . . Oh, oh! But now he won't ever . . .! Oh, I can't bear it!'

'Yes, you can, my dear,' said Polly. 'You can do anything. You're strong and you're about to have a lovely baby boy and nothing else matters at the moment.'

And to Bea she explained, 'Some fool called in here a few minutes ago to tell Tyra that her husband's been killed. The fool said she thought the police had tried to call on Tyra at home, but that knowing it was one of her days to help here, she went out of her way to come in to give the bad news. What a terrible thing! I can't believe it. Tyra's contractions started straight away. They were at ten minutes but are getting quicker, and I don't know what's best to do.'

Bea set Pip down on the floor and, with some difficulty, Bea joined him there. She stroked Tyra's cheek to get her attention. 'Listen to me. Pete might not be dead.'

Polly gaped.

The woman on the floor said, 'Not . . .? But . . .?'

Bea repeated herself. 'Sir Julian went looking for Pete and found a body. It's hard to tell from the injuries, but he doesn't think it was Pete.'

The woman gasped, 'But she said . . . the police were looking for me at home, but I'm here and . . . I don't know who to . . . But, if he's not dead, where is he?'

'Missing. And his dog.'

The woman fell back on the floor. 'That something dog. The bane of my life. But that dog wouldn't leave him, alive or dead. Would she?' She convulsed, panting.

Polly said to Bea, 'I think she should go to hospital, now!'

Bea got out her phone. 'They'll want her name.'

'Tyra. Primigravid. A first-timer, she's thirty-eight. No particular complications that I know of. Doctor's surgery in the next town. Due in three weeks. Contractions now down to seven minutes.'

Bea made the call, only to be told there'd be a delay as the police had set up a roadblock just outside town.

Typical, thought Bea. She supposed they'd closed the road looking for the tractor that broke into the amusement park. The vehicle in question was probably back in its own quarters by now, being hosed down by its owner to remove all traces of its adventure.

Tyra grabbed Bea's arm. 'You say he's not dead? He's missing? Really? Are you sure? He swore he'd see me through this. He knows how scared I am. We tried and tried and I couldn't get pregnant and now . . .' She convulsed.

Both Bea and Polly looked at their watches. Five minutes!

Polly said to Bea, 'Can you fetch Old Jenny, that used to be the midwife here? She'll be in the pub next door at this time of day. She'll tell us what to do. Leave Pip. He can't get into any trouble in this room.'

Bea scrambled to her feet, limped to the door – she was really getting too old to sit on the floor and then leap to her feet like a gazelle or whatever – made it out through a now quiet nursery and into the street. Pub. Where? Next door but one?

Open? Yes. People sitting outside, drinking at small tables.

Oh. Ian Charpentier had said he was going to the pub. Bea did not, repeat not, want to meet him and have to explain . . . Oh, bother. Was that him sitting outside, with his back to her?

She darted inside. Pleasant enough. She'd been here a couple of times, hadn't she? There's a snug. That's where Old Jenny would be. Looks like a crone, will of iron, don't cross her or she might curse you.

Where is she? Not here?

'You looking for me?' Jenny was sitting in a corner beside what used to be a fireplace, because that's where she'd sat for sixty years or so, even though the flames in the grate were now artificial. She was wearing a silvery vest under a black velvet jacket, both of which had been designed for someone in their twenties. And jeans. She was wearing them with elan.

'Yes, I was looking for you,' said Bea. 'If you'd be so kind? It's Tyra, starting in labour. She's in the back room of the hall next door.'

'Have I time to finish my pint?'

'Er, no. I'll buy you another, after.'

'Tyra's a silly fool. Can't count.' The wizened old crone hoisted herself to her feet. 'She's supposed to be helping out at the nursery, isn't she? Ha! More trouble than she's worth. Thought she'd volunteer so as to make some friends in the village, being a newcomer. Give us your arm till I'm steady on my feet.' She turned on a group of men by the bar, addressing one of them. 'You! Useless lump! Fetch me my bag. It's on the table inside the front door – door's not locked. Bring it to the hall, chop chop, right?'

To nobody's surprise, a hulking great man with a shock of blond hair wiped the back of his hand across his mouth and departed at her bidding.

Bea steadied the old woman on her way to the door, thinking that this was madness and that Old Jenny couldn't possibly be the right person to call on nowadays in an emergency. What was Polly thinking of?

'I remember you!' said Old Jenny as they cautiously braved the twenty or so steps along the pavement to the hall. 'Interfering busybody. Old friend of Sir Julian's. Can count on more than the fingers of two hands.'

Bea accepted this assessment of her character, grateful that it wasn't worse.

Jenny paused for breath. 'Pete's dead, they said. But his dog, Beauty, is missing. That's not right. How close are the contractions?'

'Five minutes. Sir Julian went looking for Pete and found a dead body but he doesn't think it's Pete and yes, Pete's dog's also missing.'

Jenny grunted. 'Pete's thick as two short planks and stubborn as a mule. He allows that fool of a wife of his to walk all over him, but he wouldn't have let the yobs in to wreck the place . . . if that's what they were up to. Here we go. And Young Useless with my bag, too.'

So saying, she detached herself from Bea, got herself balanced on her own two feet, took a deep breath, swept into and through the foyer, navigated her way round the group of children singing a nursery song, twitched a forefinger at one of the attendant women to follow her and swept into the back room as if she had wings on her feet.

One look at the perspiring, wretched Tyra, and Jenny issued her orders. 'Mrs Abbot, make yourself useful. Get some newspapers from the shop. I can't get down to her on the floor, so we'll put her on the table, and you know how water stains wood. No, you fool! Clear those books off first. Lady Polly, take Pip and get out of here. And you, girl,' she said to the woman she'd co-opted from looking after the children, 'see if there's any towels in the cloakroom or the kitchen. Get me a paper roll if necessary. And call an ambulance!'

Bea ran to obey. Newspapers. Newsagent? She'd seen one somewhere along the street. Yes, there it was.

The newsagents was agog with people, talking about Pete with indrawn breaths, saying what a dreadful thing and what was the world coming to, and that Tyra would take it hard, wouldn't she?

Bea gatecrashed the queue, made an urgent request for newspapers, lots of them, for Jenny, and could she come back and pay later as she'd left her bag somewhere and Tyra was . . . Yes, she was in labour and Old Jenny had sent her for . . .'

Newspapers were thrust into her hands, with good wishes which probably were meant; someone opened the door for her and she was out and back in the street in a trice. Which way was the hall? Ah, this way. Outside door, then inner. Rushing through the main room, she noted all was quiet. There had been changes in the short time she'd been away. The singing session was over and Kylie was sitting on the mat reading a story, with the children all around her. She had a good, clear voice and knew how to make all the animal noises. Her audience was rapt.

Bea caught a quick glimpse of Polly sitting on one side with Pip before she opened the door to the end room and had her bundle of papers snatched from her by Old Jenny who was now wearing a huge apron that had been starched in its heyday, but was now limp if still white. The woman whom Jenny had co-opted from the nursery was also there. The smell of disinfectant was reassuring.

Jenny told Bea to make herself scarce, which she was only

too happy to do. She really, really needed to sit down somewhere and . . . where was her bag with the sandwiches and flask of coffee in it? Ah. There. She collected both, reminding herself that she must go back and pay the newsagents when she had a minute. Meanwhile, she'd been sent to rescue Polly, so she went to find her.

Polly didn't look as if she needed rescuing, but was happily feeding Pip, who was now strapped into his buggy.

Bea eased herself into a seat beside her. 'I gather we're both surplus to Jenny's requirements. Want a sandwich and some coffee? How come you got involved in helping out here?'

'The people who used to run the nursery here were getting too old but now that Julian's got the farm shop and café up and running, the young mothers want to be free to apply for a job there and earn some money. Kylie's the obvious person to take over here but she needs help so I said I'd come in most mornings till the next baby's due. And, I do get the village gossip.'

Bea said, 'Julian's worried about you.'

'I'm worried about him, too. He sees things so clearly, far more quickly than anyone else, and he doesn't always get someone to cover his back before he goes into battle. Everything was all right when I set off this morning but of course everything went haywire afterwards. Julian got involved, right?'

'He found a body in the amusement park, but he says it isn't Pete. The police disagree but they want Tyra to identify the body. There were signs a group forced their way in and later retreated. No damage otherwise. Want some more news?'

'The intruders found the buried treasure?'

'No such luck. Marcus and Mona arrived by helicopter. They're engaged. He wants to buy the Hall; she wants to have a lavish wedding reception there and then swan around being Lady Muck. Is that enough news for today?'

'Mm. Julian did wonder whether Marcus was serious about Mona. I suppose his pursuit of her makes sense if he wants to join the aristocracy. But Julian won't sell. As for holding wedding receptions at the Hall, we did look at the matter briefly but decided it was a project for next year or the year after. Tell me more about the body that they found in the park.'

'Julian took a photo on his smartphone. The deceased had no earring and no dog.'

'His dog wouldn't leave him, dead or alive. Oh. Well, that's a relief. I think. But, if it wasn't Pete, then who was it, and where's Pete?'

'I suppose the dead man came with the yobs who broke down the fence, but why they should want to do so, and why he's dead, I have no idea.'

Polly said, 'People have been listening to gossip about buried treasure. Idiots! The helpers here say no one local's been reported missing, so the dead body must have come from town. Only that doesn't add up.'

Pip was eating some gooey green stuff with a spoon. It looked revolting but he seemed to like it.

Bea was thinking along different lines. 'What happens if the ambulance gets here before Tyra produces her baby? Will Jenny insist on her right to deliver the child, or will she hand her patient over without a fight?'

Polly grinned. 'My money's on Jenny. If there are no complications, she'll see that Tyra gives birth with the least possible drama.'

If Polly trusted Jenny, then everyone else could relax.

Bea said, 'I was there when the police came to the Hall this morning. What's up with them? They acted like Julian wouldn't know his left foot from his right. And that new general manager? He may be the best thing since sliced bread, but . . .'

Polly sighed. 'Local politics. It's complicated.'

Bea poured coffee. 'Drink this. Eat. I'll finish shoving food into Pip.'

They swapped over. Polly ate, hungrily, but drank from a bottle of water she had brought with her, rather than the coffee. Bea wasn't sure Pip would allow her to feed him but, after one long stare at her face, he half smiled and then opened his mouth wide for the next mouthful.

Polly said, 'If you live in a village, small events can become more important than they might do if you lived in a city with so much more going on. A couple of weeks ago there was a local derby here. A darts night at the pub. Our team were all local while the visitors were from the nearest town and included a police sergeant who likes to throw his weight about.

'Everyone turned out for it, including Julian and me. A great night. We won by a whisker. Julian presented the cup and put some money on a tab behind the bar for the two teams to have a drink. And then everything went wrong.'

FOUR

Friday afternoon

Bea said, 'It went wrong because it was town against country?'

'Sort of. That's how it ended up, anyway. What happened was that a woman who came with the visiting team screamed that she'd felt someone remove her smartphone from her back pocket. The sergeant looked around, saw an obvious outsider and nabbed him before we could say anything. The lad is a Ukrainian refugee who's been granted asylum and has recently landed his first job here. He was terrified. A couple of locals, knowing something of the boy, expressed their concern.

'You see, we could make a pretty good guess at who'd done the deed, and it wasn't the refugee. For some months now we've been plagued by three or four local scumbags, late teens, up to all sorts of mischief. Nicking a stranger's smartphone would have been just up their street. Two of them shouldn't have been in the pub anyway but their older brother had accompanied them.

'When the sergeant nicked the refugee they tried not to laugh, which was a dead giveaway. Julian was about to intervene, when the captain of our darts team spoke up, saying, "Hang about! You've got the wrong one!"

'Remember we'd just thrashed them at darts? Policeman Plod stuck to his guns and there was a lot of murmuring, on both sides. Captain Courageous said we had to uphold the law, and that it was only to be expected that refugees, coming over here, would steal from us. He made a number of other remarks which you might well consider racist, such as, "What can you expect if you let in the sweepings of foreign jails?"!'

Bea said, 'Is Captain Courageous a racist?'

Polly giggled, and then gave a little cough. 'Dear Bea, do get his name right. He's Major Charpentier, retired. Now he's in civvies, he pretends to have dropped the title. Only, if anyone forgets to use it, he frowns. If they remember it, he preens. He keeps saying that Julian will never learn if he doesn't toughen up, that he must keep the peasantry at a distance, and so on. I've heard that Mrs Maggs has taken to calling him Captain Carpenter, but that's not correct. Not at all.

'Anyway, yes, that's him. Old school. That's the way he's been brought up. You might have thought the people who live here would be the same, but we've had Mr and Mrs Patel and Imran living here for yonks and they've been brilliant and we've had a chance to see what the new lad's made of over the last few months, and we'd decided he was all right.

'And yes, we could all make a guess as to who'd actually done the deed. The only problem was that we didn't want to point the lads out to the police because they're from influential families and . . . well, it would have made things difficult. The sergeant said he was taking the lad in. He was backed up by the captain who tried to clear a path to the door for him.

'Voices were raised. That's when Old Jenny compared the sergeant's ancestry unfavourably to that of a donkey and everyone laughed. I thought the sergeant was going to have a heart attack, and the gallant captain went puce with rage. Old Jenny confronted the real culprits and made them turn out their pockets and there was the smartphone, which made the policeman and Captain Courageous extremely angry because they'd been made to look foolish.

'The landlord booted the culprits out and Julian took the floor. He was brilliant. He smoothed everything over. He congratulated the sergeant on recovering the phone, which had clearly been mislaid by its owner. He ordered another round for the two teams. And that should have been the end of it, right?'

Bea sighed. 'I think I understand. Those who'd been made to look foolish didn't forget. You're telling me that this tiny incident was enough to start a feud between town and village?'

'No. It added fuel to one that's existed for ages. Apparently they fought on opposite sides in the Wars of the Roses and again when Roundheads clashed with Cavaliers. Of course it sounds ridiculous to say that something which happened several centuries ago can influence the way we think today, but if your grandparents tell you what their grandparents said and did, then you remember. It's not sensible, but it's built into your bones.'

Bea said, 'I suppose the antagonism lies dormant till something stirs it up again. In this case, the police were shown up by Jenny, on top of the village beating the town at darts. Do they play cricket in the summer and bring in the army to umpire the games? And, oh, dear! Don't tell me they have football matches, as well?'

Polly laughed. 'Both sides have asked Julian to join their cricket team. He's pleaded his poor sight as an excuse to both.'

'Right. So what happened to the yobs? Did the sergeant arrest them?'

'He knows the families and didn't dare. What did happen was that the dear captain gave Jenny written notice to quit her cottage at the end of the month. He said she was behind with her rent, which she was because she'd stopped paying when her boiler went on the blink. You see, the captain has taken over the job of attending to the long list of repairs needed in the village, and hadn't done anything about her complaint. She alleges that he took backhanders to move people up the list of repairs that needed to be done.'

Bea said, 'Did she threaten to turn the captain into a toad overnight, or to give him piles?'

'She didn't need to. The news of his petty act of revenge came up to the Hall with Mrs Maggs and the morning milk. Julian took Major Charpentier into the library and shut the door. I don't know exactly what was said, but we could all hear the dear major bellowing with rage.'

'You think it was true about the backhanders? Did Julian give him a written warning?'

'Yes, but he couldn't sack him outright. There's no written proof, nothing that would stand up in court. It's all rumour. Tittle-tattle gets you nowhere. The major has got four months to go on his contract and powerful friends to back him up if Julian tried to get rid of him without proof.

'What Julian did was to go down to see Jenny. He told her the major had misunderstood the situation. The replacement boiler was going to be delivered and installed next week and naturally she was not expected to pay rent during the time she'd been inconvenienced by having no hot water. He said there was no question – none! – of her being asked to leave. They both knew this was a face-saving exercise and what that might mean. I gather Jenny gave Julian some of her special home-brewed beer to drink. He left his car outside her cottage and came home walking with care.'

'He handled that well,' said Bea, 'but the major must have been furious at Julian upsetting his nasty little plan.'

Polly wiped a smile off her face, saying, 'The problem is that the man has clout. He's related by marriage to the chief constable of the county and is engaged to the sister of our local MP.'

They thought about that.

Bea said, 'I think I understand. Major Charpentier believes in running an estate as in the old days when the authority of the man in charge could never be questioned. He's no sense of how the countryside works nowadays, and believes the opinion of the common man is of no importance.'

'Correct,' said Polly. 'He's got contacts but doesn't seem to have saved any money as he's living in a house in the village on a peppercorn rent. He runs a leased car which is probably more than he can afford and his intended doesn't seem to be in any hurry to tie the knot. I don't say he left his last job under a cloud because his references were good, but I think he needs this job and will cling on to it till his contract ends in a few months.'

Bea didn't like the feeling this information gave her. She remembered something else which had worried her at the time. 'Rosemary. Why did she leave at short notice? I got her the job here and I thought she was doing brilliantly. She didn't tell me she was unhappy and yet she's gone. If there'd been a problem, I'd have thought she'd have contacted me.'

Polly went all wooden. 'She decided to take another job at a moment's notice. It's caused a lot of talk. It's been quite unpleasant.'

Bea worked it out. 'You think the major contrived to get her out because she threatened his position here? Do you think he's also trying to undermine Julian by gaslighting him? Trying to make him appear a fool, someone who doesn't know how to run the Hall?'

Polly downed the last of the sandwiches. 'I must admit I'm a trifle worried about what the man can do. I'm so glad you came,

Bea. You'll see him off, won't you?' She got to her feet with some difficulty, stretching to ease her back. 'Oh, by the way. In case you didn't know. Pete is a popular member of our village darts team.'

A thin wail cut through the air like a knife. Everyone within earshot stopped what they were doing, their heads turning to the back of the hall, listening. Some of the children had now departed for the day. Half of the rest were laid out on mattresses on the floor, having a nap, while the rest were seated at low tables, occupied with colouring in each other's faces as well as the papers before them.

The children who were awake looked up, interested but not worried. The wail was repeated, and all the adults smiled. Reassured, the children went back to their colouring. Tyra's baby sounded strong, healthy and very annoyed at being pushed out into a cold world.

Polly said, 'Good-oh. You'll look after Jenny, won't you, Bea? I must go. See you later.' She removed herself and baby Philip from the hall just as a siren announced that the ambulance had arrived. Bea stayed where she was, trying to assimilate all she'd heard and what it meant.

Within minutes Kylie and her helpers were on their phones to announce the good news as Tyra, cuddling her newborn baby, was taken off in a wheelchair to the double-parked ambulance outside.

Conversation became lively and upbeat.

'Yes, a little boy, the spitting image of his father, who . . .'

'Well, no one seems to know what's happened to him, but he's bound to turn up soon, right?'

Bea listened but didn't contribute.

'You owe me a pint.' Old Jenny materialized at Bea's side, handing over her midwife's bag.

Bea took the bag and offered her arm. 'I surely do. Tyra's going to be all right?'

'Silly girl. What a fuss about nothing. There'll be all hell to pay here, us having to use all the paper towels from the toilets as well as the newspapers from the shop, though they won't create at the shop, not them. But the afterbirth came away nicely – she won't even need a stitch. In my day, she'd have gone straight home for a cuppa and a rest, but the paramedics have to make a big song and dance about it, don't they? And never a word of thanks.'

Jenny's hand trembled, and she shuffled rather than walked out of the hall and into the pub. The news of the birth had gone ahead of her, and she was congratulated by several people as she threaded her way through the afternoon crowd on her way to her usual seat.

She was touching ninety and the birth had taken it out of her, but she had enough energy left to call out to the landlord that he owed her another pint. She explained to Bea, 'He gives me a pint for every baby I've delivered. Thought I'd finished, so he did. Hah!'

Bea settled the old woman by the fireplace, and a pint and a pie was duly delivered to her by the landlord. Also a half-pint – Bea was surprised and pleased – for her as well.

Jenny took a deep draught, and nodded acknowledgement as various people in the pub raised a glass in her direction, or gave her a thumbs up.

Bea ate, drank and waited for whatever it was Jenny had to tell her.

Jenny drank her pint. Another one replaced it, though Bea declined a top-up. Jenny dozed a little. Two helpings of apple pie and cream appeared in front of them, and Jenny woke up enough to join Bea in demolishing them.

Jenny said, 'Pete's well liked, and a dab hand at the darts. You said he's not dead?'

This was Bea's cue. 'Sir Julian said that he didn't think the dead man was Pete. I believe him. What do you think happened?'

Jenny shook her head. 'Dunno, I really don't. At first I thought it might be the youngsters round here, they're daft creatures, need their bottoms tanning, up to all sorts of mischief. Now they've turned their attention to treasure hunting with metal detectors, courtesy of Amazon, no doubt. But why would they go crashing into the park at night, eh? Are they that stupid?'

Bea said, 'I suppose they believe there's buried treasure at the Hall. I know there's a legend about it, but surely any treasure would be in the house, not the grounds?'

'They're idiots, like I said. They started in the churchyard trying out their metal detectors. I blame the telly, that series about those men hunting for gold. Fat chance!'

'Yet the youngsters placed enough reliance on a legend to spend good money on metal detectors? How long has that been going on for?'

'Since the headmaster chappie, Mr Colston, gave a lecture in the church hall recently about the history of the manor. He's been looking into the archives and trying to decipher some scrolls written on vellum, if you please, with a quill pen and home-made ink. Got everyone talking that did.'

Many things now became clear to Bea.

Polly's father, Mr Colston, had originally been opposed to his daughter marrying a penniless, nameless boy like Julian and had only become reconciled to the match after his son-in-law had inherited Marston Hall. Mr Colston had then moved into a house in the village where he was well looked after and treated with respect. He spent his days studying a chest full of ancient documents found at the Hall, and might well have come across something to substantiate the old story of buried treasure.

Bea looked a question at Jenny, who blandly refused to meet her eyes. Bea had met Mr Colston and knew he was enough of a scholar to decipher ancient documents. So had that cantankerous old man been stoking the fires of curiosity? He was perfectly capable of stirring up trouble, wasn't he?

Bea said, 'What precisely did Mr Colston say?'

'He said he'd found evidence that in the old days many people came as pilgrims to this holy place and left gifts behind.'

'To the church? Or to Marston Hall? Is that what started the youngsters on their treasure hunt?'

Jenny tried to get to her feet and failed. 'My mother used to say it was best not talked about. She said it would only lead to trouble.' She raised her voice and beckoned to a hulking great man standing at the bar. He was even taller and bulkier than the one she'd summoned to do her bidding earlier, but of the same type. 'Come on, Waste of Space. Give me your arm to get home, will you?'

'Yes, Granny,' said the man. He lifted her heavy bag as if it weighed nothing, and walked the old woman away with steps carefully tailored to match her shorter stride.

Was he really her grandson, or was 'Granny' a courtesy title?

Bea tried to pay for their food and drinks. The landlord took money for hers, but refused to accept anything for Jenny's. Instead, he asked in a carefully non-interested fashion if she were staying up at the Hall.

She understood that the landlord really wanted to know how close she was to Julian and Polly. No one slept at the Hall nowadays. Water and electrics were now available, and the builders were working on creating accommodation in the top floor, but Polly had struck at the notion of sleeping on horsehair mattresses, clearing away one's personal belongings on days when the Hall was open to visitors and carrying a toddler up and down two flights of stairs.

A casual visitor might well claim to be staying at the Hall thinking that would enhance their prestige . . . and the villagers would know that it was not at all likely and dismiss them as fools. But if someone said they were invited to stay in the limited accommodation of the estate office, it meant they were real friends.

So she said, 'In the estate office, yes.'

The landlord nodded. 'Don't forget to call in on the post office.'

The post office? Oh, the local shop? Now what on earth . . .? Oh. Ah. She had to pay for the newspapers she'd swiped from there at Jenny's command. She'd nearly forgotten, but the landlord hadn't.

She looked around. Roughly half of the customers were tourists, people passing through. The rest had their eyes on her. She recognized one or two people she'd met earlier. Wasn't that the man Jenny had called 'Useless Lump'? Was he cousin or brother of 'Waste of Space'?

Whatever she did or said, word would get around. It might have felt like a threatening situation but it wasn't, because they seemed to approve of her. She was not one of them. No. She was an outsider. But she'd been given provisional status as a friend of the village.

She wondered, perhaps a little hysterically, how long it had taken Julian and Polly to achieve acceptance.

She stepped out of the pub to see that traffic was moving at its usual snail's pace through the High Street. A girl biker in helmet and black leathers – did they really have food deliveries out here? – wove her way skilfully in and out of the traffic and disappeared. Now that was the way to travel. Except that Bea hadn't been on a bike since she was in her teens, and hadn't enjoyed the experience then.

Next stop was the village shop which was also the post office. A bell tinkled as Bea pushed open the door, and everyone inside turned to see who'd entered – and fell silent.

This was the only shop in the village, selling everything from batteries to biros, cheese to umbrellas. It was crowded from floor to ceiling and the passageway between shelving was so narrow that a baby buggy could probably not proceed from jigsaws to coffee machine without snagging on something.

The only open space was in front of the post office section and that was currently occupied by four or five people plus a couple of toddlers, all staring at her.

Only a lively-looking, dark-haired lad who was shelf-filling tins of baked beans ignored her. Was he the refugee who'd been wrongly accused of theft? He didn't know who she was, but everyone else did. A bit creepy, what?

A bright-eyed middle-aged woman in a headscarf was behind the post office counter, and yes, it must be her husband behind the till on the other side of the shop. Mr and Mrs Patel, presumably. Bea hadn't had occasion to speak to them before although she'd had some dealings with their son Imran, who'd overcome local prejudice well enough for Julian to appoint as manager of the farm shop. By all accounts he was doing well and had acquired a local girlfriend.

Bea made her way to the cash register. 'You were so kind as to let me have some newspapers for Jenny this morning. I came rushing in without my money, as it was such an emergency. May I pay for them now?'

Of course Imran's family would be open-minded enough to give the refugee a job. What nationality was the boy, anyway? Had someone said he was Ukrainian?

Imran's father, Mr Patel, knew who she was, and so did at least one of the other customers. One of the children, one who Bea recognized as having been at the nursery that morning said, loudly, '*She* was helping Polly this morning. I saw her. And Tyra had a baby and it cried like our cat! Yeow!'

A shocked voice said, 'I've told you before. You call her *Lady* Polly!'

'I don't think she cares,' said Bea, looking for a stand of sweeties and finding it at her elbow. 'The children were all so good while Tyra was having her baby.' And to Mr Patel she said, 'May I have some of these bags of sweets for the children as well?'

Mr Patel accepted money for the newspapers and the sweets. He didn't smile, but she had the feeling that he was cautiously approving of her actions. Bea was about to leave when the dark-haired boy dropped a can of beans on the floor and disappeared through a door at the back.

'What the . . .!'

A large form appeared at the glass door and pushed it open. The bell tinkled and a police officer entered. Upon which the customers gathered up their children and their purchases and disappeared. The bell on the door tinkled as it shut behind the last customer. Only Bea remained.

The atmosphere inside the shop tightened.

Bea recognized the officer as one of those who'd disrespected Julian earlier. He recognized her, too, but dismissed her as of no consequence. His mind was on other prey.

'Where've you put him? We want a word, down the station.'

Were the police after the refugee boy?

Mr Patel said stolidly, 'He's free to come and go. His papers are all in order, and if he wants to help me out in the shop, then he's free to do that, too.'

The officer's jaw tightened. Was he actually chewing gum? Surely not! Oh. Yes, he was. Mm. Trying to stop smoking, perhaps? In which case, the poor man was to be pitied.

The officer leaned on the counter and tried a nose-to-nose confrontation with Mr Patel. It didn't work. Mr Patel's face was set like a stone. He said, 'Your usual cigarettes?'

The officer shook his head angrily. And then gave in. 'Oh, all right. Put them on the tab.' Which meant he wasn't going to pay for them?

Bea thought that Julian would have known what to do at that

point, and that she didn't. She said, 'What a difficult job you have, officer. Have you found Pete yet?'

He barely looked at her, saying, 'Pete's dead. His widow's not up to much at the moment—'

Mr Patel said, 'So you haven't found Pete yet? And now he has a fine boy, right? A blessing. Perhaps he'll grow up to join the darts team.'

Now that might sound like ordinary chitchat, but Bea knew – and the officer knew – that Mr Patel was reminding his customer that the village had beaten the town at the darts match.

Bea didn't know whether to scream with laughter or cringe as the officer reddened, snatched his cigarettes, said, 'I'll be back!' and exited. The doorbell tinkled happily as he left.

Bea held on to the counter, and gave way to laughter.

Mr Patel ignored her to yell out, 'Lunch time!' He turned the 'Open' sign on the door to 'Closed' and held the outer door open for Bea to leave. So she did. Apparently she'd been given only temporary status as a villager.

She didn't know what to do next. She wondered if she could find Mr Colston – that scholarly, difficult man who might or might not have unearthed something about buried treasure.

Time was getting on, and she wanted to touch base with Julian and Polly. There were questions which had been raised that morning which they might be able to answer, and one that she might be able to answer herself. So, she got into her car – no parking ticket, thank goodness – and set off back to the Hall.

On the way, she slowed down wherever a gate allowed access from the road on to farmland, to inspect the ground. The rain the previous night had softened the soil, showing whether or not a car or tractor had recently passed that way.

She looked across the fields, wondering how many farms might belong to the Hall. There seemed to be a mixture of dairy and arable farmland hereabouts and, to judge by the neatness of the hedgerows and farm buildings, all seemed to be doing well. She only spotted one set of tractor tracks on her route, but they were not recent and she didn't know if the pattern matched the ones found in the park.

Reaching the Hall, she parked outside the estate office, noting that Bruno was on guard duty. He rose to his feet when he saw her, and nudged her hand. She tried to get around him, but he wouldn't have it. He didn't want her going into the estate office.

Instead, when he'd got her attention, he led the way across the yard to the back door of the kitchen, waited for her to understand what she was supposed to do, and returned to guard the door to the estate office.

Bea followed Bruno's instructions and entered the kitchen to find not only Mrs Maggs but also Captain Courageous – no, no! She must remember to call him 'Major' – with Julian, and the baby asleep in a carrycot on the table. Both men had laptops open before them.

Julian gestured for Bea to join them, saying, 'Polly was too tired to get up the stairs so she's lying down on the settee in the office to have a nap. Helping at the nursery wears her out. Bruno's on guard.'

The major sent Bea one quick glance, dismissing her as before; an older woman of no importance. He brought his attention back to Julian. He seemed very tense, speaking through gritted teeth while he gripped his laptop as if it might try to get away from him. He was saying, 'But you must see that this sort of favouritism—'

Julian leaned back in his own chair, caressing his own laptop. 'No doubt you're right. As a general rule it's asking for trouble to give preferential treatment to any one tenant. In this particular case, I think it was the right thing to do. I owe Jenny a great deal.'

So the major is now annoyed that Julian overruled him in the matter of Jenny's boiler?

The major was indeed somewhat aerated. His colour had risen and his grip on his laptop was something fierce. 'Well! You pay me to manage the estate for you and if you're not going to take my advice . . .!'

'I know. I can see it is most upsetting for you when I don't follow the rules.' A gentle tone, an inflexible attitude.

The major rose to his feet. He said, 'Of course it must be your decision, but it's going to cause me a great deal of extra work. You realize I now have to alter all my repair schedules? Some of the other tenants will object most strongly—'

'I doubt it,' said Julian. 'Jenny's delivered half the village and is related to the other half.'

'That's feudal! Totally out of date!'

'Strong personalities do influence local matters.'

'That is . . . beyond all . . .! And now we're down a member of the security team. I'll have to phone the agency, see if they can supply anyone else.' The major grabbed his laptop and departed, banging the door to behind him.

Mrs Maggs placed a mug of tea on the table before Bea, and nodded a welcome.

Julian said, 'Do join us, Mrs Maggs. We need to talk.'

Mrs Maggs, sharp as a tack, unbelievably black hair as neat as usual, sat down somewhat reluctantly. For once, she looked worried. She said, 'I don't know anything.'

Bea thought, Uh-oh. That means she does know something. But what?

FIVE

Friday, late afternoon

Julian said, 'Let's pool our knowledge. I'll start with what I've done. I checked the roads were open again and that all is well at the farm shop and restaurant. I went into town and gave a statement to the police. I pointed out that Pete wears an earring but the corpse didn't. I said that in my book Pete was missing and we should look for him and his dog, Beauty.

'Their reaction was that I'd been overworking and as my testimony conflicted with the established facts, they couldn't take it seriously. The major has apparently identified the dead body as Pete's and the police say that they expect his wife will confirm it in due course.'

He looked a query at Bea, who said, 'I told Tyra that it likely wasn't Pete who was killed but I'm not sure she took it in. There was a delay getting an ambulance to the nursery, so Jenny delivered Tyra's baby. He's a fine boy. Mother and child were then taken to hospital to be checked out.'

Julian said, 'I'm hoping the police will put the dead man's fingerprints through the system and that this will give us his true identity. They're not looking for Pete or his dog, or for anyone local who might have gone missing. The police theory is that a treasure-hunting gang from London stole a tractor to break into the park last night, were confronted by Pete and killed him in a panic before running away. I find this hard to believe. Mrs Maggs, can you help us out here?'

Mrs Maggs repeated her line. 'I don't *know* anything.'

It was clear to Bea that she did either know or guessed at something, but that for some reason she wouldn't talk.

Julian waited a moment, then looked at Bea. 'What else did you discover?'

'The village is withholding judgement. They like Pete and are puzzled by what's happened. The landlord of the pub is open-minded on the subject. So is Mr Patel at the shop. That police officer, the one who doesn't like your story, came in looking for the refugee lad, who had made himself scarce.

'Mr Patel was almost rude to the police officer, which probably wasn't a good idea. Next, it seems that it was Mr Colston who resurrected the legend of the buried treasure. As for Captain Courageous, you're right and the villagers wouldn't dream of standing in the way of Jenny's boiler getting priority.'

Julian rubbed his eyes. 'It isn't just Jenny's cottage that needs urgent attention. Many of them do. It's a nightmare! Leases have run out and not been renewed. Some tenants have fallen into debt, or have sub-let, or moved in with relations. And the arrears! I left it to the major to sort the mess out, but I've noticed that he's using a firm of builders from town to do so, and not the local people. That may or may not be a good idea.

'Jenny is complaining one of her neighbours has had a patio built across the back of his garden while others are still waiting for basic repairs. I'm beginning to wonder if the major's list is governed by who's giving the biggest bribes. But that,' said Julian, choosing his words carefully, 'is only passing on gossip which was conveyed to me by Jenny.'

Julian looked again at Mrs Maggs, but she was looking into her mug and rolling the last drop of tea around. She wasn't reading the tea leaves, was she? Goodness gracious!

Julian looked at Bea. 'Anything else?'

'I assume the police are looking at the approaches to all the farms around here, looking for recent traces of a tractor which might have been borrowed overnight in order to be used in the raid on the park.'

'They should be, yes.' Julian turned his laptop round so that Bea could see what was on it. 'Here's a map of the area. I looked at the tracks and it occurred to me they might have been made by two different vehicles accessing the site. Perhaps not a tractor, perhaps other wide-based vehicles. I might be wrong. The rain blurred the outlines.

'I did look into the matter of tractors which might have been used. The estate has one for mowing the grass in the meadows around the Hall. It's kept under lock and key in a shed at the back of the farm shop. I've checked; it's still there, its tyres are dry and it hasn't been used recently. I wondered, if a tractor had been used to gain entrance to the amusement park, where did it come from? Tractors don't travel far or fast. Whose tractor do you think might have been used, Mrs Maggs?'

Mrs Maggs folded and refolded her hands. She made as if to speak, then shook her head. 'I don't know of any.'

Julian said, 'I'm assuming that at least two people were involved, because after the death of the unknown man, someone was still alive and able to drive their vehicle away again. Possibly with Pete chasing after them? Who do we know locally who would lend a tractor out for an invasion of the park? Or allow it to be borrowed by third parties?'

Mrs Maggs said, 'It's a mystery, innit?'

Julian was patient. 'I've managed to meet all my tenant farmers but I don't know them well. I can't, offhand, think of any of my tenants who would risk lending a tractor out for a night-time raid on a neighbour's property. And yet, that's supposed to be what's happened. What am I missing, Mrs Maggs?'

Mrs Maggs produced a tight smile. 'You thought that it might not have been a tractor, but something with a broad base? An old Land Rover, perhaps? I know the police think it was a London gang who did it, but I don't see it, either. It must be people with local knowledge.'

Julian said, 'You're thinking of those stupid lads who've been causing chaos around here? It's a big jump from petty vandalism to breaking down fences to trespass on a neighbour's property.'

Mrs Maggs said, 'It could have been them. They've been using metal detectors around the church, looking for the buried treasure. I suppose they thought it would be a lark to try them out in the park.'

Julian shook his head. 'They'd need transport, so where did they get it? Look, they're not the type that walks any distance, encumbered by metal detectors, and they aren't old enough to have driving licences, are they? No, wait a minute, I believe one of them did have a licence and lost it for drink-driving. But they have no cars of their own.

'So where would they get a heavy-duty vehicle from? They aren't farmers, are they? Farmers work all hours of the day and sometimes the night, too. These lads we're talking about have time on their hands. And if it was them, how did they meet up with a middle-aged man in heavy working clothes? I'm talking about the man who came in with them but who didn't leave the site alive. Did he drive them to the site? And if so, who drove them away again?'

Mrs Maggs twisted her hands. 'No one else local has gone missing. I'd have heard.'

'All right. Let's move on. The men who came in with the vehicle knocked down the fencing and drove across an acre or so of rough ground to where the treetop ride had collapsed on to the ground. Why? Why that particular place and what on earth did they intend to do when they got there?'

Mrs Maggs said, 'They was looking for treasure.'

Julian said, 'Mrs Maggs, I do understand that you have loyalties far beside the Hall. You have relatives living all over. Is it possible that one of them might have some information that would help us? Can you not just give me a hint of where to start looking for Pete and his dog?'

'Pete wasn't local. He come down from London, didn't he?'

'Yes, he did. He was happy here, wasn't he? He'd joined the darts team, his wife was helping in the nursery and they were looking forward to the birth of their first child. The major believes Pete let the vandals into the park. I don't agree. Pete would never have done that. The fact that they had to break down the fence to get into the park proves to me that he didn't.

'There's something else to consider. Pete was conscientious about making his rounds. It's quite some area to cover and he reckoned that it took him about an hour each time. If the invaders were local, surely they'd know when Pete would be on the far side of the park. If they'd been careful, they could have been in and out before he'd know anything was wrong.

'Were they careless or foolhardy, for they were still working on the spot when he returned? Either way, he heard something, or perhaps saw a light, and went to investigate. There was a fight and a man was left for dead. The intruders withdrew the way they'd come.

'Now, the question is did they take Pete and his dog with them? And if so, why? He wouldn't have gone with them of his own accord, not with his wife due to give birth. All I can think of is that he could identify them if left at large. Pete might have been wounded and crawled after the invaders with his dog . . . and have died somewhere en route. I'm terribly afraid they might have been left in a ditch somewhere. I can't rest till I find them, alive or . . . dead.'

Mrs Maggs's hands were tight around her mug, but she shook her head. 'No one I know would do a terrible thing like that.'

Julian said tiredly, 'Yes, yes. But when you introduce gold into the picture, you lose sight of right and wrong. It seems to me that no one intended to kill anyone. The intruders accessed the park, reached their target and worked on it before Pete realized they were there. Maybe it was his dog, Beauty, who spotted them first? He should have phoned for help and not tried to tackle them by himself, but I think he did and in the fight that followed, a man died. After that, Pete and his dog disappeared. There's no sign thereabouts of a second body or of the dog, so where are they, Mrs Maggs?'

The housekeeper made as if to rise. 'If you're quite finished, I'd best check on—'

Julian put his hand on hers to detain her. 'What of his dog? A fine collie. The last time I spoke to Pete, he said he was thinking of entering her in the next dog show. He asked if I'd enter Bruno. Where's Beauty now, Mrs Maggs? She's not lying beside the body of the dead man, because he was not her master. Alive or dead, Beauty wouldn't leave Pete.

'The raiders wouldn't want her following them because she's too easily identified. But she wouldn't give up, would she? What happened to her? Did they kill her and throw her body in the nearest ditch? What of the man they left behind? They smashed in his face and put Pete's lanyard around his neck. Was this to delay identification? Why did they do that, Mrs Maggs?'

Mrs Maggs sought for a hankie and blew her nose. 'I don't know. I don't know anything.'

It was now very clear to Bea that Mrs Maggs might not *know* something but she'd guessed, or was uneasy about . . . what?

Julian said, 'Pete was on my payroll. I owe it to him to find him if I can.'

The carrycot shook. Baby Pip was stirring. There was a yawn, a threshing of arms and legs, and Julian lifted the boy into his arms. The baby – well, he was more than a baby now, being what, nine months or so? – looked around with the same bright blue eyes as his father.

Bea wondered if she'd be asked to change and feed Pip, but Julian proceeded to do what was necessary, as to the manor born. Pip burped and wriggled to be put down on the floor. With Julian holding him up, the boy tried to walk this way and that. His concentration was excellent. That was another way in which he took after his father.

Bea thought Mrs Maggs might take the opportunity to slip away, but instead she occupied herself with warming up some goo in a jar for the little boy, who Julian installed in an ancient baby high chair which had probably been made for his great-grandfather.

Mrs Maggs decided to talk. 'They're saying now that there's a curse on the Marston-Langs. I never heard of one, growing up, but now I think there must be something in it. The day that Lady Fleur came into the house and bewitched your grandfather, the day he let her and her wicked son drive your father away . . . that was a bad day. All that side of the family is bad news, thinking of nothing but what pleased them to do. Those two girls, Mona and Celine, her granddaughters, they aren't that bad, though they're not good.

'Now Lady Fleur's son Frederick and his son Bertram, they both lied and cheated and laughed when people got hurt. And they did get hurt. We all saw it, and we couldn't do nothing about it. It's the way they're brought up. So long as they get their way, that kind are happy even with the house and everything in it going to rack and ruin. And their seed takes root and grows and then there's another generation who think they can do as they like and never be held to account for it.'

Julian thought that through. He said, 'I understand that you feel you can't help me at the moment. If circumstances change, let me know.'

Bea wondered if Julian would now give up. He didn't have anything to work on, did he? The police had made up their minds and were not going to look into the affairs of the young layabouts. What could Julian do?

What could anyone do?

Julian began to feed Pip, who laughed and banged on the tray and opened his mouth for the next mouthful, and the next. The sound of his laughter lightened the greyness of the late afternoon.

Julian said, 'I'm a lucky man, am I not?' He took the child out of the high chair, burped him, and settled him on his knee, before reaching for his laptop. 'Let's approach the problem a different way. This map shows the house and park around it, including the farm shop and café. A road surrounds the park with a drystone wall keeping trespassers out.

'Once upon a time, the Marston-Langs owned many acres beyond. Some land has been sold off over the generations but going north from here to the village it's still our land. I've tried to meet and talk to everyone in that area. Going south towards the coast is a different matter. I've no land in that direction. I've met some of my neighbours but so far have found little in common with them. They don't care about the village, but look to the coast for their entertainment.

'Looking at the map you can see the main road circles the park and then goes due south to the Downs and the coast. There are well-used tracks across the park to and from the house, each leading to a gate on to the encircling main road. Roughly, they can be said to lead north, south, east and west.

'Coming from the village, the road enters the estate and divides. One branch leads to the house. Another turns off at right angles to serve first the farm shop, car park and café, and then on to the entrance to the amusement park. There it divides again; one branch goes to the southern boundary and from there on to the coast. The other goes to the eastern gate which nowadays is not much used. Should I look for the tracks of the tractor to the north or the south, Mrs Maggs?'

'I dunno, do I? East, west . . . east's best. That's what they say, don't they?'

Bea froze. *No, they didn't. They said, 'East, west, home's best.' Is she telling us to look to the east?*

Julian said, 'You think it might be worth a try to take Bruno along the road that goes off to the east, to see if he can pick up Beauty's trail?'

'How should I know?' Mrs Maggs shrugged and closed her lips tight.

Julian checked his watch and looked out of the window. 'It's going to get dark early. I'll get going as soon as Polly can take over with Pip. I don't like the thought of Pete lying out there somewhere, either injured or dead.'

Mrs Maggs said, 'You go now. I'll see to the family and sort some supper out for you.'

Julian nodded and handed his son over to Mrs Maggs. 'Thank you, Mrs Maggs. I appreciate this. I'll take Bruno and Mrs Abbot with me.'

Julian led the way to his beat-up old car and clicked his fingers at Bruno, who leaped into the back seat with only a lingering look at the door of the estate office.

Bea said, 'Mrs Maggs is feeling guilty about not telling you what you need to know?'

'It's clear she suspects something but has no evidence. She's connected to half the neighbourhood by birth or marriage. Her brother farms at Hill Top to the south of us. His family have been tenants there for generations. Sometime over the past twenty years my grandfather sold that farm to the local bigwig, and if I understand correctly, this means that the Maggs family could be given notice to quit if they don't behave themselves. No wonder Mrs Maggs can't give us chapter and verse. But she didn't tell us to look south. She told us to go east, and that's where I'm going to have a look.'

Bea said, 'What about Rosemary?'

Did he jump in his seat? He said, 'Yes, indeed? I hope she's all right.'

Bea began to get a very bad feeling about Rosemary's abrupt departure. 'We could do with her now. Shall I try to find her?'

'No, I think not.'

Now, that's an odd thing to say. Bea had suggested Rosemary for the job in the first place. Julian and Rosemary used to be the best of friends. Mm. Has the major had anything to do with her sudden departure?

Julian said, 'Leave it, Bea. She'll surface again when she's ready.'

He took the road to the amusement park, and came to a halt outside the security guards' caravan. The police tape was still warding off curious onlookers, and there was no sign of a current security guard, who must be out and about on his rounds.

The caravan was locked, but Julian let Bruno out of the car, asking him if he could follow Beauty's trail from there.

Bruno set off, nose to ground, following the track which ran east from the amusement park. It did not look as if it had much use. However, crushed weeds on either side made it apparent that a broad-based vehicle had passed that way recently. Julian drove slowly along behind the dog. They came to a gate in a drystone wall which marked the boundary of the park or rather, to where a gate had once stood but had recently been smashed open and left in pieces.

Julian said, 'Now why hasn't that been reported to me? That gate's usually closed and padlocked. I'll have to get someone on it or we'll have the world and wife camping in the grounds, digging for treasure.'

He got out of the car to investigate various muddy tracks inside the gate and outside on the road. Returning to his seat, he said, 'We're on the right path, I think. Now, do we go left or right here?'

Ah. Bruno had taken off to the left along the encircling road, and was now waiting for them to catch up. But when they did so, he didn't want to continue round the perimeter of the park but led them off to a minor road, little more than a track, again going due east. And yes, the vehicle whose tracks they'd been following had also gone this way.

Bea asked, 'Who lives out this way? Anyone you know? Is it your land?'

'Not my land, no. Lady Knighton lives this way and between her and us there's a patchwork of small farms.'

Suddenly Bruno became distressed, nosing back and forth.

What was that dark stain on the road? Not blood? Pray it wasn't blood.

Bruno stood over a patch of trampled-down verge, and whined.

Julian left the car, followed by Bea.

There was a ditch running with water beyond the verge, and half in and half out of the water lay a muddied creature which had once been the proud Beauty. Dead? Judging by the flattened state of the grass around her, the dog had struggled to climb out of the ditch, but had only partially managed it.

Regardless of mud, Julian got down into the ditch and lifted the pathetically muddied body out and on to the grass.

Bea told herself this was no time to scream or to faint. She told herself she was not the fainting sort. She got out her smartphone and took pictures. Julian and the dog. The trampled verge. And then the lane itself. Was that a stile over there? They needed landmarks. Yes, there was the roof of a shed some way along. Good. That should pinpoint the location. Click, click.

Had Pete been thrown out here, too? No, there was no sign of him.

Julian was attending to the dog. 'Back right leg swollen, maybe broken. Been kicked in the ribs. But she's alive. Just.' He looked at Bruno. 'Pete? Search?'

Bruno was licking at Beauty's head and had no intention of continuing the search. Bruno was telling them that Pete hadn't walked along here. If he'd been carried away on the tractor, or in a car, then there wouldn't be any scent for Bruno to follow.

Bruno whined. Beauty lifted her head an inch.

Julian said, 'We must get her to the vet's. I don't want to give up on looking for Pete, but . . . I'm torn. The police must take over the search for Pete from here and our priority must be saving Beauty's life.' Julian opened the boot of the car, and with some difficulty lifted Beauty into it, covering her with an old rug kept for Bruno's use. That wise dog, unasked, leaped in after her.

Julian looked into space.

Bea said, 'What?'

'Pregnant, I think.' He looked down at Bruno, who was attending to Beauty.

Oh. Ah. Of course.

Julian looked down at himself. He was muddied to his eyeballs, his jeans were shedding dirty water and his shoes were ruined. He wiped as much dirt off himself as he could, and said, 'Can you drive, Bea? I'll do the phoning. First to the police, telling them what we've found. Then to the vet's, asking them to stay open. Do you remember where it is, in town? And I must let Polly know what's happened.'

They got back into the car, Julian squelching at every move. He started on the phone calls, while Bea put her foot down. She headed north, following the road around the park till they came to the turn-off to the village, and thence north again to the nearest town.

The call to the police didn't go well. Julian started to explain that they'd found Pete's dog and where, and then stopped. Listening. And finally clicked the phone off.

He said, 'They say they've run the dead man's fingerprints through their system and there's no match to anyone on the police database. No one else has been reported missing so as far as they're concerned, Pete's body is in the mortuary and that's that.'

Bea said, 'But we're sure the dead man wasn't Pete.'

'They like their story better. They say Pete came down from London to help a gang of criminals look for properties which they could burgle. They say thieves fell out, as they do, and that he was killed. The hunt for the criminals has shifted to London.'

'And Pete's dog?'

'They say Beauty must have run away when Pete was killed. They say she must have been injured by a passing car.'

Bea said, 'When Tyra gets to see the body found in the park, she'll explode that story.'

'They say she's being kept in hospital for a few days and is not to be tasked with having to identify her husband, so that under the circumstances they won't be asking her to see his body.'

This was not good news.

Julian applied himself to his phone again, to organize matters at the vet's. And then to tell Polly he'd be late for supper and why; to tell Mrs Maggs what had happened; to have a word with his secretary, who hadn't known what to do, to work or stay at home; and finally to update Captain Courageous – Bea told herself she really must stop calling him that! – which also didn't seem to go well.

She drove as fast as she could, being careful not to jog the precious cargo in the boot, but every now and then Beauty moaned, and Bruno whickered. Dusk was beginning to cloud the sky by the time she parked at the vet's. There were customers waiting for attention with various animals but Julian managed to get Beauty seen straight away.

He surrendered the injured dog and explained where she'd been found, that he thought she was pregnant, and that if Pete didn't appear to claim the dog, he personally would cover the costs of any treatment. Bruno sat at Julian's side, listening to every word. Well, that's what it felt like.

The receptionist said, 'We heard that Pete was dead.'

Julian explained. His voice began to fade from exhaustion.

Customers waiting for attention heard what Julian said and joined in, exclaiming this and wondering about that. What a terrible thing. The poor man and oh dear, what would happen to his dog?

A vet wearing scrubs popped out to confirm that there was a problem. Beauty was pregnant and near to term, she'd strained her right back leg but they didn't want to X-ray it because it looked as if she were about to go into labour. Pros and cons. Was it better to X-ray and perhaps lose the puppies, or leave the leg alone for the time being?

Bea felt that if she didn't sit down, she'd fall down. She'd been on the go since she left London only that morning. Was it really only that morning? So she sat. And then realized that the vet had disappeared again and Julian was looking down at his ruined clothing and apologizing to the receptionists for his condition. He said he'd like to stay till Beauty was in the clear, but didn't want to sit down and dirty the chairs in the waiting room.

Bea thought that if she didn't have a cup of tea and a lie-down soon she'd do someone an injury. Instead, she asked one of the receptionists if Julian could have a strip wash in the visitor's loo and put all his muddy clothes in a plastic bag. She personally would go to the nearest M&S or whatever and buy him whatever he needed so that he could walk out of the vet's without causing a riot.

Customers and receptionists then entered into a discussion about how to dress Julian. Someone said he could borrow some scrubs, couldn't he? Another said, 'What about shoes? And what about, you know, under things?'

Julian sat down on the floor, put his head in his hands, and whooped with laughter. Nervous reaction. At which point everyone else began to laugh, the cacophony amplified by the various cats, dogs, parrots and other birds which barked, squeaked and chortled until Bea shouted that she needed his size, please, and a big man who was attached to a tiny cat said there was an M&S if you went out of the back door and up the snicket – apparently he meant a passageway between two houses – to the main street and turned right. And a receptionist with more sense than most produced mugs of sugared tea.

So Bea had her cuppa and, leaving Bruno with Julian, followed directions to the main shopping centre and bought this and that, putting everything on her card. Shoes were the big problem. She bought three pairs of trainers, hoping that one pair would fit.

Returning to the vet's, Julian greeted her with the news that three live pups had arrived so far, and there might be another on the way. Julian was clean and dressed in some borrowed scrubs and flip-flops. He donned his new finery only to exclaim that he never wore light blue, at which Bea threatened to clout him. He ducked and apologized. And yes, one of the pairs of trainers did fit. As did the underpinnings and the jeans. And yes, his soiled clothes and his shoes had been put in a large plastic bag to be taken away and dealt with.

Then it was time to go. They had to leave Beauty and her pups at the vet's overnight to be collected next day if all went well.

Bea drove because Julian was constantly answering the phone with people wanting to know what had happened and why, and what was he going to do about it. Bruno didn't seem happy about leaving Beauty at the vet's, but when Julian spoke to him in a certain tone, the dog did agree to get into the boot of the car and be driven home.

It was almost completely dark by the time they reached the Hall, only to find the big house in its night-time sleep and only the estate office at the back lit up. And there was Polly walking a grouchy Pip up and down.

Julian managed, somehow or other, to summon up a smile, take Pip from her, and say, 'Now, then. What's the matter, eh?'

At which the reliable Polly burst into tears and Pip began to grizzle.

SIX

Friday evening

Bea could see Julian was about to give at the knees, so she plucked the boy from his father's arms. 'Feeding time? Where's his bottle?'

Polly sobbed, 'I know I'm being stupid. I shouldn't give way like this. I wanted to see Tyra. I ought to do so. She hasn't anyone else. But I can't take Pip into hospital and Mrs Maggs said she had to go off early and she's left some food for us but I forgot to turn the oven on, and . . . Julian! What on earth are you wearing!'

Julian sank on to the settee and held out his arms to his wife. 'Think of it as fancy dress. Polly, love. Come here and give me a cuddle. Bea will cope with Pip.'

Oh yeah! Dear old Bea can always be relied on to cope even when she'd prefer a lie-down in a darkened room with someone to bring her hot drinks and a tasty supper.

Bea was sensible enough to know that what she wanted was not going to happen.

She watched as Polly hiccupped herself into Julian's arms, he closed his eyes and allowed himself to relax. Probably there was a bottle and some soft food in the fridge for Pip.

Yes, there was. Heat bottle. Change nappy. Teething? Yes. Rub gum with stuff from fridge. Pop bottle into mouth. Find somewhere to sit. Aaargh. That's better. And take a moment out to pray.

Dear Lord. Thank you for dumping me in it. Really! A weekend off work sounded perfect and look what's happened! I'm in such a tizzy. Well, we all are. Is Pete really Pete or is he a London gangster? Who killed who and why? There's something very peculiar going on and I have a feeling that Mr Colston – Polly's father – quite deliberately reignited the rumour about there being buried treasure at the Hall. This has drawn a lot of undesirable attention from all sorts. Not to mention that very odd visit from Julian's cousin and her paramour.

Hm. I don't think I've ever thought of a man as a paramour before. But that is what Marcus is. I think. Probably. Not to mention Captain Courageous, who seems to want to relegate Julian to the back row so that he can run the show himself. And his way of doing things is not Julian's.

Which reminds me that Rosemary leaving Julian in the lurch like that is not right. She wouldn't. No. Unless . . . has the gallant captain been telling porkies and got her to resign? But what could he have said to her to make her turn turtle and run away? It's not like her.

Dear Lord, without being rude or anything, I could do with some help here. I mean . . . I don't know what I mean.

I'm tired and want hot food and bed.

Ah, but so do the two babes in the wood. Both of them falling asleep, which is good-oh. Except that someone has got to put Pip to bed . . . and what about Bruno? He's waited so patiently to be fed and watered . . . Dear Lord, give me strength!

Somehow or other Bea got everyone, including the dog, clean, fed and watered. The telephone was switched to messages, her host and hostess managed to perk up and, as Bea stacked plates into the dishwasher, even managed to discuss their problems.

Polly recovered first. She twitted Julian on wearing such a bright blue which matched his eyes. She said she'd long wanted to see him in something which was not sober grey, at which he almost blushed and said he blamed Bea who'd chosen it. Then he had to explain why his own clothes were in a dustbin bag in the car.

Polly clucked and kissed him and said that of course they must find someone to look after Pete's dog . . . if Pete really were dead. Or, if he wasn't dead, where was he?

Julian said, 'We'll work it out tomorrow. Now, Polly, what are we going to do about you? I don't want you wearing yourself out every day running the nursery. It's not sensible. And sit down *now*, woman! Nothing is more important than your health.'

'I know,' said Polly, sitting down for five seconds, and then getting up again to attend to Pip, who was wriggling around on the floor, trying to swim or crawl or run a marathon. Whatever.

Polly said, 'The problem is this: you've managed to get the café and the farm shop opened again, which means that at long last there are some jobs available for the villagers who would otherwise have to make the trip into town every day. They want jobs here. But, if they have small children to look after, they can't take a job unless the nursery is up and running.

'Kylie is going to be really good in time, but she's not really experienced enough to run it by herself, Tyra was only there temporarily, and in any case she's the sort to cry if you looked at her askance. There is another woman who used to run it, and she is qualified but her attendance is spotty, so they need me, who's got all the right certification. Only I'm not much use at the moment. I can't get down to the floor and if I do, I can't get up again so . . . I don't know what to do.'

Julian said, 'Ask Jenny or Mrs Maggs to find someone to help you?'

'If I do that, there'll be a battle royal about whose candidate gets the job, and it won't be anything to do with who's the best person for it.'

'All right. What about asking Lady Knighton? Somebody told me she'd had a fall which put her out of circulation for a while, but she'd know who could help.'

Bea thought, I know that name, don't I? Ah, the woman who used to run the volunteer stewards who show people round the Hall. Elderly, now living in a dower house because her son has taken over the stately home. Lives not far away. We walked near there earlier. Very bright. Connected to everyone in the country.

Polly said, 'Oh, her. Someone said she was still out of it but yes, she'd know who might help. Only, if I ask her to do this, she'll blackmail me into going on some committee or other. Says it's expected of me in my position. She's run this and that in the county for ever and expects me to follow in her footsteps, and I don't know how. Come to think of it, she left me a message about picking up some raffle tickets for a coffee morning next week. I'll pop in to see her tomorrow.'

'Dear Polly, you need to delegate some of your workload, instead of increasing it. You can't continue to run around the countryside helping everyone with everything. You need to rest, and you need some help with Pip.'

'Oh, no! I can manage.'

Julian cradled her cheek with his hand. 'You need Kylie's younger sister – or someone like her – to give you time off. I know you think you ought to be Earth Mother and solve all the problems of the world but there are only so many minutes in the day and your poor neglected husband yearns for your company for at least one hour of it.'

Polly started to laugh. 'Oh, you! All right. I hear what you say. I promise I'll be good. Well, every now and then!'

Bea, sitting in the background, thought how much Julian had grown up since she'd first stumbled over him outside her garage in town. He'd always been a clever clogs at the money business, but his expert management of people was something new.

Polly had grown, too. Now she took a good look at her husband and said, 'What's wrong, my love? It's not just Pete going missing, is it? The police will sort that. And as for Captain Courageous . . . Oh, I shouldn't say that, I've caught it from Mrs Maggs, who doesn't like him, either—'

'Nor does Bea. Nor the workmen. Nor Pete. I picked the wrong man for general manager there, didn't I? It'll take time to sort.'

Bea slammed the dishwasher shut and set it running.

There was a sharp cry from Pip who, unwatched for a minute, had succeeded in hauling himself up on to his feet, only to fall with a bump on to his behind. But Pip was like his father. A moment of pain, a frown, and then . . . he looked around for something to do next, and was diverted by Bruno nosing at his back. Pip patted Bruno. Bruno lay down, reducing himself to Pip's level.

Pip clutched at Bruno's fur, and managed to haul himself to his feet once more. Wobbled a bit. Straightened up. Looked around at the room from this different angle. Tried climbing up on to Bruno's back, slid down and landed on his side. Bruno licked Pip's hand. Pip grinned and threw his arms and legs around the dog. Warmed by his closeness to this surrogate parent, he relaxed, yawned and sighed. His eyelids fluttered, and he drifted off to sleep.

Julian picked him up, popped him into an ancient wooden cradle with the boy's favourite somewhat frayed toy giraffe, and covered him with a blanket. For one long moment Julian stayed by his son, looking down on him. Bea thought he was probably praying.

Polly was yawning. 'Shall we forget our troubles and watch something mindless on the telly? And have an early night?'

Julian said, 'Early night. Good idea. Polly, you go on up and I'll be with you in a minute. I want to check something first. I think someone's left a window open in the library. I know Mrs Maggs usually goes the rounds, but I'd like to be sure.'

Bea recognized her cue. She said, 'I'll come with you if I may.'

With Bruno at their heels, they crossed the courtyard and went into the great house. Julian switched on lights as they walked through the kitchen quarters to the library which formed the east wing of the ancient house.

Julian checked all the windows, though there was no need. Mrs Maggs might have been distracted that day, but she wouldn't have omitted to see the house was properly shut up at night.

The library had been built by someone who understood space, and light. There were windows down one side of the room and shelves of books from floor to ceiling on the other. The ceiling was high and the floorboards shone with polish.

Julian said, 'When we first came here, I couldn't understand why my ancestors built such large rooms. Now I find I need the space. I need to get away and think.'

'You're thinking that Mrs Maggs gave us a hint as to where to look for the tractor that broke into the amusement park and you're wondering what she meant by it.'

'She told us to look east. Why? What does she know that we don't? Has she heard something on the grapevine but can't be sure it can be relied on? It would be like her to hint but not actually point the finger.'

He flung himself into the chair his grandfather had always used, the throne-like one in the centre of the long oak table. When he'd first inherited the Hall, he hadn't wanted to sit in that chair but Bea noticed he'd grown into it recently.

Bea said, 'You've met all your neighbours to the east by now?'

'I've met them, yes. I can't say we hit it off. They made it clear the Hall should not have been left to a bean counter who – and I quote – doesn't understand what is expected of those fortunate enough to inherit property. They told me that I should join this and contribute to that. Unfortunately these are not causes I would choose to back. They are silkily rude to Polly. Well, all except for Lady Knighton, but she's been out of the picture recently.'

Bea said, 'Describe the neighbours you don't get along with.'

'First and foremost there's his lordship, multi-billionaire, on to his third wife and still pinching bottoms. Something in the City. He bought a Georgian mansion, added a swimming pool and a helipad, installed cameras and electronic gates. Private plane. A-lister parties. Looks rather like a vulture and acts like one too. Tried to goose Polly at a drinks party.'

'What did she do to him?'

'Made his eyes water. Got him amidships. He had to pretend he was having a coughing fit. We haven't been invited since.'

'So he's Lord Loadsa money,' said Bea. 'Influential. Mostly lives in the South of France or somewhere similar? Hordes of hangers-on?'

'Indeed. Then there's Lady Knighton's son, married to someone frosty and double-barrelled. He's our local MP, tipped for cabinet office, chair of everything in sight, on the telly every now and then. He and his wife are away somewhere at the moment. Holidays. Cayman Islands? Can't remember. He's somewhat portly and it's ludicrous to think of him or his wife, or indeed of his friend the multi-billionaire, breaking into the park at night and digging for gold.'

Bea giggled and finally Julian allowed himself to grin.

Julian's phone rang and he answered it. The call was from Lance, that expert on the restoration of old properties, who was currently guiding Julian through what could be done at the Hall. Lance wanted to talk about what had happened that day so Bea took a hike down the long room while Julian reassured Lance that the workmen could get back in on the morrow.

Bea thought it was interesting that Lance had bypassed the major to speak to Julian. Did that mean Lance didn't trust the major? Or what?

She scrolled down on her own phone to find Rosemary's smartphone number. It niggled at her that Rosemary had left Julian so abruptly. It wasn't like her.

'Rosemary? It's Bea Abbot here. I'm down at Marston Hall for a few days and Julian told me you had to leave unexpectedly. Are you all right?'

'I've been expecting your call. Are you alone? Because if not, can this wait till you are?'

Bea looked back at Julian, who was frowning as he listened to what Lance was saying. She said, 'Is all well with you?'

'Yes, of course.'

Bea said, 'Is this about Captain Courageous? He got rid of you. How?'

'With malice aforethought. Ring me when you're by yourself and out of the Hall.'

Bea rang off. That remark about the major had been a shot in the dark, but it sounded as if it had found its mark. Bea couldn't think how he'd managed to get rid of someone as competent as Rosemary, but then, she'd seen him undermining Julian, trying to make out that he couldn't cope. So . . . what was the major's aim? To be given a free hand to run the estate as he wished? To skim off backhanders here and there? It couldn't just be that he wanted to run the estate his way, could it? Surely there must be more to it than that?

Buried gold, perhaps?

Well, that was probably all in Mr Colston's imagination.

Julian could sack the major now, but needed proof of wrong-doing. The man had already had one written warning, but if taken to court, that wouldn't be sufficient reason to sack him.

Bea considered that a great many things had been happening lately, each demanding attention: the break-in and unidentified body; Pete's disappearance and that of Rosemary; the unhelpful-ness of the major, the state visit of Marcus and Mona.

None of these were connected, were they? No, of course not.

Each one must be solved separately. Pete was missing. So where was his body? And was he really a member of a London gang come down looking for buried treasure?

Was there any possible connection between the major and the break-in? No. How could there be?

Julian switched off his phone, and sat back in his chair.

Bea said, 'What made the intruders dig in the amusement

park? Have they found a map with X marking the place that hides the gold?'

'I've not heard of any such map. I can't see anything out of the ordinary where they were digging, either. There's a clump of shrubs there around a ruined stone grotto built in the eighteenth century. It's rapidly disappearing under ivy. I suppose the grotto might once have been considered a good place in which to hide treasure, but it's surely not old enough to be of that much interest. Anyway, the raiders don't seem to have unearthed anything of consequence.'

'How do you know that? Maybe they did find something and took it away with them. You think it was your local yobs who brought in their metal detectors to search the site?'

'It did cross my mind. But they're so young, so stupid. Yes, they did start off in a small way trying to nick alcohol from the farm shop, and went on to petty acts of vandalism. Yes, they do have enough money to purchase some metal detectors and I suppose I can see them daring one another to try a spot of treasure hunting in the park. But kill someone? No. They're the type who rings the bell and flees when the householder opens the door. If Pete had challenged them, I'd have expected them to run for it, not to stand and fight. And where did they come across the rough-looking man who died?'

'A clumsy attempt was made to pass the dead man off as Pete. Why? And why didn't Pete phone for reinforcements as soon as he spotted the invaders? Wouldn't you have expected him to use his phone to . . . Where is his phone, anyway? Was it on him?'

Julian rubbed his forehead. 'No, not that I've heard. Perhaps the police are right, and this was a raid plotted from London . . . although I wouldn't have thought it would be worthwhile for a London gang to bother. For a start, travel with tractor is not precisely a London gangster's usual mode of transport.'

'Perhaps someone was holidaying down here? Someone with local connections, who thought it would be fun to see if the legend were true? They borrowed a tractor—'

'From whom? A gangster on holiday doesn't have the clout to borrow an expensive piece of equipment and farmers don't rent them out for a spot of extra cash.'

Bea said, 'And would farmers hereabouts believe in buried treasure?'

'I don't believe in buried treasure, or in curses. Or rather, I believe that people like to think they exist. They fantasize that they'll become millionaires overnight. They fear that the magic might work if they were cursed. Their fear and their greed cause them to believe in both. Powerful stuff.'

Bea said, 'And you don't think it's a tractor, anyway. Something about the tyres don't look right?'

He sighed. 'I don't know all that much about tractors but yes, you're right.'

Bea tried a different tack. 'Talking of legends and curses, you've got to know the estate well. You used to ride around it first thing in the morning. Maybe you still do. Does any part of the estate speak to you in a special way? Is there anywhere you feel uneasy . . . or perhaps, joyful?'

He stared at her and through her. Started to speak. Shook his head. 'I suppose that . . . But it's half a mile from the Hall in the opposite direction to the amusement park. I've got a second-hand golf buggy for getting around the estate nowadays and I often take Pip to visit a particular meadow out to the west.

'I can't say exactly why, except that it's peaceful. It's no good for growing crops as it's on a steepish slope. There's a spring that rises there and keeps the grass green. The water trickles down the hillside into a small wood of old trees and then disappears. Lots of birdsong. It's Polly's favourite place. And Pip's. He sings to the birds and I swear they sing back. I'll take you there if we have time.'

He pulled himself to his feet with an effort. 'Time for bed?'

It had been a long day.

Bruno walked beside them as they returned through the house, crossed the yard and entered the estate office.

Polly had taken Pip upstairs, but lying at full length on the settee was a rangy, dark-haired man wearing the smug expression of a man content with life and with the whisky in the glass he was holding on his chest. Bea's husband, the portrait painter, Piers, lifted an arm in greeting.

Bea hadn't realized how much she'd missed him. 'Piers! When did you get in?'

'Just in time to help Polly up the stairs with the babe, who tried to tweak my nose and laughed when I protested.' He stood and held out his hand to Julian. 'I hear that you're coping well and have improvements going on left, right and centre. Not to mention bodies littering the landscape. You've started a local feud, I hear? Town against country?'

Julian smiled a welcome. 'Who told you that?'

'Polly. She couldn't wait for me to get through the door before she was giving me the rundown. She told me where you kept the whisky, too. Hope you don't mind. She also said you'd had a long day and I was to send you straight up to bed when you came in. She said Bea would fill me in on the detail.'

That was an order. Piers didn't often bother to exert himself for anything but the latest portrait, but he could do 'authority' when it was needed.

Julian said, 'I'm sorry to give you such a poor welcome, but it's true that it has been a difficult day. I'll go on up, then. You'll turn the lights off when you come up?'

He went up the stairs rather more slowly than usual, and Piers pulled Bea down on to the sofa beside him. 'You look tired, too.' He turned his head, listening. They heard Julian open the door to the master bedroom, greet Polly, and shut the door behind him. Then there was silence.

Piers kept his voice down. 'I wasn't going to come down today, but I had a phone call from someone who promised I'd find a weekend down here more amusing than painting a vacuous A-lister. What's going on?'

Bea jerked to attention. 'Who rang you? Surely not . . .! Rosemary rang you?'

'I felt honoured. I didn't think Rosemary ever needed to ask help from anyone. She wouldn't say why. Only that she thought you might need a helping hand and not to believe everything you're told.'

Bea laid her head on his shoulder. 'She warned me not to speak when I'm in company. Does she think these rooms have been bugged, and if so, why? I took her warning seriously, and so did you . . . which is why you were trying to work out whether or not Julian could hear us if we talked down here. Do you really think someone would take the trouble to put a bug in our bedroom here? I can't believe it. And yet . . . Oh, I don't know whether I'm on my head or my heels. Surely Julian wouldn't want to listen in on our conversations? No, I don't believe it.'

Piers finished his drink and put the glass aside. 'I learn much about my clients by observing the way they talk and either meet, or avoid my eye. In my opinion neither Julian nor Polly are guilty of anything but being tired out and worried to death about what's happening. Polly was all churned-up about local affairs and, yes, she's worried for Julian, but she was absolutely open with me. She thinks Julian is in danger. She says he can't understand what's happening and neither can she.

'Now you, my girl, are also all of a twitter. You're puzzled and angry. But you were delighted to see me, as I am to see you. So let's go to bed and get a good night's sleep. In the morning we'll walk out into the grounds and have a nice long chat about this and that and why Rosemary called me in. Right?'

SEVEN

Saturday, early morning

Early risers that they were, Bea and Piers were beaten to it by Julian, who had fed Pip and dressed him into some warm clothes by the time they got downstairs.

Julian said, 'I'm taking Pip out with me in the golf buggy for an early morning ride. Would you like to help yourselves to a drink or whatever you fancy? Polly will be down to make a big breakfast for us in half an hour or so.'

'Going somewhere special?' said Bea.

'Checking on the western gate. I have a feeling . . . It's not likely anyone's used it, but I want to be sure.' He left, taking Pip and Bruno with him.

Bea and Piers had a mug of coffee each, put on their jackets and went out for a wander. There was a light mist and a sheen of frost over the park. The sun was rising. Minute by minute the light was changing and the park emerged in all the richness of its autumn colours.

First, they inspected the work being done at the stables. Here was a work in progress, surrounded by scaffolding. On the left there was a row of boxes which used to house horses on the ground floor and living accommodation for the stable boys above. That whole block had been doubled in size by extending back into the park. Floors and roof had been extended to match, with the new roof tiles matching the old. The old frontage had been retained, together with the elegant central tower on which an ancient clock advertised the time as ten to three.

Below the clock, a new front door had been created, giving on to a hall with a staircase curling upwards to what would eventually be bedrooms on the first floor. The ancient wooden doors to the boxes had been removed awaiting the advent of new windows to replace them.

The stalls on the opposite side, backing on to the old Tithe

Barn, were only one storey high and had been left untouched for the time being. At the far end of the yard, there was a wooden gate leading to a farm track and pastures beyond.

The transformation was not yet complete, but promised to provide delightful – and private – living quarters for Julian and his family.

Piers and Bea leaned on the farm gate to look out over an empty paddock where once an animal rescue centre had kept their elderly horses. Bea wondered if Julian might one day keep a horse of his own there. Piers said he was full of admiration about the amount of electricity the Hall would generate from the solar panels on the back roof of the barn.

Bea was familiar with land to the east end of the house housing the library, but hadn't ventured as far as the park on the western side, the part which was overlooked by the long Portrait Gallery. So they went back along the length of the Tithe Barn and estate office to emerge into a scene of some neglect. Here were the crumbling brick walls of a walled garden and a wilderness of roses left to go wild. A project for next year or the one after?

The road here – it was more of a track – continued due west. As they strolled along, Bea told Piers everything she'd heard and observed.

In the end she said, 'I think all this – whatever it is – began with the appointment of the gallant major, but maybe I'm wrong. It might have been started by the lecture which Polly's father, Mr Colston, gave. I think he did it to make himself feel important. He didn't want his daughter to marry a nameless nobody, and now Julian's inherited the Hall, Mr Colston's having a hard time eating his words.

'He'd no occupation and no standing in the community till he discovered the cache of papers at the Hall and now he's writing a book and preparing scholarly papers about it. I expect he was just making mischief when he talked about there being buried treasure here. That would be like him. He's settled into the village here and enjoying his notoriety.'

Piers chuckled. 'You mean the villagers are meant to touch their caps when they see him, and call him "sir"? What happens if they don't pay him the respect he thinks is his due?'

'I presume he'd decide not to notice the omission.'

'You want me to tackle him?'

Bea put her arm through his. It was good to have him on board. 'I wonder if that awful old man would tell you if he really had found something of interest in those papers? I can't believe he made the whole thing up. He'd talk to you, especially if you said you were always pleased to come across an interesting face and looked at him in a measuring sort of way. Flattery might be the key to open that particular box.

'Perhaps he really has found mention of a long-lost holy relic from the Middle Ages, or a chest of coins buried when Roundheads were battling Cavaliers hereabouts. There must have been something to set him off on this buried treasure lark.'

Piers surveyed the sweep of parkland before them. 'Legends always accumulate about old houses. He might well have found something of interest in the old papers. The Hall itself has been pretty well pulled apart and put back together again recently. The priest's hole came to light, but nothing else of importance. I'm wondering if it's the land itself which inspired talk of wealth in the old days.'

Bea, too, looked at the park with interest. The track they were on led due west to a steep escarpment which descended into a small wood. This was Capability Brown's territory, and very picturesque it was, too.

Bea said, 'What do you mean, that the land brings wealth?'

Piers said, 'Consider what you see before you, both within and without the limits of the park. Some old woodland. Some good pasture, well watered, sheltered from the south winds by the Downs. It's been farmed for centuries for the benefit of the lord of the manor. There's a village on the doorstep to supply people to work the land and look after the lord and lady of the manor. There's easy access to an ancient town and thence to London. This is an old landscape, probably been farmed since Doomsday, or earlier. That Tithe Barn is far older than the house and its size confirms that this was land which produced a good income for whoever occupied it.'

Bea said, 'Apparently most of the farms around here did once belong to the Hall, but some were sold off over the years and I can't think there's ever been enough money around to warrant the legend of buried treasure.'

'What we think of as treasure now, might not seem so then.

Treasure comes in many shapes and sizes. Look at Cornwall. The land provided us with tin and lead. The north of England and Wales provided coal. Our shipping ports bring in fish and imports from all round the world. Each brings wealth in its wake. Has anyone been looking for a rare mineral here?'

Bea was doubtful. 'Would Mr Colston know about such things, or think they were important? Oh, do you think this is something that Marcus might have been interested in? Would a sniff of some rare metal being found here be enough to interest him? Surely, if anything like that had been going on, then someone local would have told Julian. The local yobs have been looking for buried treasure around the church, but that's all.'

Piers nodded. 'It's worth checking. I'll call on Mr Colston this morning. See if he'll open up to me.'

They walked on in silence, while Bea considered how interesting it was that one man would think of wealth as being something originating from the land, while she still thought of man-made trinkets, of gold and silver coins. She recalled stories of monks burying their church silver plate when threatened by a hostile ruler. And what of the hoard of jewellery and other precious items, hidden in a wall in London by a jeweller in Tudor times and only found recently?

Before that, hadn't hoards of coins been buried as the tide of war pushed this way and that during the Wars of the Roses? Earlier still, there'd been jewellery buried with Roman burials, and before that, precious artefacts had been put in the graves of the Angles and Saxons who'd lived hereabouts.

Was Julian a throwback to an Angle or a Saxon? And did she know the difference? Didn't the Angles occupy the east and gave their name to East Anglia, etc? Which meant that this part of the country was probably settled by the Saxons? Not that it mattered much. Well, probably if you uncovered an ancient grave, you might need to know which was which.

Piers looked at his watch. 'Do you think breakfast's ready? What are you planning to do today?'

'I'd like to set up a meeting with Rosemary, if that's possible – she left here all of a sudden and is not easy to contact – and I'll see what Polly might like me to help her with. Let's hope no other bodies have been found overnight.'

No more bodies had been found, and Polly was setting the table for breakfast when they returned. Julian was also there, stripping Pip, who'd apparently gone for a swim while they'd been out. Pip was happy about it. Julian was half amused, and half annoyed.

'All that rain the other night. Our favourite meadow has been flooded. Pip took one look and plunged into the water before I could stop him. I had to bring him straight back and we never even got as far as the western gate!'

Polly dished up a full English breakfast. 'Pip's a water baby. He's always liked water. I never know which are the water signs but whichever they are, he's one of them.'

Her mouth curved into a reminiscent smile. 'The water there is always so . . . soothing.' And she giggled.

Bea told herself not to raise her eyebrows, or show any sign of understanding what Polly and Julian had been up to. Water baby, indeed! Conceived at the spring? The very thought of it made Bea smile.

Polly said, 'Come and sit down. We need a good breakfast before we face the day. Bea, Piers? Tea is all right for you? I'm afraid I can't do coffee at the moment. I was all right when carrying Pip, but the next baby objects to coffee.'

Julian installed Pip in a high chair which looked as antique as the one in the kitchen, saying, 'He knows something's up and he's playing up.' He bent down to his son's level. 'Pip, listen to me. Mummy's a bit tired today, so we must all try to help her. Understood?'

Pip stared up at his father. Bea thought the boy understood very well what his father was saying, but was not sure that he'd agree to behave.

Julian sighed, and got out his phone. 'I've just remembered. I've got a meeting set up with the major to go through the list of repairs in the village, and Lance wants a word, too. Only, I have to collect Beauty from the vet's first. Tyra won't be able to cope with Beauty at the moment, so—'

Polly started feeding Pip with one hand and spooning scrambled egg into herself with the other. 'No, Julian, you can't bring that dog here. I simply can't cope.'

'I know that.' He spoke into the phone. 'Is that the vet's?

Julian Marston-Lang here.' He listened, clicked off. 'Beauty's fine; just the three live pups. Mother and babies all doing well. I can collect her any time. If I go now, I could be back within the hour. I'll message Ian to say I'll see him half an hour later.'

Julian scooped up another mouthful, gulped some tea and spoke into his phone again. 'Sorry I didn't get back to you last night, but . . .'

The landline rang. Bea picked it up. A quavering female voice, 'Oh, dear, oh dear. Is Sir Julian there? I'm really not up to it, you know. All these terrible things happening! My diverticulitis is playing up something . . .'

Pip had been given a spoon to bang the feeding tray with. He banged. And opened his mouth for another spoonful. Then turned his head away so that the food spattered over his cheek and clean clothes. He'd decided he was not going to behave. Oh dear.

Polly heaved, but made it to the kitchen sink in time to throw up. Julian looked anxious but she waved him away, saying, 'I'm all right.'

Pip examined the food in his plate, and tried to get some on to his spoon and then into his mouth. And spat it out.

Piers had an ability to turn off everything going on around him. Lucky Piers. He took Bea's uneaten bacon on to his own plate and reached for more toast.

Bea soothed the woman on the phone. 'I'll tell Sir Julian. Thank you for letting us know.' She switched the phone to taking messages, and reached for the last of the toast saying, 'Your secretary has just gone off sick.'

Julian was looking at his watch again. 'There's a couple of messages on my phone that I'll try to deal with on the way to collect Beauty. The pub wants to know if we'll switch on the Christmas lights at the end of November. I know that they have to think of these things in advance, but . . . that reminds me, Polly. Someone asked if we throw a party for the volunteer stewards at the Hall at Christmas. I assume we do. Can you check? And yes, I'm off. Beauty will need bedding and some food. I'll try to collect her things from Tyra, if she's back home and if not, I'll stock up at the vet. Bea, did you say Mrs Thing can't make it?'

'She says she can't. What's she supposed to be doing this morning? Can I help?'

'Can you take notes of what's decided at the meeting with the major? Otherwise, he'll alter the schedule to suit himself. Would you . . . could you . . . do it?'

'Of course.'

Polly looked pale, sipping a glass of water. Pip grinned at her, his spoon more or less in his mouth. She sat down, picked up his spoon, gagged and removed herself, breathing deeply, to stand by the window.

Piers took the last slice of toast and ladled butter on to it. He never got indigestion, no matter what he ate.

Julian drained his mug, and said, 'I must be off. Polly, my dear, this can't go on. Ring Kylie and ask her to find someone to help you. I'll leave Bruno here on guard.'

He kissed Polly and Pip – on the top of his head which was about the only part of him not liberally daubed with food – grabbed his laptop, checked he had his keys, and fled.

Bea took Polly's place and set about getting the rest of the food into Pip. Over her shoulder, she said, 'Polly, Julian's right. You can be a full-time wife and mother but not when you're expecting the next and not when you're supposed to be playing the role of Lady Bountiful on the side. Ring Kylie. Or Mrs Maggs. Or Jenny. And Julian had better find himself another Mrs Thing – that's not really her name, is it? – or I will. Or get Rosemary back.'

'I wish! Such bad timing, her going away just now. But Bea, it's not always like this. Or not every day.'

Piers started to clear the table. 'I know when I'm in the way. I'll stack the dishwasher and wander down to the village.'

Bea finished feeding Pip, and began to clean him up. Polly was right – he did like water. He actually enjoyed being cleaned up and inserted into clean clothing. Bea reckoned this was the third outfit he'd had on that day. She set him down on the floor and watched him try to work out how to walk. It wouldn't be long till he was scooting around all over the place, and then, thought Bea, the little family would have another problem on their hands.

Polly seemed too exhausted to do anything. Too exhausted even to yell for help.

Bea said, 'I'm going to organize someone to look after Pip. All right?'

The very smallest of nods from Polly. 'I know it's only sensible, but I hate the thought of letting someone else look after him. I'll take him with me this morning. I've an appointment in town at ten. The local embroidery group are showing in the church there, and I want to see the exhibition because they're thinking of setting it up here at some point. I'm sure there's something else I promised to do, but I can't think what it was for the life of me. I'll get going in a minute.' Polly closed her eyes and relaxed. It might be only nine in the morning but she was worn out.

Bea rang Mrs Maggs to explain the position. Polly was tired and pregnant. Pip was lively and about to walk. Julian was beleaguered on every side. Query: who do you think could help?

Mrs Maggs said, 'Ah. Yes. Seen that coming. My niece, not Kylie, but her younger sister. Should be doing her A levels but she's not really academic, as you might say. Good with animals and small children. Thinking of training to be a nurse but not done anything about it yet. She could leave school now, start tomorrow.'

Bea was soothing. 'Yes, of course. Very suitable. But perhaps we ought to throw the net a bit wider and interview several people? We don't want people talking of favouritism, do we? I was thinking of asking Jenny if she knew of someone who might . . .?'

She let the suggestion die on the air. There was a sound from the phone as if Mrs Maggs were tapping her teeth. Finally she said, 'I suppose it might be a good idea to spread things out a bit.'

And your protégée didn't sound all that promising, did she?

Mrs Maggs said, 'Well, I can't think of anyone else. Except . . . I suppose one of the girls who lives in Crook Cottage might do in a pinch. Never finished school due to a bad bout of something or other with a long name that I can't remember. Eighteen now, or maybe nineteen? She's been helping out at the dairy in town, but the foreman there wants the job for his girlfriend that he's got moving in with them, and that's created some tensions, I can tell you.'

'This girl is one of Jenny's extended family?'

'There's some as says so but it's a right mix-up, that lot, getting into the sack with their cousins as would have been better if they hadn't, if you see what I mean. But this girl's all right, so long as you don't shout at her. She doesn't like being shouted at. And I don't think she's on too many pills now.'

Bea told herself not to laugh. Mrs Maggs was doing her best to ensure her own relative got the job, wasn't she?

'Mrs Maggs, let's put our family feuds aside for the moment, shall we? I need your honest opinion. Without fear or favour. Which girl would be best for Lady Polly and Pip?'

'There's no denying that I'd like it for my niece . . . well, there'd be no harm giving the other a chance, like. I could get them to come up for an interview and then maybe they could have a week's trial, say. My niece has got a bicycle, could be with you quick, and the other can walk up from the village. If young Pip takes to one of them, then we could see if it would work out. And tell Lady Polly not to forget to take Jenny's mixture that she sent up last week.'

'Lady Polly would be free for interviews this afternoon, I think. Let me know if and when they can come.'

Bea shut off the phone just as young Pip tripped over his feet and landed on his face. He didn't yell. He shook his head to clear it, and then tried to get to his feet again.

Polly had fallen asleep.

Bea helped Pip up, and let him hold on to her finger while he navigated his way around the big chair till he got to his mother.

'Down!' he ordered. Did that mean 'up'?

Bea helped him up on to the settee, where he found his favourite toy giraffe. He nestled into his mother's side with the giraffe and crooned to himself.

Bea looked at her watch and set about making the room ready for the scheduled meeting about repairs in the village. She wondered what Julian would arrange for Beauty. If she knew him at all, he wouldn't dump the dog on just anybody. No, he'd probably take the dog on himself . . . which was what Polly was afraid he was going to do. Julian really was a soft touch, wasn't he?

Question? How do you have a business meeting in a room containing a sleeping mother and baby? Correction: baby about to throw himself off the settee, only to be caught just in time. What do you do with the baby? She had no idea of a baby's routine nowadays.

The phone kept recording messages, the dishwasher worked through its cycle and Bea spotted a pile of Pip's discarded clothing which could do with a wash.

And the phone . . . No, it was her own smartphone this time. She answered it with Pip in her arms.

It was Julian. 'Sorry, Bea. I rang the landline, but no answer. Is Polly there? I've been held up but Beauty's all right, lovely pups and she's coping well. Her leg isn't broken, just strained, which is good. I phoned the hospital. They're sending Tyra home; mother and baby doing well. I'll check that Jenny can get someone to look after her. Returning to an empty house with a missing husband is not going to be easy for Tyra.

'Ian is due at half nine to discuss repairs in the village. We've had to rearrange the date a couple of times and there's stuff I really want to look at. Lance is coming straight after. We can't meet in the main house, because it's open to visitors today. Can you give them some decaffeinated coffee? It doesn't upset Polly so much. Is she all right? She can be fine for a couple of days and then . . . they say it's normal, but I do worry. Tell her I'll be another half an hour. Can you cope?'

'Yes, of course.' Though she wasn't at all sure she could. Julian rang off, and Polly stirred herself, saying, 'What time is it? Where's Julian? I should be . . . where is it I'm supposed to be?'

Bea said, 'You're supposed to be meeting some people in town. Couldn't you cancel? I've arranged for a couple of young girls to come up this afternoon to apply for the post of nanny for Pip. Now, Julian rang to say he's been held up, but Ian and Lance are due to arrive any minute. What do you want to do?'

Polly heaved herself to her feet and took Pip from Bea. 'I'm still half asleep. I don't want to stay for the meeting. They're not at ease with one another. Julian says Ian is trying to get rid of Lance, and vice versa. So wearing. We need them both. If only Rosemary hadn't been called away.'

'Couldn't you get her back?'

Polly shook her head, easing her back. 'No, we can't. We'll manage, somehow. It's not ideal, living here. We should be able to move into our new quarters in the stables soon, but for now, well, it's better if I keep moving. I'll take Pip over to the kitchen, and see if Mrs Maggs will look after him till Julian gets back. And then I must be off.'

Polly tested Pip to see if he had a wet nappy, looked relieved, and departed, saying, 'Come on, my love. Mrs Maggs spoils you, doesn't she? And there's an old playpen we can put up in the corner and a mountain of toys. People will keep bringing you toys! You love it in the kitchen, don't you? You like to see people and to interact with them.'

Bea watched Polly cross the yard and into the Hall. She wondered which of the two local girls would get the job of looking after Pip. Of course Bea had nannies on her books at the agency, but under the circumstances it seemed best to employ someone local.

Also, accommodation in the village was at a premium. Rosemary had lived in her own mobile home, but if Bea had brought someone down from London, where would she live?

A tap on the door, and in came Bristles. He was early, wasn't he? And Julian wouldn't be back for a while, and the major was due. Oh dear. Whatever next?

EIGHT

Saturday morning

His name wasn't 'Bristles', of course.

Bea had called him that in her mind when she first met him because he'd been trying to grow a beard. His name was Lance and he was a renowned expert and restorer of old buildings. He had a reputation for keeping his temper and his workforce. Admittedly, he did look like a jobbing plumber, being somewhat square in body and devoted to an elderly leather jacket, but there was nothing wrong with his brains. And, they'd always got along.

'Morning, Mrs Abbot.'

'Good to see you, Lance. Julian's going to be a bit late, and the major is expected any minute.'

'He'll have to put up with me hanging around. I really need to speak to Julian today. It's good to see you. Was that your husband I passed on the way through the village? Is he down here to paint the local VIPs?'

Bea grinned. 'Possibly. He's gone to see Mr Colston.'

'Oh. Ah. You know that he's moved in with one of the Marston-Lang sisters in the village?' A guarded tone. He was being polite, wasn't he?

'It sounds most suitable. Any news of Pete?'

He shook his head. 'It's upsetting. He's well liked.'

'At least you're not pretending he's dead. Julian's having a hard time convincing the constabulary that the body he found was not Pete. We found Pete's dog . . . Ah, you know about that?'

'He rang me as I was on my way over. Asked if it would be all right to keep Beauty in one of the stalls in the stables, so that he can keep an eye on her. Sounds good. I've warned my men to keep away. Nursing mothers can bite.'

They both grinned. Was he only referring to Beauty? Or to Polly, who most certainly could bite?

He put his laptop and a file of papers on the table. 'Mrs Thing not turned up?'

'Her diverticulitis. What's her real name? I can't keep on calling her Mrs "Thing"?'

'What's that?' A sharp voice. The major had arrived, also carrying a laptop but no files. 'We have to respect our workforce at all times.'

Lance said, without emphasis, 'Her name is Mrs Tring. Did you think I was mis-calling her?'

Bea thought, Ouch! They actually hate one another!

The major took a seat at the table, and shot his cuffs. 'Well, I see Julian's late again.'

Lance took a seat opposite him. 'He shouldn't be long.'

'I suppose he's out rescuing another of his lame ducks?' He consulted his watch. 'I don't have time to waste. You may be able to leave your men to get on with things by themselves but I like to make a plan and stick to it.'

Implying that Lance wasn't doing his job properly?

Bea said, 'Coffee, gentlemen? I'm afraid it's only instant.'

Lance shook his head. 'That's kind of you, but no thank you.'

The major didn't even bother to look Bea's way. Just shook his head.

You don't like women much, do you? Did someone say you are engaged to a VIP hereabouts?

The major consulted his watch. 'You'd think common courtesy . . .! But what can you expect when you try to do everything yourself? I've told him . . . but he's losing it, I fear. Did you hear he didn't even recognize his own security guard's body? Shock, of course. Understandable, but it does make my life more difficult.'

Lance said nothing to that. Bea took a seat away from the table, and opened her own laptop. She also set her smartphone to record. Lance sat like a piece of rock. Quietly self-contained. Not making waves.

The major fidgeted. 'I'd have thought he would want to be here, if only to find out why the work on the stable block is taking so long.'

Lance stirred. 'New windows. Some delay. To be expected.'

'You should have made it clear you're only seeing this as a small concern. With another, bigger firm, we'd have been done by now.'

Lance yawned. 'Conservation area. Takes time.'

'Builders always take for ever. Well, at least I've got those two cottages in the village ready for sale. They'll fetch a pretty price.'

Lance said, 'Not my department. Have you checked their leases?'

'There were two old dears living in them, couldn't look after themselves, on their last legs, already in the care home in town. They'll be no problem. I have a waiting list of people wanting to buy down here. People who can pay far more than the locals.'

Lance sighed. 'City folk, working from home? Not wanting to mix with the locals? Causing parking problems with their big cars? Complaining that a cockerel wakes them up at five in the morning? Do we really want any more of those?'

The major fizzed with energy. 'Of course we do. Mind you, if there were only a golf course locally, we could up the price even further.'

Lance shook his head. Closed his eyes. 'Sir Julian won't want to sell.'

'Of course he will. He needs the money to get the amusement park back on track again. I understand there's someone interested in investing in new rolling stock. That should make a difference.'

Is he referring to Marcus, who wants to play with a grown-up train set? Ah. Didn't Marcus say he'd come across the major somewhere before? Is this a link set up by the major? Does Julian know about this?

A car drew up outside, and the major said, 'About time, too!'

Bruno barked, again and again. Men's voices. Bea went to see what was happening outside.

Yes, Julian had arrived. Some of Lance's workmen were crowding around his car. Bruno was darting around them, getting under their feet.

'Quiet, now,' said Julian. 'Don't distress her. Hi, Lance. Are we OK with this? There, now; Beauty, it's going to be all right. We'll look after you till your master gets back.'

One of the men lifted the beautiful black and white collie dog out of the boot of the car and carried her into the box at the far end of the stables, while a second brought a basket containing her squeaking puppies. A third brought her bedding and some tins of food and a bowl for water.

Bruno jumped up and down, whining.

Bea watched, fascinated, as Julian helped one of the workmen settle mother and babies in the end stable. It was dark in there, and warm. Beauty seemed to like it. Julian said they'd leave the top of the door closed and the bottom half open so Beauty could get in and out. Food and drink were laid out. Bruno frisked around, making it clear he was in charge of his new family.

At last Julian stood back, suggesting they all gave the new mother space. The workmen nodded, knowing whose dog this was. One volunteered to look in on Beauty and see that she was fed and watered at appropriate intervals.

'Thank you for being so understanding,' Julian said. 'And so, back to work for all of us.'

Bruno wanted to stay and guard Beauty. Julian said he might do so, but he was *not* to attack visitors. Right?

So they returned to the delayed meeting.

The three men sat around the table. Bea provided Julian with a cup of coffee – only instant, unfortunately – and settled herself in the background with her laptop and phone.

Ian harrumphed. 'Well, now we've finally—'

Julian cut across him. 'Apologies. I know you're both busy men. To bring you up to date on what's been happening: Tyra and her baby have been discharged from hospital, both doing well. Jenny is seeing to it that someone goes in to look after the new mother. There's no news of Pete, but we've rescued his dog and her pups, and will keep them here for the time being.'

The major looked pleased. 'Good news for once. This means Pete's cottage becomes free. It's in good nick. Tyra will probably go back to London or wherever it is she came from, and I'll put her place on the market. There shouldn't be any trouble getting rid of it as I have a growing list of city-dwellers gagging to buy down here.'

'Not so fast,' said Julian. 'Pete's not dead, and I'm not having Tyra upset by your suggesting she has to vacate her cottage.'

'Oh. Well, I suppose we have to wait till after the inquest.' He produced some paperwork. 'Meanwhile, the builders need paying for this last month's work in the village. If you can see to it . . .?'

Julian looked at the papers, and stiffened. 'These bills are a bit steep. They're charging almost double what the local builders quoted, aren't they?'

The major rolled his eyes. 'The builder I work with is first class. The local lot are fine to fix a dripping tap, but not in the same league as the people I've used.'

Julian steepled his fingers and looked at the major over them. 'I thought I'd made it clear that I'd prefer to use local people, wherever possible.'

The major opened his mouth to object, shot a glance at Lance, and shrugged. 'We'll discuss it when I'm not so pressed for time.'

Julian sighed. 'Yes, that would be the right thing to do.' He turned to Lance. 'I know you have a meeting this afternoon, so shall we take your report first?'

The major huffed. 'That would be most inconvenient. I have an appointment to meet with some possible buyers in the village this afternoon. I told you I could get you a good price for those two cottages. I guarantee you'll be pleased to hear the price they're willing to pay. Perhaps it will now be possible, to restock the amusement park, with help from our well-to-do friend. Congratulations are in order, right?'

Julian looked at the major through half-closed eyes. 'Sorry, Ian. I thought you understood the system. You were only able to work on those two properties because the tenants had to go into care for a while. I know they're still in the care home, but they worked as gardener and chauffeur for the Hall all their adult lives and their leases are for life.'

The major simpered. 'They're both very frail. One of them has got acute bronchitis and the other's on borrowed time, too.

I'll give them each a fifty pound note – which is more than they've seen in a while, I can tell you, but it pays to be generous – in exchange for the cancellation of the rest of their lease. That way, the properties come back on to the market.'

Lance closed his eyes and withdrew himself from the conversation.

Julian's jaw tightened. 'No, Ian. No. I said I didn't want to sell off any more property and I meant it. If my tenants are too frail to live by themselves any longer and have to go into care, then we'll have to consult our solicitor about how to end their leases, but I am not selling. I must make a note to pay them a visit soonest.'

He flicked a glance at Bea, who made a note.

The major thumped the table. 'This is the outside of enough, Julian. You employ me to guide you through territory of which you have no experience. You asked me to get the estate up and running again, and that is what I am doing. You know nothing of how these things work, but I do. You really must learn to trust me.'

'I can read a lease. I listen and I learn. I'm not selling off any more property.'

The major reddened. 'Can't you see that this is the only way forward? I heard you've recovered what your family had stashed away in foreign banks, but that's gone to pay for what was needed to be done at the Hall itself. You've got the farm shop and the restaurant working again, but it's going to be a while before you recover all the money you've had to lay out.

'Instead of concentrating on getting the amusement park restarted, you've chosen to splash out on converting the stables, and getting a crew to make a film there, for heaven's sake! You're deep in debt, running around in a car that's only fit for the junk yard, and you turn down the money the cottages will bring you? This is not reasonable.'

Julian said, in the mildest of tones, 'But Ian, you agreed with me that making a film would be an excellent advertisement for the Hall. It only takes a day or two every now and then.'

What's this? Julian really is bringing in a camera crew? Marcus said something about that, didn't he? My word, a camera crew! That would be expensive and I suppose it does seem a little strange that he's going ahead with all the work at the stables when so much else needs doing. So where is he getting the money from?

The major's colour had risen. 'Tchah! More expense! I'm beginning to wonder . . . oh, of course you've had a bad time . . . we must all make allowances . . . but you really should ask yourself if you are quite up to the job.'

There was a very nasty silence.

Lance hadn't stirred. Hadn't heard? Had decided not to hear?

Julian steepled his fingers. In a quiet voice, he said, 'You are questioning my judgement?'

'I think anyone would. It's my job to run the estate, and you are preventing me from doing so.'

'No,' said Julian. 'It's your job to carry out my decisions. You may consider my judgement ill-advised, and you may give me your opinion, but I carry the can, not you. If I drive the estate bankrupt because I have not cared to follow your advice, then that's on my head, not yours.'

'I would not wish to be associated with . . .' The major stopped, seeing where this might lead. He backtracked. 'Of course you're the boss and entitled to be, well, eccentric. Naturally I obey your orders. Very well, the cottages remain in the tenants' hands. Though how I'm going to explain that to the people who are arriving this afternoon for a viewing, I do not know. I can't just say that you've decided to withdraw them from the market for personal reasons. Perhaps I could show them around, save them the journey . . .?'

Julian shook his head. 'No. They mustn't be given false hopes.'

The major slammed his laptop shut, and stood. 'I implore you to take my advice, Julian. For your own sake.'

Julian didn't react. 'I hear you.'

The major picked up his laptop. 'Well, if you will excuse me, I have to go and disappoint some people who wanted to give us a king's ransom.'

'Of course.' Julian dipped his head.

The major showed his teeth. All of them. And shot out of the room, barely holding on to his temper.

There was a silence which gradually became warmer. Lance

opened his eyes, and his file of papers. Julian indicated that Bea join them around the table, which she did.

Lance said, 'The major needs this job. I made enquiries. He's had similar jobs to this in the past and always been passed on with the highest of references. He's from a decent, middle-class family. Well educated, well connected. Engaged to a woman with her own business. The only thing I could find that raised a question is that the wedding date has been deferred, twice.'

Julian nodded. 'Agreed. Also, he's not interested in other women. I haven't had a single complaint about him trying to flirt with any of the village girls, or any of the older women either. Lance, give me your feelings, your wild suspicions, whatever. Things that wouldn't stand up in court.'

Lance said, 'My men don't like to talk to him. There's an unease whenever he's around. There's gossip which they aren't passing on to me, because I'm the boss. I suspect – but cannot prove – that he's taking a backhander whenever he arranges a repair in the village, and he will take a cut as and when he can sell one of the cottages that might come on to the market.'

'That's my understanding, too. That bill from his builder is grossly inflated and yes, I suspect he's taking a rake-off on it. But so far I can't prove it. No one will talk because they think he has the power to turn them out of their cottages if they do. Jenny's set a good example; perhaps they'll follow her lead in future. Now, let's have your report. Do you know when the windows for the stables' conversion are expected? And, mustn't forget, I have another date for filming. The fifth. They're very pleased with what they've got so far. How does that fit in with your schedule?'

Lance looked over at Bea. 'Mrs Abbot is trying to hide shock horror at your extravagance. She's worrying that you've been getting into debt.'

Bea closed her mouth and made up her mind. She trusted Julian's expertise. 'No, I trust him implicitly with regard to money. He'll have a good reason for doing . . . whatever it is.'

Julian laughed. 'Yes, I do. I'll tell you later. Meanwhile, Lance, have we a possible date for moving into at least part of our new quarters in the stables? Polly is having difficulty with the stairs, and doing office work here is proving tricky. Something else to add to your list. Do you have the name of a decent landscape gardener? Polly would like to beautify the stable yard, make it into a pretty courtyard. The film people would like that, too. Also, what are we going to do to make the stables private? We don't really want the world and his wife gawking at us as we let Pip out to play in the yard.'

Lance said, 'I was thinking you need electronic gates at either end. Expensive, but should give you the privacy you need. I'll get some quotes. Now, the windows . . .'

The meeting proceeded as planned. A quick overview; questions raised and dealt with. Decisions made on this and that. Dates suggested; possible and more probable. Lance said his men should be out of the top floor at the Hall any day now, but he wanted to check on the fitments for . . . this and that.

Bea took notes. She hadn't had to do this for many a long year, and found herself having to concentrate to keep up with these two lively minds. When they'd run through everything, she said, 'It's none of my business, I know, but you need a good PA. Your Mrs Tring is not much cop. What really happened to Rosemary?'

The two men looked away from one another. Lance shook his head. 'She was called away. Family matter.'

Julian said, 'The major got at her and she decided to leave. She was in a difficult position.'

Lance's eyes met Bea's, and looked away, quickly. A certain suspicion formed in her mind. Bea blinked. Could it possibly be that the major had suggested that Rosemary and Julian might have . . .? No, surely not! But something pretty important must have happened to cause Rosemary to turn tail and run for the hills. Whatever it was, Lance knew. Or suspected that he knew. And wasn't going to put it into words.

Bea said, 'Can we get her back?'

Lance shot a look at Julian and then shook his head. 'Let sleeping dogs lie.'

Bea said, 'Very well. But you must have someone to sort you out, Julian. Someone local, who knows what's really going on.'

'I agree. Ideally they should be local and understand local

affairs because I don't think I'm halfway to understanding what's going on in the neighbourhood at the moment. I do know of someone who might well be perfect for the job, but I'm not sure she'd want it. Also, if she did take over here, she'd probably need somewhere to live and the major would be against letting someone from the village rent one of the newly done-up cottages, wouldn't he?'

Lance smiled. 'An interesting thought.'

Julian consulted his watch. 'Now, I must check on Beauty, remind Bruno that his main duty is to look after us and not to guard the new mother. And then I want to get down to the village to see what the major's up to. I don't trust him an inch.'

He stood up, and stretched. And laughed. 'Do you know, when I took Bruno into the vet's this morning and he saw that Beauty had pupped, well, you never saw a dog look so astonished! I'm not sure he realizes he's a father. Beauty is recovering well from her ordeal and it looks as if she's going to be a good mother. Her leg isn't broken but she needs rest.'

'Good, good,' said Lance, also rising to his feet. 'My men will look after her.'

Julian said, 'Bea, our apologies; we invite you down to the country for a quiet weekend and look what happens. Would you mind if I leave you to your own devices for a bit? I'm not sure that Polly's up to much today. Fortunately it's a Saturday so she won't have to worry about the nursery and can take it easy. Wait a minute; didn't she say she needed to go somewhere . . . and see Lady Knighton. Was that today?'

Bea said she would check on Polly. She said she had plans of her own and not to worry. Somewhat relieved, Julian followed Lance out.

Once the men had gone, Bea tidied up and went across to the Hall to check on Pip. Polly had gone about her own business, but Pip was happily playing in an antique playpen, with a couple of Mrs Maggs's entourage keeping an eye on him.

Bea sorted out in her mind what she wanted to do first. She got on her phone and arranged to meet up with Piers in the village in a couple of hours' time, and then she drove to the farm shop and restaurant. The car park was almost full, which augured well for business.

What a difference there was from her first sight of this place under the old regime! Not a scrap of litter to be seen! Paintwork shining. Notices all in order. Saplings had been planted around the patio outside the restaurant, and people were sitting at the outdoor benches in the autumn sunshine.

Bea ate at the restaurant, which was so clean, it sparkled. There was a limited menu – freshly prepared food, good quality, reasonably priced. The pastries were out of this world and the coffee was acceptable if not to die for. There was excellent service by local young people. Almost every table was taken, not only by tourists, but by families and older people who had travelled from the town and surrounding countryside to eat there.

Who was in charge? Bea looked for the manager, that wonderful baker, Kate, but there was no sign of her. A middle-aged woman who looked very much like Kate but who was probably a little younger seemed to be in charge. Had something happened to Kate?

Bea left the restaurant to find the car park was full with an overflow on the verges. Mm. Hadn't she heard that Julian was having a tussle with the local council about expanding the car park?

Bea made her way to the farm shop, which was also busy. Imran's father and mother ran the village store and post office, and their only son had gone to university and worked in many different jobs till Julian had appointed him manager of the farm shop.

Bea looked around the shop, noting the buzz of success here. The shelves were well stocked by someone who understood how to lay out goods to attract customers, and there were plenty of them around. Ching! Ching! Cash flowed and debit cards were flashed. All the tills were busy.

She spotted Imran talking to someone who was shelf-filling a new consignment of Christmas cakes. He looked much as she remembered: dark, sharp, civilized and intelligent. He caught sight of Bea, and excused himself.

'Mrs Abbot, good to see you again. Would you like to have a

look at what we're planning for Christmas? Hampers of different sizes, filled with different products. Gift tags attached. We're thinking about a raffle, too, to benefit a children's charity. What do you think?'

'Excellent. Might I have five minutes of your time in private?'

He gave her an old-fashioned look and led her up some stairs, through a busy office which had a large window overlooking the shop floor below, into a smaller one which was clearly the centre of the operation. He offered her a chair, tea and coffee, and waited for her to explain herself.

She said, 'You know how much the neighbourhood needs the income from the farm shop, restaurant and visits to the Hall itself. You and your family are part of it now. If the estate prospers, so does everyone who lives in the village, who works here and on the surrounding farms. You understand, perhaps better than anyone else here, what Sir Julian and Lady Polly are trying to do.'

He was wary. He said, 'They gave me the opportunity to do this job. I love it. I hope they are pleased with me.'

'You know they are.'

A slight smile. 'Sir Julian drops in every now and again, never at the same time of day. He talks to all the staff, knows their names, who's related to who. He knows what sells best, and who is off form. He leaves me to get on with things, rarely makes any suggestions. He's a good boss.'

Bea said, 'Yes, I think he is. This problem with those yobs trying to steal from you, messing you around. Has that stopped now?'

A wary look. 'Yes, the security men have made a big difference.'

'It's terrible about the missing security man.'

'Pete. And his dog. Beauty is an excellent rat catcher and Pete is always ready to lend a hand when we need the odd job done. They are both great favourites with us. Even now the staff are putting together a box of goodies to take to Tyra.'

And that was code for saying he believed Julian when he said the dead man wasn't Pete. Good.

'Did you see the body of the dead man?'

'Yes. The major didn't want us trampling over the site before the police arrived, but I couldn't let Sir Julian go into the site alone, so I went with him and the major followed. The corpse was a mess, you understand. It was a shock, seeing him lying there, hand outstretched as if . . . But the mud! The rain had . . . it looked as if his face had been beaten in. They found a tyre iron nearby. Horrible!'

'You didn't recognize him?'

'You couldn't. The major said it was Pete, and I thought that if he said so, it must be. Only Sir Julian said it wasn't Pete, and I looked again, and I couldn't be sure. But if Sir Julian said it wasn't Pete, then I believe him.'

'Pete had a gold stud in his ear. The dead man didn't.'

'Ah. Yes. So who was he?'

'I don't know.'

'Have you any idea why that particular part of the park was invaded?'

A shrug. 'There's been these rumours recently. Some people believe in fairy gold. My father says they talk about it in the post office. Weird and wonderful stories, nothing in them.'

Bea said, 'When families live in the same place for generations, they pass tall tales down from father to son. They exaggerate this detail or that to make a better story. You should have heard my mother about her father's miraculous escapes from the bombing during the war! I suppose it gives us hope for the future when things are bad.'

He shrugged.

He was a practical man and not interested in treasure seeking.

Bea said, 'I had lunch in the restaurant. It was good, but I didn't see Kate. Is she off sick? She is the manager now, isn't she?'

His face became expressionless. 'She is an excellent manager, indeed.'

Bea waited.

He said, 'She has varicose veins which trouble her a little. She has to rest and has hospital visits. She's appointed her cousin to deputize for her. She is a good second-in-command and I keep an eye open as well. She brings me any problems that may arise, and sometimes I allow myself to suggest this or that. Sir Julian knows this and says nothing. He is the sort of boss who sees much and says little.'

'And the major?'

He shook his head, looked away.

Was this code for 'I don't like the man, but it's not my place to say so.' Time to press for an explanation?

NINE

Saturday midday

Bea said, 'What did he do to Rosemary?'

Imran looked uncomfortable. 'He told us . . . he spread a rumour . . . some believed it. I am not sure that I do. She was an exceptional person.'

Bea sighed. 'Well, Rosemary was only supposed to be with us for a short time, and Sir Julian desperately needs someone better than Mrs Tring to deal with the paperwork. Any ideas?'

He shook his head. 'Not really.'

'You have someone in mind?'

'Surely you will bring in someone from London?'

'There's a question of where that person would live. Rosemary lived in her own mobile home, but where would an incomer stay?'

He hesitated, shook his head. Opened his mouth. Closed it. He had something to say but wasn't sure of her reaction.

She said, 'I wonder . . . you know all the local people. Is there anyone you've come across here who might have what it takes to do the job?'

'I have wondered if I might suggest . . . But, no. It would not be right to . . .'

Bea said, 'You know someone who might do? Ah, wait a minute, you have a girlfriend who—?'

'My fiancée, Francine, is the practice manager at the doctor's surgery in town. She enjoys bringing order out of chaos. She's been at the surgery for five years and would like to move on, but to get a better job she would have to travel up to London every day, and she is already tired of the commute into the town. We did think she might come here to work for me, but there would not be enough for her to do.'

He waited to see if she'd follow his lead, which she did, saying, 'Have you a picture of your Francine?'

He showed her on his phone. A strong face, intelligent. Dark hair, well groomed. No Botox. Slightly undisciplined eyebrows. Not flashing the flesh. Casual knitwear in a deep blue.

Bea considered what she would surmise about this girl if she'd come to the agency looking for a job.

Well, she'd be a bossy boots, a stickler for rules and regulations . . . but then that long upper lip signalled a sense of humour. She would have strong likes and dislikes, be conscientious, trustworthy and either a pain in the butt or an indispensable aide.

Bea asked, 'Has it occurred to Francine that there might be a job going here after Rosemary left?'

'She heard the rumours about Sir Julian and Rosemary and said she didn't want anything to do with him.'

'Do you have a date set for your marriage?'

Imran was careful with his words. 'We do want to marry but we will have to wait till we can find somewhere to live. Currently she lives with her parents – he's a retired solicitor – in a small house just above the village and I live above the shop. I did ask . . .'

He cut himself off.

Bea said, 'You asked the major if there were any possibility of renting one of the cottages which have just been renovated, and his response was . . .?'

'That he had orders they were to go on the open market. Then he said he had an opportunity to invest in a racehorse, which he said would bring him in a lot of prize money. He wondered if I would like to put some money into such a fail-safe proposition. I said that with regret, I had sworn to my father that I would never gamble.'

'How much did he want you to "invest"?'

'Ten thousand. I understood what he was at and thought of complaining to Sir Julian, but the major said that if I ever brought up the subject again he would, with regret, have to inform Sir Julian that *I'd* offered *him* a bribe. The major said it would be my word against his, and he would be very sorry but that might cause me to lose my job.'

Bea said, 'Ouch. He's a clever man, the major, but he's not clever enough to understand how Sir Julian thinks, or to realize how highly he regards you. Sir Julian told me he is against selling any property in the village, so I imagine he is thinking of keeping them for local people.'

She watched that sink in. 'May I ask if he and Francine have ever met?'

'Yes, at the darts match. They had a good chat in general terms and he introduced her to Lady Polly. I could see Francine revising her opinion of him. He asked what her plans are for the future. She said it depended on where she could get a good job and where we could buy or rent a house.'

'This was code on his part for asking if she were interested in a job, and on hers for saying it depended on your getting somewhere to live.'

He said, 'Yes, that's what we thought. It would solve so many problems if she went to work for him and we could find somewhere to live in the village. But, wouldn't people say I'd taken undue advantage if I pushed Francine forward?'

Bea smiled. 'I don't think your Francine would let you push her into a job she didn't want and likewise, Sir Julian may wear a velvet glove, but I'm sure you've worked out by now what's inside it.'

Imran grinned. 'Pure steel.'

'So may I ask whom you think wears the pants in your relationship with Francine?'

He was serious. 'We've talked it through. We want the same things in life. There's no arguments.'

'Sir Julian's got a lot going on at the moment,' said Bea. 'Let's see what tomorrow brings. Thank you for showing me around. I do like your ideas for Christmas. Are you and Kate planning something special for the restaurant? Special rates for pensioners perhaps? A new sideline in Christmas goodies produced to Kate's own family recipes?'

He grinned. 'I'm ahead of you, Mrs Abbot. I have a meeting scheduled with Sir Julian to discuss Christmas events and menus.'

He showed her out and she managed to retrieve her car from an overflowing car park before her smartphone rang. It was Piers.

'Where are you, Bea? I've just left Mr Colston and am in urgent need of a restorative. I'm in sight of the pub and I'm famished. Meet you there?'

* * *

Bea had some difficulty finding a parking space in the village but finally managed it in front of the church hall. The one and only High Street was buzzing with locals going about their business, plus tourists graciously admiring the scenery while telling their unruly children to behave. Both sets were double-parking their cars.

Bea realized she was looking at the place with the jaundiced eye of a local. She could see the people who lived there needed the visitors who brought money to the place, but she could also see that they would resent them taking up all the parking spaces *and* most of the outdoor seating in front of the pub.

She shouldered her way into the crowded main bar to look for Piers. And couldn't see him at first. With her 'local' eye she saw that there was an almost visible line drawn across the main bar; on one side were the visitors, praising the beer and the food, and laughing a little too loudly.

On the other half, large men such as Jenny's Waste of Space were edging their way out through the back door into the garden. They weren't talking much, or only in low tones.

Bea glimpsed Old Jenny in her usual corner next to the chimney breast. Jenny was wearing a top ornamented with purple sequins. Next to her was Piers with an empty plate of food before him, finishing off a pint of beer and sketching someone or something with his free hand, while a couple of locals crowded around, breathing heavily, wanting to see what he was doing.

Bea reflected that Piers could make himself at home anywhere. And wouldn't it have been nice if he'd ordered a drink for her as well as for himself?

Then she saw that, propped up behind the bar, was a caricature of the landlord himself. Ah-ha! So Piers had been busy here already, had he? Currying favour with the locals? Well, it wasn't a bad way of getting yourself at least tolerated if not actively welcomed. Annoyingly, he might well have learned more than her.

She slid through the throng until she caught Piers' eye, and he made space for her along the settle on which he was sitting. A half of shandy was waiting for her on the table. Good for him.

She was greeted with some warmth by Old Jenny. 'So you

made it. Been poking your nose into somebody else's business up at the farm shop, have you?'

Old Jenny had a better news-gathering service than most. How on earth did she do it? She'd be enquiring Imran's intentions with regard to his fiancée next. And she'd know, oh yes, she'd know what the major had been up to.

Bea said, 'Thank you,' to Piers, and 'Hello, Jenny. How's Tyra doing?'

'I sent my youngest granddaughter to fend off prying folk as should know better. Drat it, the girl had promised to dig up some leeks for me this afternoon and she'll have forgotten all about that now, won't she? There's no news of Pete, I gather? But sir's found Pete's dog and she's doing all right. New mothers can bite. I told Tyra, she'll see Pete again soon.'

'So you don't believe he's dead?'

'Sir Julian said not. The police here have passed the buck up to London Town, thinking Pete – or rather, the man they think was Pete – will have gone to ground up there. They've no more idea where he is than my youngest great-grandchild who is, I'm sorry to say, a trifle lacking.'

'Look east?' suggested Bea. A pool of silence formed around them. Did she imagine it or did people move slightly away from her?

Piers tore off the page he'd been working on and handed it to Jenny. She gave a cackle of laughter and held the caricature of herself up for all to see. 'Not bad, my lad. Your wife may have no more sense than to let you go traipsing around the world while she works hard to earn a decent penny, but you've eyes to see . . . which is more than I can say about certain people I know.' She tried to get to her feet and failed. Tried again and made it.

She flicked a glance at an elderly man sitting nearby, saying, 'You can help me home now. I won't ask you to lift my leeks, but you've had your quota for today, and your granddaughter will be waiting for you back home with your dinner on the table, which is more than you deserve, right?'

A passageway opened through the throng, right up to the door. Exit Jenny and escort.

Piers collected his glass and said, 'Do you want anything to eat, Bea? No? I've ordered a dessert for myself but suggest we might move to the garden. I can't think in here. Too many unspoken thoughts colliding with one another.'

The garden was well furnished with outdoor tables and a sunny corner fenced off for a children's play area. They took the last unoccupied table, and the sun went behind a cloud. Bea shivered. The afternoon was turning colder. Maybe there'd be more rain?

A harassed-looking woman brought out a dessert for Piers, collected half a dozen glasses – how did she manage to carry so many at once? – and disappeared back into the pub.

Piers tackled a large sticky toffee pudding with real custard. 'Mm,' he said. 'Better than Mother makes.'

Bea ignored that provocation and took a sip of her shandy. 'How did you get on with Mr Colston?'

'You said he was a lonely, difficult, old man, and he is. He's got himself into a pleasant niche here in the village by moving into the house which Julian turned over to his cousins. Now that Mona has gone to live with her billionaire Marcus, only one of the girls is still living there, and that's Celine, the one who believes she's going to be the next bestseller of purple romances.

'The old man is encouraging her and maybe she'll make it and maybe she won't, but at the moment they're very happy playing master and pupil and being waited on by someone from the village who feeds them stodgy food, keeps the dust down and sends the laundry out.

'Mr Colston was pleased to see me because he thinks it fitting that people should call on him, as in the old days. It adds to his feeling that he's one of the elite. When I told him who I'd been painting recently, he assumed I was down here to do a portrait of him and that Julian would pay for it!'

'The nerve of the man.' Bea was half laughing and half annoyed.

'Yes, but it broke the ice and he told me his life story, how his wife let him down by dying young and how his daughter's betrayal of him by marrying a nobody had frustrated his goal of becoming the headmaster of an elite school. It's all Polly's fault, you know. He'd always assumed she'd marry someone suitable – another teacher of course – and that his dutiful daughter and her husband would sit at his feet and spend the rest of his life looking after him.

'Instead, the ungrateful child went and married a fellow student, a man without a name or connections and worst still, not even an English scholar! Julian's always had a bent for maths, hasn't he? If Mr Colston had been able to say he'd nurtured another English prodigy, it might have been easier for him to accept Julian's undeserved rise to the aristocracy.'

Bea said, 'It was through his own folly that he lost the chance of a good headmastership and without Julian's backing, he'd be stuck in a rest home without anything to do. Instead, his life has been changed for the better because Julian has made it so. How hard it must be to be grateful to someone you used to write off as beneath your notice!'

Piers said, 'It's an interesting situation. He's something of a scholar but has a chip on his shoulder to rival Ben Nevis. When I enquired about the treasure hunt that he'd set off, he laughed till he choked but didn't deny that he'd been stirring the pot. I asked if I could see some of the papers he'd been working on, and he was happy to let me do so. All in Latin and undecipherable to yours truly.'

'But he can read them and make sense of what they say?'

'I would say so, yes. He's translated all the papers taken from the priest hole which were written in Latin, and has been comparing his results with what's known of the history of this area. He's preparing a book for publication about his findings, which he says will ensure his name goes down in history as a mover and shaker in academic circles. He's envisaging a bright future for himself, being asked to lecture here and submit papers there.'

'But has he actually found anything of value?'

'Annoyingly, I think he probably has. He's being very careful in what he says. It does look as though something happened here in the Middle Ages which brought an increase of wealth to the Hall and village. He's now working on the Hall's accounts which give details of who was paid what and why. From this you can build a picture of a change in lifestyle at that time. There's a surge in the number of labourers building the Tithe Barn – which predates the present house – and for a row of cottages in the village. A different lot of builders were taken on to build a lady chapel for the church in the village, which almost doubled its size. I must have a look at that some time.

'There's a licence for a change of ownership at the inn and building some stables at the back. There's payments for cloth and tableware from Flanders, also for the purchase of some fine glassware. What Mr Colston doesn't explain is why this happened.'

Bea thought about it. 'In the Middle Ages pilgrims did bring offerings of money to shrines which held the relics of saints. Mr Colston is guessing that there was something found at the Hall, or kept at the Hall, which had people wanting to travel to see it? Some holy cup? Perhaps it's some relic or other which one of Julian's ancestors brought back from the Crusades?'

'I asked him that. He tapped his nose and said I'd have to wait till his book came out. He's excited to have found something which will bring him kudos but hasn't forgiven Julian for his good fortune and is therefore paying him out by not telling him what it is.'

'If he can get one up on Julian, he'll do so?'

'He bears a grudge. Julian is aware of it but can't take the easy way out by shoving his father-in-law off to a rest home.' He scraped up the last of the pudding, and patted his stomach. 'Coffee, do you think? Shall I get some for you, too?' He disappeared to order some.

The lunchtime rush was over. The sun had stayed out though there were clouds on the horizon. Most people were leaving the garden now but a few were still arriving. Bea unbuttoned her jacket.

A braying laugh caused her to stiffen. She knew that laugh! What was the major doing here? He appeared in the pub doorway, looking pleased with himself. Behind him were a well-dressed couple in their forties. Not local. They were also looking pleased with themselves.

Uh-oh. He was meeting people who were interested in one of the newly refurbished houses in the village?

Hadn't Julian made himself clear when he said he didn't want to sell? Yes, he had.

The major didn't see, or perhaps didn't recognize Bea, but indicated a table which had just become vacant. 'The food here is excellent. When you don't want to cook at home, you'll always find a meal here.'

Bea took out her phone and got through to Julian. 'The major's here showing a youngish couple the sights.'

'I'm in the village. Be with you in a sec.'

Piers returned with two coffees, and checked the whereabouts of the sun. 'It looks like rain later, but we should be all right for a bit.'

The major brayed out another of his laughs. 'Shall we make it a toast to a happy future in your new home?'

Piers said, 'What?' And swivelled around to see what was up.

'Yes,' said Bea. 'That's the major with a couple of people who are seemingly interested in buying a house in the village. Julian's said he doesn't want to sell, but I think the major is going to try to force his hand. And here comes Julian, prompt on cue.'

Julian appeared in the pub doorway with Pip strapped into a harness in front of him and Bruno at his side. Pip was asleep. Julian was very wide awake. He surveyed the scene, beckoned to Bea and Piers to join him, and took them over to the table at which the major had seated himself and his customers.

'Hello, there! Fancy meeting you here, Ian. Do you know my good friend Piers, the portrait painter? And you've met Mrs Abbot already.' He held out his hand to the newcomers. 'Julian Marston-Lang. You're visiting for the day? It's quite some place, this village, isn't it? All mod cons. Well, some of them. The traffic is quite appalling, isn't it? I had to park at the back of the church and that's in the slot marked for the vicar.'

The major did not look pleased to see Julian, but hid it well enough. 'Mr and Mrs Thomas, down from London. Going to settle in the village.'

'Such a pretty place!' said the wife, 'Just what we've always wanted now the children have left home. A little piece of Eden.'

'Without the snake, ha-ha,' said her husband. 'The major here has managed to get the price down so that we can just about manage it. We'll have to have a survey done, of course, though we can see for ourselves everything's been done to tip-top quality.'

'Delighted!' Julian beamed at them. 'It's the double garage

that did it for you, I suppose? Up there?' He waved his hand at the stony hillside above the pub. There were no garages there. No houses, either.

Bea understood what Julian was up to quicker than the others. He'd invented a new-build, a cluster of modern houses on the hillside above, which would suit newcomers better than what was actually on offer down in the village.

She chirruped, 'And of course there's the private lane, winding up the hill which will avoid the hurly-burly in the village street. You've seen for yourselves how difficult it is to find a parking space in the village, but up there . . .'

'And the view,' said Piers, who was also quick to follow Julian's lead. 'No late-night carousing from the pub to disturb your sleep as it does in the village itself.'

'And the Wi-Fi is a little better up there,' said Julian. 'I must admit, down here it's so poor it puts potential buyers off, whereas up there . . .' He waved his hand at the rocky rise above them. 'It's not perfect, of course. We can't expect that, but it should be better.'

The major wiped his neck with a tissue. 'But they're wanting the end cottage down here! There's no houses up there!'

'Not yet, no. Of course not.' Julian beamed. 'So wise to get in on the ground floor. We're thinking of calling the new development "Village View". It's going to be quite something. Of course the developers are worrying themselves sick about planning permission, but I'm sure we can get it through soon.'

'But . . .!'

Julian said, 'We're one big family down here. You'll want to get involved in village affairs, won't you? Of course you will. All the coffee mornings and fundraising that goes on. And the food bank. Hard graft, but so worthwhile. And then there's the sport. We're very keen on sport here. Everyone takes part. Do you play darts? Our team has just won a local match, defeating our old enemies from town. No? But you play cricket, of course, Mr . . .? The pavilion burned down last year but we're having a fundraising event and I'm sure you'll want to pull your weight there.'

Mr and Mrs Thomas consulted without words, their eyes wide with shock. Mr looked at his watch, saying, 'Well, that's just . . .

I don't think we quite understood that . . . Major, we'll be in touch.'

Mrs chimed in, 'Yes, that's it. Such a big step. We have to consider the distance from town and what the children will say . . .'

'Yes, yes. Be in touch.' They wafted themselves away, leaving their half-full glasses of wine on the table, untouched.

The major was tight-lipped with fury. 'They were prepared to pay . . .! You need the money! That land up there . . .' He gestured widely. 'It's not possible to build up there. You're having me on! You're heading straight for bankruptcy! You don't take my advice! I wash my hands of you!'

Oh, if only he would!

Wonder dog Bruno didn't like the major's tone. He remained sitting at his master's side, but allowed himself a tiny growl, checking to see if he might express himself further.

'Quiet, Bruno,' said Julian.

Silence while the major considered resigning his post.

Resign! Resign!

But no, he thought better of it. He said, 'I hope you know what you're doing.'

Julian was smooth as silk. 'I hope so, too.'

The major rose to his feet, holding on to the table. He made his way somewhat unsteadily into the pub. Bruno settled down again.

'What a waste of a good drink,' said Piers. He picked up an untouched glass and sniffed. He put it down again. 'How like the man. Can't even buy them a decent vintage.'

Julian tipped all three glasses of wine on to the grass. 'It is quite true that I have been considering how to increase the housing stock hereabouts. The youngsters are having to leave because there's nowhere for them to live. We need a mix of two- and three-bedroomed houses or perhaps a row of bungalows for the older folk. I've been wondering for some time about that field at the back here. It might do. Fortunately I do still own it.

'I'll have to get a couple of developers in to have a look at the site. Lance won't touch it, but he'll know someone who will. We'd need a new road. Maybe we can get the council to create a car park at the end of the village. Now that would be good for business.'

A toy giraffe's head poked out from the harness Julian was wearing. Pip was waking up. Julian held the boy up high. Pip dropped his toy giraffe to crow with delight.

'Down!' he said. And maybe this time he meant it.

Julian laughed. He lifted his son down on to the grass and, holding his hand, helped him to walk a few paces this way and that. 'He's getting the hang of it.'

He helped the boy move from one table to the next. Bea saw it wasn't the first time Julian had brought his son to the pub's garden, for there were many people there who smiled on the lad, and had a word with his father.

Jenny's grandsons, Waste of Space and Useless Lump, lifted the boy on to their table and let him walk along it to be caught at the other end by another big lad, whom Bea recognized from earlier visits; what was his name? Big-Teddy-with-the-bad teeth? Odd-job man, willing, but not too bright? Were they friends? Or cousins, perhaps?

Piers murmured, 'Excellent PR to bring the boy here. A good way for Julian to get to know people.'

Bea picked up the toy giraffe. It hadn't been new when Pip had taken to it, and his legs and neck were getting floppy.

She smoothed the toy out, and stilled. There was something hard in the giraffe's body. A few stitches at the back had been done in a darker colour.

What's this? It's not a squeaker. The giraffe never had a sound box. Who would place something inside a toy? Julian? No. Why would he? Ah, Rosemary might. It's the sort of thing she might do to keep a much-loved toy safe. Has she put a device in the giraffe so that it can be located if Pip loses it? People can trace their lost smartphones by ringing from another instrument. Is this what it is?

Which made her think of contacting Rosemary again. 'Rosemary? I haven't had a minute, but where are you, my dear? Can we talk now? Or better still, meet?'

'I'm up north. Returning south tomorrow.'

'I need to know what you've discovered about the major's murky past.'

'Not murky. Sunshine all the way.'

'There must be something. He's changed jobs far too many times for an estate manager. Has he a criminal record?'

'No! Definitely not. You haven't told anyone you're in touch with me, have you?'

'Only Piers. And you contacted him first, didn't you? Listen, have you put a tracer device in Pip's giraffe?'

'Tell no one. And, yes.' Rosemary switched off.

'What was that?' Piers wasn't really interested. 'Shall we make a move?'

Julian had been stopped by an elderly man in a wheelchair, asking for . . . what? A bottle of water? How odd was that?

Julian returned, looking thoughtful. 'Poor man. Got a nasty rash.' He began to hoist Pip into the harness. He said, 'Can you smell anything? That old man says he can always tell when Pip and I have been in the water. Some herbal smell? I wonder what herb's growing up there. Shall we get going now?' He looked up at the sky. 'There's more rain on the way. Where did I leave my car?'

The first drops of rain thudded down and phones began to ring.

Running for the pub, Bea ignored her phone till she was safely under cover.

Piers was just behind her, on his phone. 'What . . .!'

Waste of Space shouted, 'Fire! Someone's set alight to the Hall!'

TEN

Saturday teatime

Julian was right behind them. Also on his phone. He said, 'On my way! Bea, take Pip, will you?' He swung the harness to Bea and made for the door, followed by Bruno and . . .

Waste of Space – what was the man's real name? – and Useless Lump, who crashed through to the door after him, shouting, 'Wait! We've got the lorry outside!'

Pip struggled. Bea held him with difficulty while still on her phone. She recognized Mrs Maggs's voice. 'Mrs Abbot, do you know where Sir Julian is? Lady Polly's not here, either. It's the stables. On fire! That poor dog . . .'

'Make way! Fire at the Hall!' shouted Piers, helping Bea through to the door.

'Where's your car?' Big-Teddy-with-the-bad-teeth was right behind them.

'Outside the church hall,' said Bea.

They stepped out into a downpour. Rain was bouncing off the pavement. The sky was dark as midnight. Teddy had one arm around Piers, rushing them along the street, cars hooting, someone shouting, brakes squealing. Their car was still there, and there was – almost – enough space to manoeuvre out.

Piers held out his hand for the keys. 'I'll drive.'

Teddy got in the front passenger seat.

Bea got in the back with Pip. She was shivering. Her teeth chattered and she firmed her jaw.

Pip was restless, mewling, picking up the tension. Thunder rolled across the sky. Raindrops pounded the roof of the car. She was already wet through.

Not that that mattered.

Teddy put his hand on the horn as Piers went backwards and forwards . . . It was going to take too long to reach . . . the fire brigade would have to come from town? Who else might be able to . . .?

Bea said, 'Teddy, what's Imran's phone number? He's closer, might be able to . . .'

He gave it. She got through. Explained. 'Fire at the Hall. Stables. Can you get someone there to help?'

Imran wouldn't lose his head. 'On my way!'

A shape loomed ahead on the road. Spray shot over the windscreen, causing Piers to curse. A lorry, half in and out of a ditch. The road, slippery.

Piers was doing his best imitation of a racing driver, which in normal circumstances would have her reaching for the door handle, but in this case . . . well, he was making good time.

Was it only the stables that had been set alight?

They reached the boundary of the estate.

Was that another lorry ahead?

Teddy wasn't one to lose his head, either. 'Ignore the road. Go straight across the grass. Aim for the stables, to the left of the Hall.'

A lorry was ploughing on some way ahead of them. The grass tugged at their wheels, slowing them down. There would be ruts there, where they had driven over sodden ground.

Pip whimpered.

Bea whispered a prayer. *Dear Lord above, dear Lord above, dear Lord!*

She peered out of the window. Through the driving rain she could glimpse the bulk of the Hall, which appeared intact. At the front, anyway.

She could feel Pip's heart beating against hers.

A swish of tyres and they stopped under the east wing, still short of the stable yard. Just behind the lorry. Parked askew across the road.

She saw Julian swing down from the lorry in front of them, followed by the two brothers.

Were they brothers, or cousins or . . . What did it matter! They were Jenny's grandchildren and they were helping Julian.

Bully for them.

Piers and Teddy jumped out of the car, leaving their doors open. Leaving her with Pip. Rain shot in. Pip burrowed deep into her arms.

Honestly! Men!

Here she was, stuck in the back of her car with a fretful baby, while the men got on with whatever they were going to do. It wouldn't help to break down and have hysterics, which is what she felt like doing. It was probably best to look after Pip and not get in the way of the people who were helping to quench the fire.

Mind you, the rainstorm would probably help.

Only, it stopped raining. Just like that.

How very . . . inappropriate.

She was so wet she'd probably stick to the seat if she tried to move. She shifted left and right. Pip mumbled but she inched her way to the door, swung it open and got out. With some difficulty. Pip was getting heavy.

Fresh air. Nice.

Not so fresh. Smell of burning.

Shadows passed her. They yelled to one another. 'Where's the buckets?'

'We've had the lot!'

'Where's the fire brigade?'

People being helpful, no doubt.

The sky was lightening. The storm had passed overhead, leaving what? The Hall itself seemed to be intact. So where was the fire?

She sniffed. Burning wood.

She inched her way round the car and splashed her way between parked cars and lorries, around the bulk of the east wing till she came to the stable yard. Here was action, all right. Men milled around. Women, too. Julian carried a bucket from the tap . . .

What tap? Where?

Did it matter?

A fire was burning brightly in the stable block opposite to where the builders had been working to provide a new home for Julian and his family.

How come there was still a fire alight after that deluge?

Ah. Yes. The fire had been set inside one of the stalls, the one next door to the one occupied by Beauty and her pups. It was under cover, so not affected by the rain. It had been aimed to kill the dog? And, to make sure she would die, the bottom part of her door had been shut so that she couldn't get out.

Why? So she couldn't identify her attackers?

That was a nasty thought.

People with buckets threw water at the burning wall of the stall and others wielded fire extinguishers. Neither seemed to have any effect on the flames which licked away, appreciating the taste of the old wood. Ah, now the flames were climbing up the wooden partition separating the stall next door from the one in which Beauty and her pups lay. The flames started on the roof.

If they got to the top, they'd be able to leap to the ancient Tithe Barn and then there'd be hell and all to pay!

Dogs barked. Not just Bruno but a frantic Beauty as well.

Men and women shouted, grimly focused on fighting the fire.

Activity. Slightly despairing. The fire was gaining ground.

A man stumbled into the middle of the yard, holding his head. Blood oozed between his fingers.

One of the guards?

Someone shouted, 'What happened? You all right?'

The man gasped, 'I heard Beauty barking . . . Something hit me . . .'

Julian guided the guard to one side. 'Well done. You sounded the alarm, so the other guards could take over.'

'I couldn't see!' He was shaking.

Julian said, 'Someone take him into the kitchen.'

A woman steered him away.

Julian and Waste of Space conferred. Julian shouted orders while holding on to Bruno's collar. The lorry inched across the yard towards the fire.

Bruno slipped his collar and leaped for the stall . . . as a sunburst of flame rose up and up . . . And Julian . . . Oh no! . . . No, Julian, no!

Someone was screaming.

Julian held his jacket up before him and attacked the lower door, which refused to open.

He struggled with it.

Flames licked along the bottom of the door. He trod them down.

'Come away!' One of the brothers shouted. 'You can't . . .!'

Everyone shouting.

Bea's throat stung.

An arm went around Bea's waist. Someone was weeping at Bea's shoulder. Mrs Maggs? 'He'll do himself an injury! Where's that blimming fire brigade when it's needed? Oh, I do hate fire!'

'Padlocked!' Julian tackled the lower door again. One of the brothers brought a crowbar out of the lorry and together . . . the flames seemed to enjoy the attention . . . both men fell back, coughing.

Where was Piers? Was he in danger?

No. He was safe. Standing at the side. He had his phone out, recording the scene. Sensible, but not exactly helpful in dowsing the fire, which seemed to be . . .

Bea turned her head away. Too, too bright!

Pip stirred in her arms. 'Hush, Pip! Hush!'

Mrs Maggs sobbed out her worries. 'Pip's hungry. Where's Lady Polly? She should be back by now, shouldn't she? Don't say she's been stuck behind all those cars in the driveway! Someone should clear them!'

True. The fire brigade wouldn't be able to get through. But who could be spared to organize the clearing of the drive?

Bea thought of something that might help later on. 'Will you get Jenny up here?'

'What? What could she . . .? Oh. Burns. Yes.' Mrs Maggs got her own phone out. Spoke. Listened. Shut off. 'She's heard. She's sending her daughter up to help us. I told her, take the west road.'

At the third try, Julian and Waste of Space attached a chain to the lower door and led it to the lorry, which backed slowly away, finally wrenching the lower door away from its frame until it lay, flickering wildly, some way from the building.

Julian ducked into the inferno. He disappeared from sight.

Bea prayed aloud, 'Please God, please God, please God . . .!'

Julian reappeared, carrying the basket which contained the puppies, with Beauty and Bruno at his heels. He carried the pups into the middle of the yard and put it down. Heavily. 'I think one of them may be alive . . .'

There was a solid 'Thump!'

The roof of the stall which had sheltered Beauty and her pups fell in. The flames concentrated on the fallen timbers. Enjoying themselves. At least they were now away from the wall of the Tithe Barn.

The flames lit up the scene and warmed the air.

Julian knelt by the puppies. Beauty dragged her damaged leg along. And coughed. Bruno whined and coughed, and growled. Julian quietened both with hand and voice.

A thin woman dressed in black appeared from the estate office end of the barn, dumped a large black bag on the floor and knelt beside the pups. She pushed Julian away. 'Let me.' She picked up one of the puppies and blew into its mouth. It convulsed, legs waving. She gave it to Beauty, who lay down to let it suckle.

Bruno whined, but allowed Julian to put his collar back on.

Bea felt her knees give way and told herself not to fall down. Not now. Not yet. She took a step back and found a clear bit of wall to lean against.

Julian stood up, slowly, favouring his leg. He looked around him.

The woman in black worked on the puppies.

No one else moved.

They all looked at Julian, who took his time looking at them. One of his sleeves had burned away. There was a red streak down his cheek, and another down his arm. Yes, burns.

Bea thought it was like looking at a stage set. The villagers' livelihood depended on Julian, who'd just risked his life to go into a burning building to rescue a dog . . . whose owner might or might not be alive . . .

Julian turned his attention to the lorry.

He considered the wide old tyres.

He looked back at Waste of Space, who stood four square, hands clenched at his sides, looking up at Julian from under his brows. Waiting for a verdict.

Did Julian think the lorry's tyres were a match to those which had been left in the amusement park on the night a man died and Pete disappeared?

Was Julian going to accuse Waste of Space of murder?

Bea held her breath. There were a lot of people in the stable yard from the village and, on Julian's side, only Bea and Piers.

And yes, Imran had arrived, too. Perhaps he would be on Julian's side?

Julian said, in a mild voice, 'Henry, you would like to explain?'

Henry – aka Waste of Space – uncurled his fists. And nodded. 'It's not what it looks like.'

A police siren in the distance broke the tension. Everyone started and looked around.

Julian didn't move, and neither did Henry.

Julian said, still in that quiet tone, 'Did you have anything to do with the attack on Pete?'

Hal shook his head. 'No. Are you going to tell the police? If they see the lorry . . .'

'Yes, they'll think it was you who . . .'

'It wasn't.'

The police siren became more and more agitated.

Julian said, 'It will take time for the police and the fire brigade to get through the cars parked along the drive. Take the lorry out through the western gate. Perhaps you'd care to call in here tonight to explain?' He glanced around. 'And anyone else who has seen or heard something?'

'The western gate?' Henry hesitated. 'It will be padlocked. It isn't used.'

Julian said, 'I think you can manage to get round that.'

Of course he will. Look what he did to the perimeter fencing and the northern gate! Or . . . No, he says it wasn't him. But if not him, then who?

Henry jumped up into the lorry and started it. His brother and Big Teddy scrambled in after him. The lorry backfired and made for the western exit, round the end of the Tithe Barn and out into the park beyond the Hall itself.

The flames were sullen, licking around the debris of the stall. Not quite defeated, but sensing their day was over.

The woman in black, who'd paid no attention to the lorry or the discussion afterwards, rose to her feet. She had a hawk-face and a straight up-and-down figure. Jenny's daughter? She said, 'The pups will live. Beauty needs watching. She may need antibiotics. And what I'm doing, treating animals in the open air on my day off, I do not know! Who's looking after the dog tonight?

Make up your minds. I haven't got all day.' She advanced on Julian. 'Let me look at that arm.'

Piers said, 'I hear a police car and the fire brigade.'

Men moved quickly, this way and that. Beauty and her pups disappeared in the care of two of the workmen.

Piers put his smartphone away and said, conversationally, 'Did I leave my car keys in the car out there? Perhaps I should rescue it.' He disappeared in that direction.

Bea felt that if she took a step away from the wall, she'd fall down. Someone – a woman? – took the sleeping Pip off her.

Bea tried to stand. A hand at her elbow, and she didn't fall. Oh, goody. Was that Kate? That was most helpful of her.

The woman in black shooed Julian into the kitchen. 'You need to sit down before you fall down and I need a basin to put your arm in. I've no time to waste, even if you have. Chop, chop!'

Kate put her free arm around Bea and urged her in the same direction. 'I don't know about you, but I could do with a cuppa.'

Somehow Bea managed to put one foot in front of the other and with the woman's help, made it to the kitchen. Mrs Maggs and two of her team were already busy making pots of tea and a mountain of sandwiches. One was cleaning a large bowl, big enough to make Christmas puddings in.

The sirens outside continued to blow their eerie note, but inside the kitchen everyone got ready to feed the five thousand while the doctor – was she really a doctor, or a vet? – took two large bottles of water from her bag and poured it into the bowl, telling Julian he should have some sugared tea to counteract the shock.

A sweetish smell pervaded the kitchen. Herbs?

Pip grizzled. He was in someone's brawny arms. It was Kate from the restaurant, wasn't it? Or her lookalike. She tidied Pip up, and put him in a high chair to feed him.

Julian sat at the table and tried to take off his shirt. The movement was obviously too much for him. He hung his head down.

The doctor – or whatever she was – produced a sharp pair of scissors and proceeded to cut his shirt off him. His arm from elbow to wrist was red raw. So was the side of his face.

Bea had a mug of tea placed before her and was told to drink it. She obeyed.

Julian began to shiver.

The sirens continued. And then stopped. Lots of shouting, mostly from the major, but from others as well.

The doctor plunged Julian's forearm into the basin of water, and held it there. 'Don't move.'

Julian's breathing became rapid . . . and then began to slow. Finally, he tried a smile. 'You've used the water before, haven't you?'

'Never you mind. Leave your arm where it is. Let me bathe your face. I don't think we've met. I'm Trisha, Jenny's daughter. She rang me just as I was settling down to watch the rugby. You don't play rugby, do you? Too lightweight.'

Bea drank her tea and was handed a ham sandwich, plus a slab of fruit cake with side slices of cheddar cheese. And another mug of tea. She started on them with gusto.

Piers arrived, saying he'd parked the car round the front of the Hall and there was all hell to pay out there. He took one look at Julian, and got out his camera again. He took photos of Julian's injuries and sent them somewhere. To his computer?

Pip seemed to inhale the food which one of the women placed in front of him. He'd also been given some gooey stuff on a dish, and his wooden spoon. He was handling the spoon better, sometimes managing to get the food into his mouth rather than on to the floor.

A loud voice announced the coming of the major, braying out displeasure in all directions. 'What in God's name do you think . . .?'

Julian tried to smile. 'He calls on God, but doesn't know Him.'

The door was violently flung open, and the major charged in, red in the face. 'What the hell's been going on here? What idiot called the fire brigade and the police out for a bonfire in the stables?'

Dr Trisha removed Julian's arm from the basin and thrust his head down into it. And held it there. Julian's shoulders heaved.

He was trying not to laugh, wasn't he?

The major wasn't receiving the attention he thought he deserved. No one bothered to reply to his questions. Except Mrs Maggs, who said, 'That fire might have set the Hall alight, and then where would we be, eh? Cuppa, Major?'

'Tcha! This has gone way past a jest! Who rang them, eh? I want to know who was responsible! When they rang me to ask where the fire was . . . I'd no idea what they were talking about! I told them, someone's having you on, and they should disregard the call. Then they called me back within ten minutes saying they'd got calls from all over and when I get here, which by the way was made extremely difficult because there's cars left all over the drive and on the grass, which means someone's going to have to dig out the ruts they've made. More expense! So I follow the fire brigade and the police, and there's nothing to show for it but a piddling pile of ashes and nobody to answer my questions!'

Julian lifted his head from the water to ask, 'Is Polly back?'

Dr Trisha shoved Julian's head back into the water again. 'Are there any other injuries? Didn't someone say one of the security men had been knocked out? I'd better have a look at him before I go. I only hope I remembered to record the rugby match. I look forward to it all week and then this happens.'

'What!' The major was almost at screeching pitch. 'Security knocked out? On a Saturday? What's he thinking of? Stupid, stupid . . .! I'll have his guts for garters! Where is he? Has he gone off sick? If so, who's he got to take over? He's fired! I'm not having incompetents working for me. Well? Do I have to do everything around here?'

Mrs Maggs said, 'It's Jock, and he's lying down in my sitting room next door. He says he did press his alarm so someone else must have taken over. He says he's all right, but he looks cross-eyed to me.'

Dr Trisha consulted her watch. 'If that's so, I might have to take him into A & E. Sir Julian, keep your face in the water. When you've counted up to a hundred, you can get up. Mrs Maggs, see that he behaves himself. Here's another bottle of the water, and he knows where to get more. See that he has another ten minutes or so of it before he goes to bed. My mother's sending along some of my salve and a sleeve to keep that arm sterile. Let me know how he is in the morning. Where's the guard? Through here?'

Dr Trisha disappeared into the back quarters, and Julian warily lifted his head from the bowl. The side of his face no longer looked red raw, but pink. He said, 'We'd better talk to the police. Or rather, Jock should. He was attacked and knocked out by intruders. The police will need his statement.'

'What for?' demanded the major. 'I told them, my apologies for your having been brought out here for a piddling little bonfire, obviously the workmen lit a fire where they shouldn't, and this is the result. As for that useless security man, I suppose he tripped over his own feet and knocked himself out. I can only hope that the police accept my apologies and write it off as another false alarm. Anyway, at least they've gone.'

'They've gone?' said Julian, pushing the basin away and reaching for his own plateful of cake and cheese. 'A pity. We need to get a crime report number from them, or we won't be able to get anything from the insurance. And I'd like to have spoken to them.'

'What for? They remember all too clearly that you made a wrong identification of the body in the park. I suggest you let sleeping dogs lie.'

Julian passed his empty mug to Mrs Maggs, saying, 'Thank you.' He turned back to the major. 'Any idea where Polly might be?'

The major couldn't care less. 'Women do lose track of time when they go shopping for clothes.'

Bea, Mrs Maggs and Kate all looked at the major with identical expressions. *He thought Polly had taken time off to go shopping? Is this man for real?*

Julian got out his smartphone. 'Messages. One from Polly? Ah . . .' He listened to it, and clicked off. 'On her way back. She's been advised to take the western gate. Very sensible.'

The major was stamping around, still fizzing with fury. 'The western gate? That hasn't been used for ever. It's completely overgrown. She'll have to go all the way round and in by the northern gate. What a waste of time.'

Bea almost smiled. The major hadn't a clue, had he?

Mrs Maggs was putting the basin, still with the water in it, up on a high shelf. Why? Did it matter? Mm. Yes, probably. What was in that water? Herbs?

'Well? Don't you want to thank me?'

The major was not as sure of himself as he tried to pretend, was he? For the first time Bea felt a little sorry for him. Not much. Just a little. He'd made himself thoroughly disliked and he must know it.

'Yes, indeed,' said Julian.

The major harrumphed and left.

Dr Trisha swept through, looking at her watch, saying Jock had a head made of teak but he should rest a while and someone should see him home tonight.

Bea thought that there were many questions still unanswered, but that certain things were becoming clearer. Or were they?

ELEVEN

Saturday evening

Imran popped his head around the door. 'The major had a word with the policemen. They did take some notes and gave me a crime number, but they didn't stick around for more than five minutes. The fire brigade's still here, making sure the flames don't start up again. Bit of a mess out there, but not to worry, soon be put right. Have you got your car keys, Sir Julian? You left your Toyota somewhere in the village? I'm on my way back to the farm shop to close up for the night, but I'll get someone to bring your car back here.'

'Thank you, Imran. I am much obliged to you.'

Old-fashioned words conveying sincere thanks, and Imran accepted them as such.

Julian said, 'And, will we see you this evening with Francine?'

A hesitation. 'Without the major?'

A nod. 'Without the major.'

Imran nodded and disappeared.

Kate picked a tired Pip up, and cradled him. Bea blinked. It wasn't Kate, but someone who looked like her. Probably a sister or cousin or aunt or . . .

Polly swept into the room, and everyone was galvanized into sitting straight. 'I did my bits and pieces in town and made my excuses to Lady Knighton, so that I could call on Tyra on the way back. She's back home and doing fine and so is the baby, thank goodness. Then Old Jenny came in and she said there was trouble at the Hall but it was being taken care of and I'd better return by the western gate which so far as I know has never been open in living memory, but today it is . . . What's going on? Julian! What's happened to your face . . . and heaven's sake! Your arm!'

Julian said, half laughing and half concerned, 'It's all right! Honestly! Look, you're worn out! Sit down and relax. And we will a tale unfold . . . or rather, we're having a meeting here tonight at which a tale will unfold.'

Polly subsided on to a chair, rubbing her back. 'If someone doesn't tell me what's happening, I shall scream!'

'There, there,' said Mrs Maggs. 'We've all had a very trying day, but Sir Julian's got it all in hand and don't you worry your little head now.'

Polly was incensed. 'That is not a satisfactory answer, and I am not going to accept it. Something's been going on. I know it. Julian, have you still got all your fingers and toes?'

Julian managed to put his arm around her. 'Yes, I do. It's all right. Really, it is. I'm sorry about wrecking another shirt but it's not as bad as it looks. I can't even feel it now. Now, tell me, has Tyra heard from Pete?'

'What! What? Did Tyra hear from . . .? Oh! You think . . .? It's true she was much calmer than I expected to find her, and she did say something about—'

'Moving back up to London?'

'Well, yes. She said that some relative or other – a brother or uncle of Pete's – had rung to say he was going to take her back up to London to live with his family, but she was to keep quiet about it. How did you know?'

'Guesswork,' said Julian. 'Pete's phone's missing.' Turning to Mrs Maggs and the Kate lookalike, he said, 'I know this is asking a lot of you, but would you like to attend the meeting this evening, too? There'll be too many coming to accommodate in the estate office present quarters, so I'm going to suggest we use the library. Also, can you find someone to look after Pip for the evening?'

Mrs Maggs gave him a look which was half pleasure at being invited, and half a frown because she didn't understand why. However, she dealt with the next matter to hand, as she always did.

'Been thinking about that. I'll get Kylie's younger sister over. She may or may not suit in the long run but she'll be all right for now. She would have come this afternoon but Lady Polly was out, so she didn't bother. Lady Polly will be herself again when she's had a bit of a lie-down and got some food down her. I've got a steak and kidney pie in the oven that'll do nicely for you and your guests.' She nodded to the Kate lookalike, 'You'll stay as well, will you?'

'Try to get me to leave! They've had it all their own way for far too long. Supper at six? Meeting at seven?'

Julian got Polly to her feet. 'Come on, my love. I've got to check on this and that, and you must have a rest till supper. Bea? Piers? Shall we retire to our own quarters and leave Mrs Maggs to her preparations?'

Bea exchanged a look with Piers. She said she'd like to see if she'd left her phone in the car first. Piers said he'd left the car at the front of the Hall and he'd show her where it was.

Once safely inside the car, Piers got out his keys but didn't start the engine. He said, 'I wonder if the estate office really is bugged, and that's why Julian wants to meet in the library?'

'I don't know,' said Bea. 'But it's more important than ever that I speak with Rosemary. We're safe here, aren't we?'

Piers got out of the car and looked around. He shut Bea into the car and stood a little way away, on guard.

Bea phoned Rosemary, who said, 'Where are you, Bea?'

'In my car. Alone. Am I right in thinking you're still working for Julian?'

'Yes, of course. I've been up and down the country, finding out things.'

'Such as, are the major's references as golden as he makes out?'

'His two previous employers were apparently only too happy to pass him on with an excellent reference. I suspect that was so he didn't make too much of a fuss about his being asked to leave, but I can't prove it. It's . . . irritating.'

'You started to look into his background only after he began spreading rumours about you and Julian; rumours which are circulating to this day?'

'That man is pure poison. We told Polly straight away, of course. She screamed with laughter, and then she wanted to take a knife and do the major a nasty injury. It was she who suggested I delve into his past, but so far I've had no luck. The only thing I've dug up is that he seems to move on regularly after only two or three years in the job. Sometimes less. Oh, and his engagement to a woman down your way has been an on-and-off affair and nobody wants to talk about it.'

Bea said, 'Well, I may be wrong, but it has occurred to me – maybe it has to you, too? – that the reason everyone is happy to get rid of him is something no one wants to talk about.'

Rosemary didn't get it. 'He makes passes at women? I've seen no signs of that.'

'Me, neither. I don't think he's highly sexed, in either direction. No, it's not that, but . . . I'm not sure what I mean. One thing I know: he takes a cut of whatever business he transacts on Julian's behalf, and to stop him complaining, he feeds the police the line about Julian going off his rocker so they don't take anything he says seriously. Now someone set fire to the stables, and I'm wondering what happens next?'

'A fire? No!'

Bea said, 'Fire is a useful servant but a wicked master. It was arson, all right. Someone knocked the security man out and set fire to the stables. Julian did get some burns but nothing to put him in hospital. He rescued Pete's dog and her pups and got the fire under control. I don't *know* that the major was involved but when he spoke to the police, he played the incident down from arson to an accident, so they didn't investigate. Julian is planning a meeting of some of the villagers this evening in the library to discuss the situation. Will you be there?'

'No. I'm in Birmingham tonight, meeting a man who served in the same regiment as the major. Let me know what happens?'

Two dark shapes loomed out of the gloaming. Julian, with Bruno at his side. Piers and Julian did that high five thing with their hands, and they all got into the car, Julian and Bruno in the back.

Julian said, 'Bruno found a bug in the estate office. I threw it out into the meadow at the back. Probably the wrong thing to do. I assume the major put it there but I have no proof of that. Any news from Rosemary?'

Bea shook her head. 'Nothing yet. What are you going to do this evening?'

'I've been taking a good look at what's been happening here

and two things stand out. One, the police are not going to believe that we are having real problems unless we provide them with proof, and two, Henry says he was not of the raiding party and I believe him.'

Bea said, 'He's one of Jenny's family? The one she calls "Waste of Space"? And is it his brother who's "Useless Lump"?'

'Henry and Hal. Local builders. So, it's not them. I cannot accept the idea that everything that's happened is due to a raiding party down for a spree from London. Looking at the situation logically, I can only conclude that it's our local layabouts who're responsible.'

Bea said, 'But you can't prove it.'

'That is, indeed, the problem. There's three young lads locally who come from good families and are way out of control. Two are under eighteen and don't have a driving licence. The third is older and did have a licence once, but lost it due to dangerous driving.

'They started in a small way with petty theft and vandalism. They got interested in treasure hunting with metal detectors which kept them occupied for a while but then wanted to try their luck in the park. As none of them had a licence they co-opted an older man to drive them, in order to get them and their equipment into the park. Their trespass resulted in a death. I don't think they set out to kill anyone. I think they're probably as horrified by what happened as we are.

'The point is that nothing has happened to them as a result of anything they've done so far. Nada. Zilch. Their fame spreads in the community and will soon attract followers if it hasn't done so already. Today they set the stables on fire, attacked Jock and fled. And again, nothing happens to them. I'm convening this meeting in the hope that we can pin down witnesses to what they've done. If we can only do that, the police will be forced to take action.'

Bea said, 'The villagers are between the devil and the deep blue sea. If they name names, the men who run this part of the world will come down on them like a ton of bricks.'

Julian said, 'And they don't fear the deep blue sea because—'

'They've studied you and think you'd always play fair . . . which the other side doesn't.'

They thought about that. Piers said, 'I think you're right to forget the supposed London gang, but could everything that's happened so far have been managed by local lads high on excitement? Surely that's a bit of a stretch? And why did they set the stables alight?'

Bea said, 'They wanted to get rid of Beauty because she can identify who committed murder and whisked her master away. She followed their vehicle out of the park till they spotted her, and put her in the ditch.'

Julian said, 'I'm wondering about the message Tyra said she'd got from a relative of Pete's. No one's found Pete's phone, have they? Is he up in London now? If he's alive and free, why didn't he contact her himself? And if not, who's using his phone?'

That was a nasty thought.

Bea asked, 'If he's dead, why bother to send her messages?'

Piers said, 'To make us think he was part of the raiding party? To keep her quiet, maybe? Ensure she goes along with the lie that he's dead?'

Julian said, 'Could "they" – whoever "they" are – be keeping him prisoner somewhere? How do you keep a grown man prisoner in these parts? I don't get it. The worst of it is that this whole thing is escalating. A man died and the police aren't looking for a local victim. Firing the stables and knocking Jock out says the raiders are not giving up. So how do we stop them?'

Bea said, half serious and wanting to lighten the mood, 'Get Jenny to put a curse on them?'

Julian smiled, but shook his head. 'Let's try something legal first. Let's get statements from everyone who's been affected by what the lads have done, statements we can take to the police which will force them to act. I don't want hearsay because that's not allowable in court. I realize that might be difficult. Some people have already tried to name them and failed to get justice. But this is the right way, the legal way to deal with this. If it fails, then I must admit I'm out of ideas.'

Bea said, 'I did have an idea, but I don't think you'd like it very much.' She explained. Twice.

The men concentrated. Piers laughed out loud. 'I like it!'

Julian said, 'You want me to suggest . . .? No, that's entrapment.'

Bea opened her eyes wide. 'You don't have to *lie.* You say you'd heard on good authority, that you are beginning to wonder if this or that . . . you act as if you think the rumours might be based on reality, but you really aren't sure they should be taken seriously.'

Julian was dubious. 'Yes, I suppose it might work, but . . . who knows where it might lead? They are so volatile they might descend to violence again. Can we risk another death? Who might be the target for them next time? Let's try the legal way first. Let's see if we can scrape together enough evidence to get them convicted. We meet at seven in the library in the Hall.'

Saturday evening, 7 p.m.

Dusk fell. Solidly. The volunteer stewards left, shutters were closed, lights were switched off. The workmen drove off. The stable yard seemed very quiet without their constant coming and going.

It had stopped raining, almost. The air smelled clean and green.

Time to go on parade. The lighting in the yard flickered on and off as people arrived.

Kylie's younger sister arrived to look after Pip and was installed in the estate office, with Polly's phone number on speed dial to ring if anything disturbing happened.

Bea spotted not just one but two security men patrolling the grounds, working in pairs. One had a dog that you wouldn't like to meet if it didn't like the look of you. The other man carried a hefty stick which gave the same impression.

Cars and a lorry drew up outside the estate office and parked in orderly fashion. Shadowy figures made their way to the kitchen door and disappeared inside the Hall. The corridors inside also had a number of security lights which were activated by movement. They came on now as various figures made their way to the library, which was fully lit tonight. Blinds had been pulled down over the windows. Some windows had shutters, and they had been closed, too.

Piers chose to sit at the far end of the library, with his sketch pad at the ready, observing all that happened.

Bea was asked to sit beside Julian and Polly to record what happened at the meeting. She prepared her laptop and smartphone accordingly.

Mrs Maggs fussed around Polly, putting her in a comfortable chair with arms, finding her cushions to help her relax, and making her put her feet up. The Kate lookalike arrived; surely she must be a close relation?

Julian had shed his fire-stained clothes and was – hurray! – in the deep blue shirt Bea had bought him. And jeans and so on.

He had a file of papers beside him, and his laptop. His phone was also set to record.

Imran arrived early; good.

Henry and Hal brought nothing but themselves and an air of tension only just under control.

The security guard, Jock, arrived. He looked as if he'd been knocked down in a rough and tumble but was about to get back up off the floor and do someone an injury.

At the last moment a dark-haired girl with striking good looks slid into the room and took a seat beside Imran, who re-aligned his own chair to be nearer hers. This would be Francine, his fiancée, the practice manager at the doctors' surgery in town and a possible replacement for Rosemary.

'Shall we begin?' said Julian. 'Henry, this all started before my time, so perhaps you could do the honours?'

Henry – aka Waste of Space – wasted no words. 'I don't see that we can do anything about it. It's hopeless. And I don't see what these two Londoners are here for.'

Julian said, 'They are people who make things happen. Like Rosemary.'

A growl of laughter. 'Well, we all know . . .!'

Julian raised his hand. 'Perhaps you do. Perhaps you don't. All right. I'll start. Let's begin with the problems of the neighbourhood. The village and the Marston Hall estate form only a small part of the county. The town and the village haven't been getting on recently. I'm told this is an historic matter dating back to the Middle Ages when they took part in the Wars of the Roses on opposite sides. Local sports events such as cricket, football and darts tend to exacerbate ancient grudges.

'For many years now this area has been ruled by local magnates whose families have been here for generations. Our local MP is firmly entrenched in society and going up the ladder in Parliament. He is great friends with his neighbour, a newly made member of the House of Lords, who has enough money to run a battleship, never mind a private jet, and who spreads his patronage widely. Between them they pretty well own the nearest town. Their influence in matters high and low is not to be trifled with.

'Then we get recent shifts in the local population. Incomers sometimes benefit the community, and sometimes don't. Because there was no work locally, young people have been leaving for the town. If they stayed here, there was nowhere to live. The Marston-Langs did make some attempt to deal with the situation by opening part of the house to the public and setting up the farm shop, the restaurant and the amusement park, but their management was not professional and their projects were bound to fail. Henry; I'd welcome your input here.'

Henry inched forward on his chair, looking as if he wished he were elsewhere. 'Well, it's like you said: incomers. They buy our houses and work from home. They don't spend much locally, they have everything delivered, and they ignore village events.

'Then come the refugees. Some people thought it was all right to take in those that didn't look like them. Some didn't. Imran and his parents, they did good by us. They ran the shop when the old folk retired and that helped us all, kept the village alive, like. They weren't like us . . . beg pardon, Imran . . . but that's how the older lot – our parents and such – how they felt. But they was accepted. And they was bright. Imran was bright.'

Julian nodded. 'And that's where some more trouble started, right?'

'Well, it weren't us,' said Henry, carefully choosing his words. 'But yes, there were those that thought it was all right to make fun of the newcomers. Some of us had been brought up to believe they shouldn't be coming here and taking our jobs and our housing, but mostly we got used to them. And yes, there were those who didn't. They said things, and sometimes they threw things. And the rest of us, we didn't say nothing.'

Imran leaned forward to speak. 'That's not quite true. When I was twelve, you fought two of them when they threw me off my bike and broke the frame.'

Henry said, 'Yeah. And straight after my dad got fined for something he hadn't done. Lesson learned. Let 'em get on with it. Not our fight.'

Julian smiled. 'But you did make it your fight, didn't you, Henry? You and Jenny and the Maggs family and many others fought fair. Over the years, Imran and his family continued to do all right, and on the whole village opinion swung behind him and his parents, right?'

'Right. Yeah. They did all right.'

Julian said, 'Then my grandfather died and things changed. My wife and I were Londoners with careers of our own but in our well-meaning, ignorant way, we thought we could do some good here. There were problems: lack of money, difficulties with planning permissions and some rotten apples in the workforce. Also, we had to learn in what way current trends were affecting country life.

'We took advice from all and sundry. We understood that we needed professional help to run the estate. Now Mrs Abbot here had already found me Rosemary' – there was a ripple of subdued amusement through the room –'who came on a short-term contract to deal with various problems left over from the previous regime. And boy! Did she deal with them! What you didn't know was that Rosemary is a professional bodyguard . . .'

Another ripple, this time of astonishment.

'. . . and her private life is just that. Private.'

Henry tried to work it out. 'You mean, she prefers women?'

Julian shook his head. 'As I said, her private life is private. Now it was clear that I needed a general manager with experience. Lady Knighton, who used to run the volunteer stewards in the house – you all know her, don't you? She's been unwell recently, so had to give that up. Anyway, she recommended that we take the major on. He had all the right qualifications, and knew many of the landowners locally because he originally came from these parts.'

Was there a draught from one of the windows? The air seemed chilly.

Julian sighed. 'I interviewed three no-hopers and the major. I was not entirely convinced that he and I would see eye to eye on the problems we faced here and I only gave him a contract for six months. He moved into one of the vacant properties in the village and set to work. I listened and learned. I discovered that each time I made a decision for myself, the major had good reasons why I'd done the wrong thing.

'For instance, one of my first acts had been to put Imran in charge of the farm shop. I'm glad I did because he has more than proved his worth. But at a personal cost to him. Eh, Imran?'

Imran looked at the girl beside him. She put out her hand and he took it, bracing himself to face the room. He said, 'It's my ideal job. I love it. I hand-picked my team. Every week, the profits increase and we reckon the signs are good for the Christmas trade.'

'And the cost to you?' said Julian.

'Yeah. The three lads came round to the farm shop the second week I was there, and tried to steal some bottles of booze. My staff chased them away, but they came back in force a couple of days later, upsetting tables, sending piles of merchandise all over the floor. We drove them out, and I told them they were banned.

'They waited a week and returned, scrawling filthy words on the cabinets, and picking out some specialist beers to take away with them. In and out in five minutes. They'd disappeared by the time I phoned the police. I took photos of the wreckage. The police came and told me I shouldn't make a mountain out of a molehill, that boys would be boys and so on.

'We cleaned up again. My staff were pretty good about it. They said they knew what we were up against, and they said they backed me a hundred per cent. One woman left, but I took on a hefty young man who said he didn't agree with stealing and that that was what it was, and they couldn't do nothing to him because he lived out to the east and not here.'

Julian turned to the Kate lookalike, saying, 'Your cousin had some trouble at the restaurant, too?'

'She had a visit from an inspector who wanted to condemn her gas cooker which was working perfectly, so she told him she'd seen his daughter slap her toddler in the town square and was thinking of telling the authorities about it, and he backed down straight away. She didn't tell the authorities but perhaps she should have done. The next night they were back, tipping the rubbish bins out all over the car park. It made her that mad she had to go to the doctor to get her blood pressure checked. But they haven't been back since.'

Julian said, 'Imran?'

'Yes, they came back again, scaring some punters, ripping up some placards and overturning the benches outside the restaurant. Then I had a visit from someone from the council about illegal parking on the verges. And that's when Sir Julian took on some security.'

Julian said, 'Yes, I did. The major said I was crazy. He said that we wouldn't have had a problem if I hadn't put Imran in charge. He said I didn't know what trouble I was storing up for myself if I didn't pay attention to his advice. He said it was a waste of money to employ security staff. Would you like to give me the names of the boys you saw doing the damage, Imran?'

Imran looked at the girl. He looked round the room. 'I've already tried that and got nowhere. The law won't do nothing, not when they're under eighteen. You saw what happened at the darts match. They pinched that woman's phone, and the policeman tried to blame it on the refugee lad that we've taken in. It was only Old Jenny who dared to stop them, and they couldn't touch her. But there's others . . . I wouldn't wonder if the innkeeper doesn't get a visit from some official or other, complaining about the opening hours or the state of the kitchens or something.'

Henry broke in, seething with suppressed rage. 'Don't forget Major Carpenter backed them up in the pub. But who are we to point the finger at him, when he's been appointed law and order around here? He could turn us out of our cottages tomorrow!'

'No, he couldn't,' said Julian. 'He tried that with Jenny and failed, remember?'

They remembered. Heads nodded.

Julian said, 'I can't sack him without proof of wrongdoing. I took him on because I needed his expertise. I didn't understand that his definition of law is not mine. He has many years of experience running estates, but it's taken me a while to understand that he thinks his job is to fleece the poorest in order to provide his boss with a good income.'

More heads nodded. Someone said, quietly, 'And the dosh didn't only go to the boss. Henry shoulda had the contract to do the repairs in the village. He and his brother, and his father before him, they always did the building work round the village and in the town, too. It's a something disgrace the major gave the contract to one of his buddies.'

'Yeah, it is,' said Henry, clenching his huge fists. 'He gave it to that lot from town that doesn't know how to deal with wood. They slap on a bit of MDF and think it'll do the job, which it doesn't. And we've had to advertise and go miles away to pick up what work we could find.'

'I know,' said Julian. 'And when I found out that there were backhanders being given for work done in the village I gave the major a written warning. He was amazed. He said it has always been understood that the middleman was paid for arranging contracts. And then he – or someone in cahoots with him – began to circulate a rumour that Rosemary and I were having extra-curricular relations. This made Lady Polly and I very sad.'

A murmur ran round the room. Heads were shaken, but no one dared look straight at Julian.

Julian said, 'It was not true.' He smiled across at Polly, who smiled back.

Polly said, 'Believe me, I would have known if there had been any truth in it. That poor girl. The major made her position here most uncomfortable, which is why she left the Hall, and will not return.'

Julian said, 'So. There was vandalism which the police didn't attend to, and dicey contracts. We had a security team and the major had one written notice. Stalemate. Moving on, we come to the terrible night when a man died. Henry, over to you to explain why your lorry went in and out of the amusement park.'

Henry shifted, uncomfortable in his chair. 'Easy. We got there too late. You see, after what happened at the farm shop and at the darts match, we understood the police and the major weren't going to be much help, and some of us from the village, including Pete and two other security guards, got together to talk the matter over down at the pub.

'We arranged among ourselves that at the slightest sign of trouble, whoever was on duty would text the rest of us for help even before he notified the police. But then it all went quiet. The scumbags moved on to metal detecting in the churchyard. We had a laugh or two about that. Treasure, my Aunt Fanny! And we, sort of, not exactly forgot about it, but perhaps we weren't as quick off the mark as we should have been on the night they broke in.

'Pete texted us late that night, and we weren't well prepared. Jock and another of the guards were watching football in a pub in town, Teddy had one of his throats and had gone to bed early. Imran had his phone switched off.'

He didn't look at Imran as he said this, but both Imran and Francine looked self-conscious. Everyone could guess what they'd been up to that night.

Henry cleared his throat. 'We – my brother and I – were in the pub in the village. I nearly didn't see the text. I rang Pete and he said there were lights moving around inside the amusement park, at the start of the tree walk. He said he'd rung the police and was going to see what was up. We got into the lorry and raced up there. Pete kept on the line, reporting to us as we drove along. He said he could see the three or four lads, laughing and drinking—'

'Three, or four?' Julian was sharp.

'Four, he said. Maybe more. But they was moving around and he couldn't be sure. There was an older man, too. Pete could tell he was different by the way he moved. That'd be the one who died, I suppose. Anyway, Pete said the lads had all got head torches on and a couple were carrying metal detectors and maybe, he wasn't sure, but maybe a spade as well. He said he could see a big car – he thought it was an SUV – with its headlights full on.

'He said he'd hang back and wait for us to come as there was too many for him to tackle. But they must have spotted him or seen his dog, because while we were still on the way, we heard him shouting and Beauty barking and it sounded like people fighting. And then his phone got turned off.

'We reached the entrance to the amusement park, and stopped to listen. But it was all quiet. Really, deathly quiet. The guards' caravan at the entrance was empty. No sign of Pete or his dog. No lights. Then we saw the fence round the site was down. We took the lorry in to where he said he'd been, but there was nothing there. No Pete. No body. It began to rain, hard. We didn't know what to think. We thought Pete must have scared them off and gone about his rounds, but then he should have told us, shouldn't he? We kept ringing his mobile but it went to voicemail. In the end, we just went home.'

TWELVE

Saturday evening, continued

Silence. Eyes were directed to the floor or the ceiling, because no one believed that that was how the night had ended.

Julian sighed. 'You arrived at the site of the action. You saw the body, didn't recognize it, knew there'd been a fight and concluded that Pete had killed the stranger. You thought that, realizing what he'd done, Pete had fled the scene?'

Henry flushed. 'That's what it looked like.'

Julian said, 'I get it that you didn't want to ring the police because you were trying to protect Pete.'

'It would have been self-defence—'

'Perhaps. Yes. But you didn't go home straight away, did you? The tracks from the lorry showed us that you followed the SUV out of the park through the south gate that had been smashed-in earlier, thinking . . .?'

'Well, it didn't seem right, Pete going off with them. If that's what he had done. So we went after him, thinking, hoping. But we didn't find him. We went near on a mile down the road to the south, and we didn't see nothing. We was running short of gas. So we come back, thinking the police would have to sort it out.'

Bea understood that if they'd taken the road to the east they'd have seen the body of Beauty . . . But they hadn't had Bruno to show them the way, and they'd taken the wrong turning.

Julian said, 'You must have realized the tyres on your lorry would be inspected at some point. Did you think of changing them?'

'We hoped the rain would wash the marks away. We couldn't afford a new set and even if we had, the police would have found where we'd taken the lorry to get new tyres. So we did nothing and hoped for the best.'

'What did you think this morning when you heard that

I'd found Beauty near to death, and had installed her in the stables?'

'We didn't know what to think. I mean, Pete wouldn't have left her if he'd still been alive, would he?'

'I'm hoping he is, but his wife has had a message from his phone. Someone rang, claiming to be a member of Pete's family in London, saying they were coming down soon to get her and she was to keep quiet about it. Fortunately, she told Lady Polly. It looks as if the invaders have Pete's phone, even if they haven't got the man himself. I don't think they'd have contacted her unless they were trying to stop her telling the police that Pete's not dead. I'm hoping they're keeping him alive somewhere, even though he's a danger to them. He could identify them, you see. The point is, can you do the same?'

Heads were shaken. 'No,' said Henry. 'We got there too late. We only know what Pete told us, and that's hearsay, isn't it?'

'You didn't keep his call on your phone?'

'Well, no. We didn't think . . .' He shifted his feet. He'd deleted Pete's call, thinking in some muddled way that he was helping his friend.

Depression settled on the room.

Bea said, 'Without identification, we don't have anything to take to the police.'

'One last chance,' said Julian. He turned to Jock, the security guard, who'd copped the worst of the 'incident' that day. 'What did you see today, and what action did you take?'

'You said to vary the time I start on my rounds, and not always go round the same way. So today I started early and went west first . . . and you know what? I forgot to log it, but the western meadow's flooded again. The water will flow over the track soon, and then what are we going to do, I ask myself? Then when I got to the south gate it was hanging open which I thought had been put right, but there it was, open.

'Then I heard a dog barking and thought it might be Beauty, so I come back down to the back of the stables, careful like, and spotted an SUV parked in the meadow at the back of the Tithe Barn. There wasn't no one in it.'

Bea said, 'Did you get the number?'

'I was too far off. So I pressed my alarm to alert the major and I phoned the police and I got to the far side of the stables and poked me head round the corner and something hit me on the back of the head and that was me out of it.

'When I come round, the stables was on fire and the SUV was gone. Then you all came and dealt with it. The doc says I've a hard head but ought to take it easy and I will, and all. The major said he'd rearrange the schedule so's I wouldn't be on for a couple of days and that's all right with me, except that I'm so blimming angry that I could do someone an injury, I really could. That poor dog. I liked Pete. He was so looking forward to the baby being born.'

'Let's be quite clear,' said Julian. 'You didn't actually see anyone at the stables. Not even out of the corner of your eye?'

Jock hesitated. 'Dunno. Might have. Just a movement. Maybe I imagined it.'

'But you recognized the SUV?' said Julian.

A long silence. Eyes sought the floor. Or the ceiling. They did know – or guess – who it belonged to, but for some reason couldn't – or wouldn't – say.

Julian said, 'There aren't that many of those around. So let's approach this a different way. None of the three lads I'm thinking of have a driving licence at the moment. The eldest boy, Nicholas – known as Nick to his friends and family – did have one, but lost it. The others are too young even to apply.'

Nods all round.

'Which means that, if they took the SUV out, either they were driving illegally, or they had an older person with them.'

Henry burst out, 'It's no good. They're untouchable. Look, anyone who complains gets a visit from the council to cut off their gas supply as being dangerous, or served with parking tickets which they don't remember having caused. Council taxes can rise because you've suddenly been transferred to a higher band, and there's been threats of children being removed from their families for bad behaviour which never happened.

'We're at the mercy of the council and that's run for the benefit of the multi-billionaires and our wonderful MP who's aiming for the House of Lords. Pete called them the Untouchables, and that's what they are.'

Julian said, in his soft voice, 'No, they're not untouchable.

They've got you thinking that way, but they're not.' He looked around, checking for signs of defeatism. And found them.

He said, 'Look, when the lads needed transport to take themselves and their metal detectors to the amusement park they had access to big cars – like the SUV that Jock saw – but no one with a licence to drive them.

'They were sensible enough not to let Nick get behind the wheel, so they co-opted someone with a licence. Someone local who worked for their parents? To judge by his clothing, this was a man who worked outside. Perhaps he was an odd-job man or a gardener? That's the older man Pete saw. I think that could be the man whose body we found in the park the next day.

'Now did someone else drive the SUV to the stables today? Someone older who had a licence? Or did Nick drive, taking the risk that he might be seen? Even the police would take notice of that, wouldn't they?'

There was a ripple of understanding throughout the room.

Julian said, 'Who drove them? That's the question. I've made enquiries. Our respected Member of Parliament has two sons and a small fleet of cars from an SUV downwards. The eldest boy, Nick, had an expensive education at a series of boarding schools, never lasting more than a year at any. He left without taking any exams and is probably unemployable.

'He was given a twenty-first birthday party in the Canary Islands, with guests being jet-setted in from all over the world. Nick is a bully, has left a trail of young girls with bruised bodies all over the place, claiming they came on to him because of his money. He's never been had up in court because Daddy can afford the very best of lawyers. Officially he's an intern working for his father, not that he spends much time on the job.

'Nick's younger brother, Boris, has only been asked to remove himself from two schools although his parents have made donations to a new library to make sure he doesn't have anything formal on his record. He's dropped out of education for the time being. He's said to be taking a gap year before deciding what to do next.

'The father of the third boy, Clement, is our very own multi-billionaire, friend of the great and mighty, tipped for upping to the House of Lords, on the board of umpteen different companies.

His wife is a multi-million heiress in her own right, and is president of this charity and that. They also have several cars. I haven't yet worked out how many. Their son Clement is reputed to have more brains than the other two put together, and to think up lots of amusing things to do . . . like tormenting cats, dogs and anyone who can't fight back. He's also dropped out of school and is taking a gap year. Both Boris and Clement are under eighteen and neither has yet applied for driving lessons, never mind taking a test.

'Both families keep a skeleton staff at their mansions in this neighbourhood, even when they themselves are staying at one of their other residences. The MP and his wife mostly reside at their London house, returning to their constituency here now and then. He and his wife are currently on holiday abroad, and his mother – that's Lady Knighton – is supposed to be keeping an eye on the house and the two boys. I'm told she's not been well lately and, by all reports, the boys are running wild.'

Someone hissed. 'Lady Knighton? But . . .! She's—'

'Untouchable,' said Julian. 'Yes, she's lovely and much loved. But she's getting on and not been well. The boys are, it seems, for the most part unsupervised. I'm told she hasn't left the dower house for some weeks, and the live-in staff at her son's house are left to their own devices. I made some enquiries and discovered that most live-in staff are couples employed by an agency. Lady Knighton is looked after by a housekeeper and her two adult children, who come and go as they please. If the boys needed a driver and someone to help them cart their metal-detecting gear around, they could take their pick from staff employed by one or other of the local houses.

'I suggest our dead man was an employee at one of these houses, who had no ties locally. He probably thought it a great lark to accept a tenner or two to take the boys out for a spot of treasure hunting. Why they chose that spot in the amusement park to dig I cannot imagine, except that yes, I believe there was once a small stone building there which had a good view over that side of the park. A folly of sorts. Eighteenth century, according to the old maps.

'The boys either knew roughly when Pete should be passing that way on his rounds or they didn't care. He spotted them, raised the alarm, and there was a melee in which their driver got hit on the head and died. The boys hadn't set out to kill anyone but their driver was dead and Pete was still alive and, if he were left on the spot, could identify them. So they panicked. They couldn't face killing Pete in cold blood, so they swapped identities to confuse matters. They put Pete's lanyard round their man's neck, bundled Pete into the SUV and one of them – I assume it was Nick – drove it back the way they came . . . just before Henry arrived in his lorry.

'Only, Beauty followed the SUV. That's how we can tell that Pete was taken away with them under duress. If Pete had thrown in his lot with the boys, then Beauty wouldn't have followed the SUV on foot because she'd have been in the car with him. But she did follow. They realized that her presence would give them away so stopped the SUV long enough to get out, to beat her up and throw her body in a ditch. And then they drove home—'

'With Pete?'

'Hopefully, yes. You may ask why he hasn't come forward? Either he was so badly hurt he's not able to get out, or he's being kept quiet by threats to harm his wife and new son if he makes waves. Either way, at the moment he can't help us. Where are they keeping him? In some outbuilding at one of their big houses? Perhaps they are pretending that he is their driver, who injured himself and they're getting someone to look after him? We need to tap into local news. Who's been engaged at the big houses recently. Who's disappeared?'

Awkward shifting on seats. Silence while they all thought about it.

Someone said, 'That's a job for the police. We're not right for it.'

Henry said, 'They win, every time. Everything they touch . . . no one dares say anything. The police won't act. We've seen that. They're underage and their parents pull the strings around here. There's nothing we can do.'

There was a stir around the room. Looks were exchanged. Watches were consulted. They considered the meeting was over.

Julian sighed and lifted his hand to gain attention. 'Very well. Let's put that aside for the moment. There's something else I have to tell you before you go. There's a rumour doing the rounds again about buried treasure at the Hall. It's nonsense, of course. I know you're all sensible enough to realize what harm it would do to let that rumour become general knowledge. Meanwhile, I'll make some discreet enquiries to find out if there really is something to worry about. Piers, you discovered what the treasure is. Tell them.'

Piers picked up the ball and ran with it. 'It's all there, in the material Mr Colston's researching, but of course he's not going to let anyone in on it until he's finished his book. What's more, if you ask him about it, he'll deny that he's discovered anything at all.'

Henry said, 'I don't get it. There is no treasure.'

Julian said, 'The legend says there is. Some say it's a gold cup filled with coins. Something gold, anyway, hidden in some secret place at Marston Hall. Mr Colston hints that it may not be in the house itself, but hidden at some landmark site in the park. Think of the civil wars. There were heavy fines for landowners who belonged to the losing side.

'Mr Colston thinks that my ancestors may have buried some gold or gold object in the grounds, intending to dig it up again when times changed. Only, they died before that happened, and so the knowledge of where the treasure had been hidden was lost.'

Mouths gaped. Henry said, 'You mean, it was true?'

Julian kept a straight face. 'It's happened in other places. Why not here? There was certainly something going on in the Middle Ages which brought money and kudos to the Hall.'

Polly said, 'Julian and I have been delving into local history records and trying to match it up with what my father has discovered. Whether it was a cache of gold coins in a golden cup, or a relic from a local saint we don't know, but there was something.'

Henry muttered, 'Well, there's a turn-up for the books. The buried treasure's for real? Where is it, then? What are you going to do about it?'

Polly said, 'We wanted you to be the first to hear our plans. We're going to bring in the experts. Perhaps an aerial survey might help, using a drone. We want to keep the whole thing under wraps for the time being, or we'll have the park crawling with amateur detectorists.'

Julian said, 'Pip and I are fond of the spring in the western meadow which does – as Jenny has demonstrated – ease some skin conditions.'

Polly said, 'In fun, we've been calling it St Julian's well.' She laughed, to show she was joking.

Julian was horrified. 'No, no. Certainly not.'

Bea noticed that most people smiled. They liked Julian and they thought it might indeed be appropriate to call the well after him.

Henry licked dry lips. 'You mean, one of the old Marstons really did hide a cache of gold in the park?'

'We've no idea,' said Julian, 'but we're going to investigate. There's a reference to a holy well on a very old map my father-in-law found. There's a cross marked on the western meadow. Perhaps in the old days there was a pathway leading down from the meadow through the trees to the road that circles the estate? We're talking about centuries ago, of course. Long before the present wall was built around the park.'

A stir of excitement. They'd bought the story hook, line and sinker. Except for Francine, who looked at Julian with narrowed eyes, and then checked with Imran, who was also looking thoughtful . . . and then he looked at Francine . . . their eyes met and both smiled slightly. Both settled back in their chairs. Those two hadn't bought the story, but they understood what Julian was trying to do.

Jock rubbed the back of his neck. 'It's true, it's a bit odd, that place. Look at the way it floods every now and then, and next day the water's gone.'

Julian said, 'Probably goes into an underground stream. I'm really looking forward to finding out what's there, though I'm pretty sure it won't be a gold cup!'

Uneasy laughter. Julian brought the meeting to a close by standing up. 'Tomorrow is Sunday and most professionals take the day off, but on Monday I'm going to find out which firms I should contact to look at the site. So, if you hear the subject raised anywhere, I'd be grateful if you'd say that there really is no such treasure, no gold cup, no gold coins. We do not want the Untouchables rushing in and perhaps muddying evidence of what may or may not become a historical site.'

He shook hands with the brothers Henry and Hal, who volunteered to take Jock safely back home. Mrs Maggs busied herself putting the chairs back where they should be for the public to see on the morrow, before whisking off, taking the Kate lookalike with her.

Imran and Francine lingered. 'May we . . . at some point . . . have a word?' Imran was nervous.

Francine said, 'Dr Trisha has already reminded me that I've got six weeks holiday due to me, and only need to give a month's notice. If you'd like to consider . . .?'

Julian checked with Polly, who nodded approval. He said, 'There's church in the morning. Come and see me tomorrow afternoon about three? The house itself will be open to the public but I think we can use the kitchen as Mrs Maggs doesn't work on Sundays. Imran, you have something to tell me, too?'

Imran said, 'Yes. About the restaurant. We didn't want to make it formal and say that Kate is having to have time off and her cousin's taking over, not till we could work out what we could do about it. Her cousin's worked at a restaurant in town for years and she's a brilliant baker but she doesn't know how to manage staff and the computer frightens her silly. She's asked me to help her out.'

He took a deep breath, and continued. 'My second-in-command at the farm shop is a local man and is working out well. Once we've decided what to do each day, he can be left to get on with it and ring me if there's a problem. This means I can get over to the restaurant a couple of hours a day to make sure everything works smoothly there. We'd like to continue that way, if it meets with your approval?'

Julian was pleased. 'Yes, I'd heard, and was waiting for you to tell me about it. I know you're running both farm shop and restaurant and that all is going well. At some point you'll need under-managers at the farm shop and the restaurant, but we can discuss this later. There'll have to be an adjustment to your terms of employment, Kate's cousin must be paid appropriately, and Kate herself must get the usual sick leave. Thank you, Imran. And Francine. I look forward to seeing you both tomorrow.'

* * *

Shadows regained their hold on the old building as they retraced their steps to the estate office, collecting the special water in the bottle and the bowl on the way.

Back at the ranch they found that a young woman had laid herself out on the settee and gone to sleep while Pip, still in his cradle, was wide awake, trying to stuff the legs of his toy giraffe into his mouth.

Polly sniffed the air, said, 'His nappy needs changing. So much for babysitting.' She woke the sleeping beauty, paid her off, changed Pip and gave him a late evening bottle.

Julian set the bottle of water and the still half-full basin on the table. He bathed his face and bared his arm to deal with his burns which had paled from raw red to a blushing pink.

Polly burped Pip, saying, 'You're going to appoint Francine in Mrs Tring's place? Are you sure you can manage her? She's run the doctor's practice with an iron hand. She'll want to run the Hall the same way. She's a ball-breaker. Goodness knows how Imran copes.'

Julian said, 'They've both got good brains, but he's the one who sees a problem and decides what to do about it while she's the one who carries out his decisions. They respect one another's talents. We'll have to find them a place to live in the village. I'm thinking of the very end cottage, the one the major was planning to sell to the visitors.'

Piers said, 'Push comes to shove, he'll always think faster than her. He's aiming to take the major's place, isn't he? Not now. He knows he isn't ready yet. Maybe five years hence?'

Julian said, 'I wish it were sooner. I'll have to get someone in to fill the gap till he's ready for it.'

Piers inspected the kitchen cabinets. 'It's a good trap. Well set. What can we use for the holy golden cup? I could cover some suitable earthenware dish with gold paint, which would fool the treasure hunters for a while.'

Polly said, 'There's some old earthenware mugs on the top shelf of one of the cupboards in the kitchen. Would one of them do?'

Julian shook his head. 'Metal detectors respond to metal. We have to use gold to fool the treasure hunters. I've got my grandfather's old gold watch and chain in my bedside drawer upstairs.

The chain is broken and the watch doesn't work, but it amuses me to think the old man's things could be used to bait the trap. I'll wrap it in some old sacking and bury it beside the spring at dawn tomorrow.'

Bea said, 'What's this meadow like? You were going to take me to see it, remember?'

'It's on the hillside over by the western gate. A spring rises at the foot of a bluff into a shallow pool. The water trickles down a short way and disappears into a stand of trees below. Sometimes the pool overflows and saturates the meadow, so it's always green. I must bury the treasure without disturbing the earth too much, as that would be a dead giveaway.'

Piers said, 'You reckon they'll come tomorrow night?'

Julian turned his forearm in the water with a sigh of relief. 'After tonight, the word will be everywhere. Even as we speak, they'll be discussing it in the pub. Tomorrow is Sunday. Polly and I will go to church as usual and, as usual, the farm shop and restaurant will be open. There'll be even more opportunity then for the word to spread.

'We shall act innocent. It would be only natural that Polly and I might take a trip out to the western meadow to show our guests where X marks the spot. We will look around, we will chatter and return to the Hall, giving observers the chance to see we are not carrying metal detectors or spades.'

Bea said, 'Yes, but how are you going to record the lads breaking in? Oh, what about the film crew you're having round every now and again?'

Julian grinned. 'The major thinks I'm off my rocker, but I do have lots of contacts which he doesn't know about. A small independent firm is making a film for television about converting old buildings – like the stables – into liveable accommodation. They're paying us a fee, not the other way round. But don't tell the major or he'll want a cut.'

'Well done, you,' said Piers. 'But Bea's right. How are you going to record what happens if the lads come digging at the spring? We can't rely on our smartphones to capture anything, or can we?'

Julian said, 'I know where I can hire a video camera and tripod, plus a machine to record voices. I'll collect them from town tomorrow . . . No, I can't, can I? It's Sunday and they won't be open. Monday, then.'

Bea said, 'You won't want to challenge the youngsters, for fear of their turning violent. I assume you wish to do the filming from a distance. Is there any cover for those recording their intrusion?'

'It's very dark under the trees. We could set up there and hope there'll be enough moonlight to illuminate what they're doing. If they use the SUV again, I expect their headlights will provide sufficient light. I can't think of any other way of doing it.'

Bea said, 'What about Rosemary? I know she's still on your payroll.'

Julian said, 'Yes, she's been going around the countryside trying to find evidence of the major's past, and she comes back this way every few days. You may even have seen her around. She's wearing leathers and a helmet, and drives one of those food delivery bikes. She's put her mobile home in a caravan park the other side of the town, and travels around on her bike.'

'Well done,' said Piers.

Bea thought that she personally wouldn't have asked Rosemary to perform detective work. It really wasn't her cup of tea. But the girl would definitely come into her own if fisticuffs were to be the order of the day. Perhaps they'd actually see some action the following night?

Polly said, 'I'm too tired to think. Someone will have to help me carry Pip up the stairs. Bring on the day when we move to the stables. Julian, who's looking after Beauty and her pups?'

Julian yawned. 'I asked Big Teddy to take them. He's so soft he's probably giving them a hot water bottle and feeding Beauty by hand. I'll help you up the stairs. Tomorrow looks like being another busy day. Let's hope it's the day we catch the Untouchables.'

THIRTEEN

Sunday morning

Bea slept late, only waking when Piers said he could smell bacon cooking. They went downstairs to find Julian bathing his arm again while Pip was banging on the tray in his high chair, and Polly cooked up a full English breakfast. Julian said he'd been up for hours, and had already managed to insert his watch and chain into a crevice beside the spring.

It was a fine, sunny day which promised to be warm, with no more rain forecast for the time being. Everyone was relaxed on the surface, but underneath they were counting the hours till sundown when the Untouchables would – or would not – descend on the meadow. Maybe they hadn't heard of the 'find' or maybe their parents had come home and they couldn't get a car. Maybe nothing would happen at all.

They were all sitting around with a coffee, discussing what time they should leave for the Sunday church service when several things happened at once. Pip fell over and banged his head which alarmed Polly, a mutter in the distance grew into a roar as Marcus's helicopter flew over the house and came in to land, and Julian took a call on his phone which set him pacing up and down, with one finger in his ear, trying to hear what the caller was screaming at him about.

The helicopter's noise did not cease, but after a long few minutes of unbearable noise, grumbled off into the distance.

Pip was soothed into silence and Julian could finally hear what was being said on his phone.

Mrs Maggs appeared in the doorway saying, 'I can't be expected to cope, especially as it's my day off, but with so much going on I thought I'd just pop in to make sure all was hunky-dory, and then she arrives by helicopter, if you please, and says she needs to go over the place in peace and quiet and she's not letting the rest of the stewards come in although some are here already, of course. I told her that the public aren't allowed in till half past ten but she told me to make myself scarce so someone else is going to have to read the riot act because I tried that and got nowhere.'

'What?' said Polly, nursing a tearful Pip. 'We're off to church in a minute.'

Mrs Maggs folded her arms at them. 'Madam Mona, that's what. With a wedding planner, if you please! Taking photos and measurements and moving the furniture around which I told her she must not do, and she called me several names that I'm not accustomed to hearing, so someone else will have to talk to her, right?'

Julian covered his phone with his hand. 'I need to take this phone call. Can you . . .?'

'I'll go,' said Piers, rather amused than otherwise.

Bea went with him. They followed Mrs Maggs into the kitchen, where some of the volunteer stewards had gathered, looking as if they'd rather be elsewhere. Rules were rules and they should be getting ready to open the Hall to visitors. On the other hand, no one wanted to upset Mona who'd been brought up there, expected everyone to fall in with her wishes and had a nasty temper when crossed.

One steward said, 'We don't know what to do. People will be arriving in the car park and walking up to the house soon, and she's turned the notice on the door to "closed".'

Other stewards chimed in. 'And she's measuring the staircase and—'

'Shifted the reception desk and—'

'We had all that trouble earlier in the week, being closed because that man died—'

'Leave it to me,' said Piers and led the way along the corridor followed by Bea, Mrs Maggs and the handful of faithful stewards.

There in the hall was Mona flashing her diamond ring. Also, a businesswoman in a black suit and black-rimmed glasses, smartphone to the fore, saying, 'No, no, no! Marcus said there must be a chapel. It may be too small for such an important wedding, and we have to consider how it will look in *Hello!* magazine, but a chapel there must be.'

Mona bleated, 'Marcus doesn't own this place yet, and he doesn't know its history. I tell you there is no chapel—'

The wedding planner was not listening, but looking around at the hall. 'Yes, now we've moved the reception desk, I can see . . . the grand piano will go . . . here! The video team will be partly up in the gallery and partly by the entrance doors . . . which, by the way, will have to be removed and more suitable wooden doors put in their place. Something Victorian Gothic, I think. As for the stairs, we'll take up the carpeting and polish the wood – they'll look so much better that way – and we'll have loops of white roses and orchids threaded through the banisters and there will be an archway of flowers at the bottom.

'Now, how many bridesmaids did you say there would be? At least eight, I hope, including flower girls. Children need extra minders but you have to have them for the photographs. And quite possibly a dog as well. Dogs press the "Aaah!" button. If you don't have one or can't borrow one, we'll arrange for a rental.'

Piers took a deep breath and tried to interrupt. 'There is a slight problem . . .!'

The woman whirled round on him. 'Who are you? Not the owner, I assume! Now, if you're one of the staff here, you can point me in the direction of the chapel. Marcus says there's a chapel, and a chapel I must have!'

Mona was lost in her dream of being Bride of the Year. 'I've always thought I could have a cage of white doves—'

A sotto voce from Mrs Maggs. 'Not if they're going to pee on my floor, you won't.'

The wedding planner clapped her hands and everyone jumped. 'Chapel!' she said, through her teeth.

Mona descended from her dream enough to say, 'I don't know where Marcus got the idea, but really there isn't one. I suppose there might have been one here centuries ago, but there's nothing like that here now.'

The wedding planner said, 'I was told that guns had taken the place of the cross.'

Mona was confused. 'What do you mean? You think the room

where we kept the guns . . . but that's an office! Yes, it's in the oldest part of the house but it's—'

'Take me there! Is it this way?'

Mrs Maggs said, 'I'll show you,' and led the way.

'Yes, but . . .' Mona hurried after the wedding planner, with Piers and Bea following.

A twist and a turn, a short corridor, and Mona threw open the door of the room that had been used as an office for many a long year. The family's collection of guns had been kept there at one time. Later, it had become a junk room into which anything not immediately needed had been thrown.

All traces of its recent incarnations had disappeared. The room was an oblong with a ceiling somewhat higher than other rooms on that floor. The walls had been painted magnolia, new lighting installed and the wide wooden planks on the floor cleaned but not polished. There was no furniture at all.

High up on the side facing the Tithe Barn across the yard, there were two windows of ancient, greenish glass. There were uneven levels in the plaster where a doorway to the outside world had been boarded over.

'The chapel! At last!' said the wedding planner. 'But what is this? It's far too small for our needs. Eight or ten bridesmaids, two hundred guests. I fear we cannot use it unless . . . We could have you and Marcus plighting your troth here at the rehearsal the night before. Yes, why not? Some pews here, we'll find a cross somewhere; they can be rented, of course. Perhaps an old religious picture or two? If not in the collection, they can also be hired for the day. Yes, yes. It will do nicely.'

There was a growl in the sky, and Mona started. 'That'll be Marcus returning for me. He hates to be kept waiting and we've hardly touched on—'

The wedding planner waved her hand. 'Off you go. You can safely leave everything to me now. I've seen enough to make a start, but I shall need to return soon when the house is quiet, bring an assistant or two, take photographs. Then I can give you some idea of how we shall plan the event.

'The house itself is photogenic, the park attractive, but the gardens have been left to nature which is not a great look for the magazine trade, and it's clear the kitchens are quite inadequate.

We will have to bring in personnel and food for the whole weekend. Another thing: the guests will not be prepared to walk half a mile from the official car park. I assume there's a field at the back we can take over for another car park, and a space nearer the kitchens for delivery vans, and so on?'

She waved her hand at Bea and Piers, saying, 'These good people can introduce me to the master of the Hall. I must say that I was a trifle disappointed that he was not here to meet me, but Marcus did warn me he's rather touchy about having to sell the place. One understands. The upkeep of this old house must require money, and I gather that's in short supply. However, if he's prepared to pay for the wedding of the year, then we mustn't look gift horses in the mouth. Hah, hah.'

Mona gave one wild look around, and fled.

Piers said, with awe in his voice, 'The chapel . . .' And looked up at those telltale, ancient glass windows. 'You found the chapel!'

'Yes, yes,' said the wedding planner. 'Given a hint as to where to look. Been at this lark for years. Know my onions. It should scrub up nicely.'

'Yes,' said Piers, his hands moving over the wall opposite the door. 'You have the eye. I can see it now. By the way, I'm Piers. I paint portraits.'

'Have I heard of you? I don't think I've come across you before, have I? You're here to paint the happy couple? And this is your wife? What does she do? Never mind that. I must see the man who's going to pay the bills before I depart.'

Piers said, 'The guns were placed here, against this wall? With the sun shining through those windows most of the day, lighting up the altar, which would be here . . .' He ran his fingers over the wall which was bumpy with many layers of paint and wallpaper.

Bea took a deep breath and addressed the wedding planner. 'To start at the beginning, the Hall is not licensed for weddings.'

'Really? Sir Julian will have to arrange that. And of course the house will have to be closed to the public for at least a week.'

'That may well be a problem, and I don't believe Sir Julian

has any idea of the scope of the arrangements you wish to make. Who has retained you to plan the wedding?'

'Marcus indicated that it is the Marston-Langs' wish to honour the joining together of the two branches of the family.'

'Papering over recent developments? It is possible that Sir Julian might be prepared to host a small family wedding reception but nothing on the lines you suggest.'

Piers scrutinized the wall under the window. 'There's been several layers of paint over some layers of wallpaper. I wonder what's under them?'

The wedding planner's voice grew sharp. 'Are you hinting that Sir Julian would duck his obligations to his family?'

'Since they tried to kill him several times, yes.'

'What! Well, as Marcus is buying him out, there shouldn't be any problem in the long run.'

Bea wanted nothing more than to throttle the wedding planner but managed to say, 'We need to talk. Piers, leave that wallpaper alone! I believe Julian has everything under control and won't thank you for tackling a job which needs to be done by experts.'

She led the way back to the kitchen but there was no one there. Of course, Mrs Maggs would have shooed the volunteer stewards out of there and into their usual stations before the doors were opened to the public.

The wedding planner looked at her watch. 'I don't think I have time for this. I have another appointment in the City at noon.'

Bea decided that this was an occasion on which it would be permissible to start another rumour. Why not? Everyone else did. She said, 'Even on a Sunday you can use your laptop to enquire about Marcus's finances. Yes, he did make an offer to buy the Hall but that offer was declined and someone told me his finances are not all as healthy as they might be. Your time is valuable and shouldn't be wasted on those who can't afford to pay for it. Sir Julian and Lady Polly did look into the possibility of hosting wedding receptions here but decided that's a project for the distant future.'

Piers said, 'Mona didn't seem to know about the chapel, but Marcus told you there was one. Where did he get that information?'

The wedding planner looked uncertain of herself for the first time. 'He said he'd been wining and dining an old man who's something to do with the family, some scholar who's writing a book about the Hall.'

'Mr Colston,' said Bea and Piers together.

Bea groaned. 'Of course. He wouldn't tell Julian about the chapel but he told a complete stranger who treated him to a good meal.'

'But anyone who has eyes to see . . .' The wedding planner was on safer ground. 'You only have to look at the dimensions, its smell. I'm sensitive that way. I can always tell.'

Bea said, 'Yes, I believe you can. I think you're right. But the chapel has been decommissioned for many, many years, and must be carefully studied by experts before it can be used again.'

Piers said, 'I could—'

Bea cut him off. 'No, you couldn't. It's up to Julian to get the experts in.'

The wedding planner took a deep breath. 'Well, I must be on my way. Time is money and I have a great deal of research to do. I'm thinking gold and silver for the tableware. White is so last year. And if Mona wants to have a cageful of doves, then I really don't see why not. I left my car at the front. Can I get out through the kitchen?' And out went she.

Piers said, 'I could just peel away the top layer of wallpaper?'

'Leave it alone,' said Bea. 'It's time for church. We're all going, remember? And you can talk to Julian about your find afterward. In the open air. Not in the estate office. Remember Bruno found a bug there? So be careful what you say and where. Right?'

Out in the yard, there was no time to update Julian as they could hear the church bells summoning the faithful to the service.

'Speak later,' Julian said, as he helped Polly into the better of their two old cars. 'Or we'll be late, and that will never do.'

Piers and Bea followed in their own car and had the usual struggle to find a parking place in the village.

The church was very old with a slightly musty smell as if candles had been used to light the place until recently. An old harmonium stood, neglected, in one corner, having been replaced by an organ which had subsequently been updated to respond to electricity instead of being hand-pumped.

The pews were solid, as were the brightly coloured hassocks upon them, and there were some rather beautiful flower arrangements on either side of the chancel and on the ancient stone font. The font, in fact, looked to be even older than the church itself.

A woman minister, sensibly short on chatter, presided over the service, giving a short, thoughtful address. She sang the hymns with fervour and picked up a straying toddler and gave him a cuddle before returning him to his parents in the front pew.

The church was a good third full, mostly of older people, but several young families were following the example of Sir Julian and Lady Polly and had brought their young to hear the word of God, and to pray for themselves and others.

Mr Colston was there, importantly reading a lesson. He nodded to those who recognized him and ignored the rest. Buxom Kate with-the-troublesome-legs was there, with her lookalike cousin. Bea was surprised to see Jenny sitting alone in a pew at the back. No one sat near her, which perhaps was not surprising.

After the service, Julian and Polly made a point of greeting everyone. There was some talk of a children's service being started. Here and there people put their heads together and looked sideways at Julian and Polly. Repeating the story of the lost gold? Or that of Rosemary and Julian?

Bea noticed that Jenny ensconced herself on a bench in the churchyard, and went to sit beside her, saying, 'You knew about the chapel and where it was to be found?'

'I heard from my gran that she heard from her gran that they Roundheads brought a curse to the place, destroying the chapel and blocking up the spring. She said it was best to forget it, that it was all nonsense. Which it may well be, for all I know. Worshipping idols. Worshipping gold. I don't hold with any of that. I speak to the Big Man and he tells me to follow Him, and that's enough for me to be going on with.'

'But you believe in whatever's in the water? You've been

making up salves using the water from the spring, and you sent your daughter up to the Hall to attend to Julian's burns with bottles of it.'

'It's an old, old story about the spring that my gran used to tell me. I misremember what she used to call it. Some saint's name? It'll be St Julian's well from now on, no doubt. My gran said as her granny used to say there was something good for the skin in the water, and so there is. In the old days one of my family nearly got burned for a witch because she cured the Marston's baby of a nasty rash. Best keep it as a story. I'm not keen on being burned alive. Or drowned, neither.'

'Julian knows about the water, though. Or guesses.'

'Young Pip knows, and all. He knows all sorts, does young Pip. He'll be a good 'un. Lift the curse and all.'

A giant frame loomed in front of them. Henry – aka Waste of Space – had come to collect his gran. He bobbed his head to Bea, lifted Jenny to her feet, and took her away.

Julian called out to Bea that he'd booked lunch at the inn, if she and Piers would like to join them? The subtext was that there might well be another bug back at the ranch, so it was safer to meet and talk elsewhere.

Bea saw Mr Colston hovering, awaiting an invitation for lunch. When Julian asked him to join them in the pub instead of sweeping him back to the Hall in order to provide a three-course luncheon served by flunkeys in the dining room, that difficult old man said he'd a ready meal in the fridge and stalked off, emanating wounded disappointment.

Looking at the sky, Bea saw that there was more rain on the way, but inside the pub all was cheerful. And busy. The landlord apologized for putting them in a side room which had only just been cleared of years of junk, but he was rushed off his feet nowadays and they'd only thought that week to use the end room for serving meals and the furniture was a bit odds and sods if he didn't mind them saying so.

A high chair was brought for Pip, and everyone else squeezed around an old table in one corner while cheerful tourists and some slightly startled locals claimed all the other tables. The landlord was going to be able to fill his new dining room with ease, wasn't he?

The food came, hot and lively, and they all tucked in. Beer was offered and the men each drank a half. The women declined. The landlord said he was thinking of stocking a couple of good wines to serve with the food in future, and there'd be a dessert of hot chocolate sauce over vanilla ice cream for young Pip if Lady Polly thought he could manage it. Which she, and he, did.

Replete, with good coffee on the table, they updated one another.

Julian said the phone call that morning was from Jock, who'd had a text message on his phone from Pete. Yes, from Pete! Jock had phoned back straight away but by that time Pete's phone had been switched off again.

In his text, Pete had said Jock was not to worry, but to phone Tyra and tell her he was safe. He said that he couldn't stick around since he'd killed a man, but some friends were helping him get away out of the country and when he was safe he'd send for his wife and child.

'At least he's still alive,' said Polly.

Julian said, 'I told Jock that he had to tell the police. He didn't want to. I insisted. Finally he said he would, but I'm not sure he will. He's wondering if the text really came from Pete and I'm inclined to agree. I don't believe Pete killed anyone, but someone made him confess. I did ask Jock to get Pete to ring me if he contacts him again. Maybe he will.'

Next, Piers. 'We found the chapel.'

If he expected exclamations of pleased surprise, he was disappointed. Polly said, 'It took you that long? Julian suspected it ages ago. He got Lance to have a look, and Lance got all excited and promised to locate the right people who will be needed to restore it. They hope to start quite soon. Next month, is it, Julian?'

Piers couldn't let it rest. 'You wouldn't mind if I just lifted the wallpaper a bit, here or there? Just to see if there's any wall paintings underneath?'

Julian said, 'We can't afford to do anything till the experts have had a look at it. Everything has to be photographed and notes taken. When we're sure we've really got something, then we can have a Grand Opening. It would be good if you could keep coming down, keeping an eye on things. Maybe even paint Polly in there?'

'Ah,' said Piers, successfully diverted from the meddling he'd proposed. 'Now there's a good idea. The pair of you, against the old wall paintings. With any luck we'll find something juicy like a Last Judgement under the wallpaper.'

'No, no,' said Julian, laughing. 'That's for cathedrals. Our little chapel wouldn't have anything as big as that. We might have an angel or two? Or just a cross and perhaps a pattern? That's more usual for smaller chapels, isn't it?'

Piers looked as if he'd had his Christmas present snatched away.

'My turn to share,' said Bea. 'The wedding planner was ordered by Mona to look the place over. She's in a dream of white tulle and orchids and can't be brought to think sensibly about the arrangements. Marcus has another agenda. He's been buttering up Mr Colston who's unearthed the information that there was once a chapel at the Hall, and that guns replaced the cross. An excellent slogan, don't you think?'

She went on. 'The information about there being a chapel had been passed on to the wedding planner who, to give her credit, really does know her business. She is under the impression that you would be paying for everything, even though you were about to go bankrupt. Oh yes, and Marcus has told her he's buying the place.'

Neither Julian nor Polly looked upset. Julian said, 'Yeah, yeah. I feel sorry for Mona. Well, a little bit. Polly doesn't think Marcus will marry her if he can't get the Hall. The story that I'm going bankrupt is wishful thinking on his part.'

Bea said, 'I told the wedding planner that she might like to look at Marcus's finances, and I think she will. Her plan is to make Mona's nuptials the wedding of the year. Two hundred guests, food and lodging for the whole weekend, live music, eight or ten bridesmaids, including children and a pet dog for sentimental value. A new car park, orchids and roses, a cage full of doves, gold and silver the order of the day. Expense no object.'

'Poor girl,' said Polly. 'A wedding is not about having an expensive party. Ours was so lovely, making our vows to one another and to God, with just our family and friends around us. Oh, I'm going to cry.'

'No, you're not,' said Julian. 'Look at the time. We're meeting with Imran and Francine in half an hour, it's raining hard and we haven't an umbrella between us.'

Sunday evening

Yes, it rained. The wind got up and the sky grew dark, but Imran and Francine were waiting for Julian when they returned. He took them into the kitchen to discuss what might happen in the future while Bea settled Polly and made tea.

Bea asked Polly, 'You think Francine will work out all right?'

'She'll be fine. Rosemary was a wonder but we always knew she wouldn't be with us for long. Francine will try to bully Julian, discover she can't, and settle down to serve twenty years as his invaluable aid, with time off for producing one or two children, who will be as clever as their parents. And there'll be no more talk of Julian playing away.'

Bea foraged for biscuits but the tin was empty. Polly said she'd order more food in tomorrow.

They listened to the rain.

'Those bad lads won't come out in this,' said Polly. 'Neither will the punters. We have to keep the house open for visitors till five, but I'd better make sure all the volunteers have a lift home.'

Julian appeared, saying all was satisfactory and Francine would extricate herself from her current job as soon as possible and take over where Mrs Tring left off.

He was restless. He and Bruno went over all the walls and the furniture in their quarters looking for another bug and didn't find anything.

He said, 'Which is not to say there's nothing there. Let's be careful what we talk about. I think I heard somewhere that playing music on the radio or smartphone makes it impossible for the listener to hear any conversation. Do you fancy Bach or the Beatles?'

It rained. They ran out of milk and had to raid the fridge in Mrs Maggs's kitchen opposite. When all the stewards and Mrs Maggs had gone home, Julian and Bea made the rounds of the

Hall, making sure all the shutters were closed and lights turned off.

Polly chanted to Pip, 'Rain, rain, go away. Come again another day.'

Piers tried a sketch or two. Tore them up.

'It's all right,' said Polly. 'We can relax. They won't come in this.'

Julian made phone calls. Business as usual.

Piers found an old backgammon set, and began to play against himself.

Darkness descended.

The rain ceased. And started again after half an hour.

Nothing was going to happen that night, was it? Julian and Bea got some sort of light meal on the table. Polly had backache and was helped up to bed. Pip was fed and watered and also taken upstairs.

Bruno was quiet, a little concerned that his master was not settling down for the night in a chair, but not alerting them of any interlopers.

Bea wished she'd taken up knitting. Or Sudoku. Or playing patience. Piers reminded her she used to know how to play backgammon so she indulged him in a game. And then he was annoyed when she beat him.

At eleven, Piers said, 'They're not coming. I'm off to bed.' And went.

Julian said, 'No, they won't come out in this weather. I thought they might because the word at church was that our MP and his wife are due back from their holidays tomorrow, and that might cramp their style.'

Bruno groaned in his sleep.

Midnight. The witching hour.

Bea thought they ought all to be in bed by now, sleeping the sleep of the just, dreaming of pastures new, or travelling through a snowy landscape or confronting a large brown bear which had opened its jaws to devour her . . .

She woke up, shivering. She was lying on the settee with a blanket thrown over her. Julian lay in his big chair, also asleep.

The central heating had gone off. The house was cold.

There was a flicker of light showing on Julian's laptop. What time was it? What was that noise? Oh, it was an owl. Maybe. Or a car?

No, it wasn't anything.

Four o'clock in the morning. Still dark. Still raining.

Nothing was going to happen.

Bother!

She went back to sleep and dreamed of a clock ticking . . . ticking . . . ticking . . . the minutes away till the morrow.

FOURTEEN

Monday morning

Bea woke at eight to find Julian, freshly showered and shaved, dressed in all-weather gear, fitting Pip into an all-in-one rainsuit. Pip was enjoying himself.

Bea struggled to orientate herself. She remembered that Julian liked to go out on his rounds in the early mornings. She seemed to remember he used a golf buggy for these forays.

Sooner him than her.

He said, 'All's quiet on the western front. The guards report nothing unusual.' He hesitated, then said, 'Look, I know you planned to return to London today but Polly and I have been wondering, if it wouldn't cause you too much trouble, whether or not you could stay on for a while?'

Bea smiled. 'You just try to prise us loose! I'll check with the office, of course, but they haven't screamed for me yet so it should be all right for me to take a couple more days off. And if you think you can get Piers to leave that chapel alone, you've got another think coming.'

Julian grinned. 'Thank you. It's still raining. Polly will be down in half an hour to make breakfast. Get yourself something to eat and drink if you can't wait.'

He pulled the hood of his mac over his head and disappeared with his son tucked under his arm.

Bea staggered upstairs to shower and get into clean clothes. What a disappointment that nothing had happened last night! Today was Monday, the toddlers' group would be starting up again in the village hall, Tyra would be struggling with her new baby, not knowing where Pete might be, and Polly would be trying to do too much. The babysitter supplied by Mrs Maggs hadn't been any good, had she? And the bad boys hadn't shown their faces.

Piers was still sound asleep, so she left him there.

Leaving the bedroom, she found Polly gently lowering herself down the stairs and starting to cook breakfast. Her colour was poor and she kept easing her back. She said, 'Another day of rain. I wish the boys had come last night but I suppose they didn't fancy driving in those conditions.'

Bea took the spatula out of Polly's hands, and told her to go and sit down and nurse her bump.

Polly protested, 'I can't sit around doing nothing for another two months.'

Bea said, 'Won't they take you in early? You look ready to give birth now.'

Polly sighed. 'I wish! I must admit I'm feeling rather tired. I can't decide what to do today. I should be at the toddlers' group. They're going to be short-handed. I need to find someone to take Tyra's place, and I was supposed to drop in to see Lady Knighton to collect some raffle tickets, but I didn't manage to get there. There's fifteen other things I ought to be doing.'

'Number one is looking after yourself,' said Bea. 'Weave a cocoon around you and Julian and Pip, and let everything else go hang. Let me help. Piers and I are going to stay as long as you need us.' She crossed her fingers. 'Well, as long as I'm not needed back at the office. I know I'm no relative but perhaps you'll let me be an adopted grandmother.'

'Gladly,' said Polly. 'Oh, very much so. Mine, too. I mean, my mother died when I was in my teens and I don't have anybody else's shoulder to cry on.'

'You and Julian, both. You're both very strong and you look after one another.'

At this point both turned aside to blow their noses.

'Well,' said Bea, 'my first act as Granny is to say you need a nanny. Not one of those young things the village would like to foist on you, but an experienced woman with the ability to know how to manage you and Julian and Pip, someone who can cope with the baby who's expected soon. I can find you someone but there's a problem. Rosemary brought her own accommodation with her, but where would your nanny live? In the village?'

'A properly trained nanny?' Polly pushed herself upright in her chair. 'That would be perfect. Only, can we afford it?'

'If necessary, I'll pay for her to be with you for a short period of time, say, three months.'

'I couldn't possibly allow you to—'

'Yes, you could. Ask Julian, and I think he'll agree rather than have you drive yourself into the ground. So where could she live?'

'Well, Julian's been doing up the top floor at the Hall. It used to be servants' quarters and he's made them into not one but three self-contained flats, each with their own front door. I think one of them is going to be ready at the end of this week. We must ask Lance. He's been putting extra men on the job, worrying about how much there is still to do. I do like Lance.'

'Yes. We're also united in disliking the major, right?'

'It's a Monday morning and he'll be here bright and early with his schedules for this and a list of new dramas. It seems to me that he really enjoys reporting fresh disasters, all of which he'll contrive to say are Julian's fault for not listening to his advice.'

'Perhaps Rosemary has found something to take the shine off his medals?'

'I wish. So far he seems to have led a charmed life, going from one post to another with the good wishes of his employers. She's visited five so far, and not one has a word to say against him.'

'Which is odd in itself. This isn't the sort of job which you only do for a couple of years and then move on. Perhaps I'm old-fashioned but I thought such jobs were mostly for life. I wonder . . . I must speak with Rosemary. Perhaps she hasn't asked the right questions. What is he hoping to get out of this job? Why is he gaslighting Julian?'

Polly sighed. 'I don't know. It's a worry. Sometimes I have nightmares of him and Marcus and the MP and Lord High Everything circling the Hall, waiting for Julian to make a misstep. To be honest, Julian has borrowed money but when I asked him about it, he said that if an accountant doesn't know where to borrow money on reasonable terms, they shouldn't have passed their exams. So I suppose I must believe him.'

Bea smiled. 'Come on, Polly! Wasn't he on fast track for promotion in his firm? Yes. Didn't he rub shoulders with multi-billionaires in the City? Yes. Does he hold his nerve, or have panic attacks?'

Polly giggled. 'Only when I tickle him.'

At which both started to laugh so hard that they had to reach for the box of tissues.

Julian returned with Pip in his arms, both smelling of whatever it was that made the spring in the western meadow so good for the skin. Father and son were hungry, and Julian was bearing news.

'Mrs Maggs says the MP and his wife returned home late last night and are off up to London almost immediately, which perhaps explains why nothing happened last night. Jock hasn't heard from Pete again. Tyra had a bit of a hiccup feeding the baby but Jenny has sorted someone out to look after her.

'The western meadow is squelchy but the rain has stopped, at last. The gates to the north and west are roughly back in place but not yet padlocked shut. Pip found a bird's nest and wanted to bring it home, so we had a battle royal about that, which he won. And we're both starving.'

Pip was holding part of a bird's nest in both hands and growled when Polly tried to take it from him. Bruno sniffed at the sodden mess, took it off Pip, shook it a couple of times to make sure it was quite dead, and dropped it on the floor next to the rubbish bin.

Julian said, 'He's like Nana in *Peter Pan*. A proper nanny.'

'Now that's my cue to find him a nanny,' said Bea, and reached for her laptop. Scrolling down, she said, 'A suitable name springs to mind. She's just finished a stint with a family, been there for years and so is available for another job. If it's one that appeals to her. I know she wants to get out of London. If she's back from holiday, she might consider . . . Her phone number? Yes. Let's see if she's in.'

She was indeed in. Bea wandered out into the yard – a little chilly but not too bad – and asked the nanny if she'd fancy a stay in a historical residence with lots of drama attached.

Nanny was a quiet woman, who took most things in her stride. Well, everything except chewing gum to which she had an aversion and the sight of which was almost the only thing that would cause her to raise her voice.

Bea explained the problem attached to this new position. Or problems, rather. She did not try to hide the possibility of fisticuffs, or make little of any of the rather terrible things that had happened so far. She detailed the lack of finished accommodation, the semi-polite war with the major and the animosity which existed between the village and the nearest town.

'Dear me,' said Nanny. 'And the little boy?'

'Physically and mentally he's fine, pretty advanced for his years. His father is short-sighted and he may have inherited that. He's trying to walk but hasn't said many words as yet. He has charm. He's intelligent, patient, thoughtful and takes his time judging people. He explores. He's attached to a toy giraffe, eats and sleeps well. Is much loved. His father is training him to take over the estate and I should say he'll be good at it.'

'And when is the next baby due?'

'Just short of Christmas. Everything seems to be in order but Polly is getting rather tired and the stairs are becoming difficult.'

'What staff do they keep?'

'A housekeeper for the house. Mrs Maggs. A wonderful woman who is balancing the demands of her family with those of the Hall. Talks a blue streak but it's as well to listen to the subtext. Do you fancy the situation? It is not something I'd suggest to anyone less experienced.'

'I'll interview the family this afternoon.'

Bea said, 'If I'm not here when you arrive, make the acquaintance of Mrs Maggs. She'll look after you.'

As Bea clicked off her phone, Mrs Maggs herself drove into the yard and parked. Seizing the moment, Bea explained to the housekeeper that she was worried that Polly was doing rather too much, and they should really take on an older woman who could look after her as well as the child.

Mrs Maggs looked as if she'd taken a mouthful of lemon juice, but had the good sense to say that Bea might have the right idea, though the girls would probably try their luck anyway. If that was all right with Bea? Which it was.

So Bea returned to the estate office to find that breakfast was ready to put on the table, while Polly was saying, 'I've decided. This morning I have to see to setting up the toddlers' club and then I'll go on to visit Lady Knighton, which I should have done yesterday. Bea, would you like to come with me? I could do with backup. Julian, what have you on?'

'Monday morning miseries, brought to us courtesy of the major. Check on Beauty. Then a whizz round various projects, not forgetting I must fetch that video camera and other equipment from the shop at the back of the old town hall. Then I've a meeting this afternoon with someone from the planning authority to discuss parking in the village and a change of use for a couple of cottages who want to apply to turn their front rooms into cafés or sell local crafts or something. Working from home can mean different things nowadays, right?'

Polly perked up. 'That means more trade into the village. Good.'

Julian said, 'The council don't want to hear about their doing well. I shall shake my head and say I'm not sure another shop here would succeed, and they'd be so delighted that I'm pushing a lost cause that they'll pass the proposed changes without hesitation.'

Piers wandered down the stairs, sketchbook in hand. 'I know I need your permission to tackle the wallpaper in the chapel, but surely—'

'No,' said Julian, Polly and Bea together.

'Come with me on my rounds,' said Julian. 'Polly and I have almost come to blows over the colour we want on the walls in our new accommodation in the stables, so I'd welcome your opinion. I'll play fair; I won't tell you which of two or three colours she wants, and I'll abide by your choice.'

'And if you believe that, Piers,' said Polly, 'you're not as savvy as I thought. He'll have the last word. He always does.'

Bea drove Polly's car because there was a child seat fitted in the back of Polly's car and there wasn't one in her own.

First stop the village hall. Pip was fastened into his buggy with a warning from Polly to Bea that the boy was just like his father, working quietly away to solve problems and that one of these days he'd manage to work out how to escape the buggy, and then what were they going to do?

Inside the building, Kylie was setting out toddlers' equipment, helped by two women who'd been with her last week, and a strapping lass Bea hadn't met before, but who was introduced as 'someone's cousin on a visit, quite useful if you keep an eye on her'.

Kylie said Jenny had sent word that Tyra was doing fine and talking of moving back to London, which everyone understood might well be best, under the circumstances. Kylie also said that she could cope with the toddlers that day, no problem, so Bea, Polly and Pip returned to the car and drove sedately out of the village to take a road to the east.

Polly said, 'You heard that Lady Knighton had a bad fall a while ago? She's not been herself since. She is over eighty, you know. I expect you heard that her son's the local MP and on the board of this and that. He shifted her out of the family home into the much smaller dower house when he was elected to Parliament, and he pays for live-in staff to look after her. Lady Knighton doesn't drive any more or go out much. She used to be so active and into everything, but no longer.'

Bea said, 'I met her once. She struck me as being very competent, running the stewards at the Hall and the food bank and, well, everything in sight.'

Polly said, 'The stewards have agreed which one of them is to be in charge in future, and I think someone at church has taken over the food bank.'

'Your father?'

At this, Polly started to giggle. 'Oh, oh! How cross he'd be if you thought he should be handing out packets of rice and tea to those who haven't had the gumption – as he sees it – to save for a rainy day. Oh, dear, oh dear!'

Bea said, 'So it's Lady Knighton's grandsons and a school friend who are the bad lads who've been causing all the trouble lately?'

'Afraid so. They've been brought up with a sense of entitlement, went to private boarding schools and have never been reprimanded. Lady Knighton's daughter-in-law, the MP's wife, hasn't a maternal bone in her body. She's an expensive, Botoxed beauty who lends her name to the board of various charities but doesn't lift a finger to help them. Their father has his head in the political clouds, dreaming of cabinet status.

'The eldest lad, that's Nick, is supposed to be working on one of his father's political campaigns but prefers a social life twenty-four seven. He and his brother, who's a pale copy of him, are supposed to move in with Lady Knighton when their parents are away, but they prefer to stay in the big house where nobody is going to question what they do.

'The third member of the trio lives not far away over the hill in a similar situation. He and Nick's younger brother have just left school and are taking a gap year to do something or other, though nobody seems to know what. I heard they proposed to visit various war zones, thinking it would be "fun", but the parents vetoed that idea and I'm not sure how they're actually spending their time . . . except with metal detectors.'

'And the police turn a blind eye?'

'So far, yes. You've seen for yourself what happens. The police line is that Pete died because he didn't wait for backup before challenging some interlopers. You understand that his lordship is generously funding a new community centre in the town and everyone treads very carefully when that amount of money is involved.'

They drew up in front of a small but elegant eighteenth-century house set back from the road behind a semi-circular drive. On one side there was what used to be a coach house, converted into a garage on the ground floor with living quarters above. The lawn within the driveway needed mowing, and weeds were beginning to grow up through the gravel around it.

Polly put her hand on Bea's arm. 'It's all my fault, this. If I hadn't been so stupid and got upset . . . nothing would have happened.'

Bea made the connection. Julian had said the bad lads had been rude to Polly. 'What did they do?'

'I'd parked the car in the village. They surrounded me and started to sing that silly nursery song, "Polly put the kettle on". They were laughing, ordering me to get them a cup of tea and . . . they twirled me round and I nearly fell. There were people around. Some looked away and some looked shocked, and I was shaking so hard that I . . . I didn't cry, I didn't! One of them said, "Give us a kiss!".

'I didn't know what to do. Then Big Teddy appeared and glowered at them, and he helped me into my car and asked if I were all right to drive, and I nodded and said I was, though I wasn't, really. I stopped when I got out of the village and did some deep breathing, and I thought about ringing the police and lodging a complaint, but honestly . . . would it be worth it? I decided I would just have to be more careful in future. So I drove home and I didn't tell Julian because I was afraid what he might do. I didn't want him ending up in jail for assault. Rosemary got me a pepper spray and I always carry that with me nowadays.'

But Julian knew! Someone told him. I thought it was overreaction on his part to employ security guards, but it wasn't. He knew!

Polly took a deep breath, said, 'Well, onwards and upwards.' She extracted Pip from the car and fastened him into the buggy. She said, 'Such a shame. Lady Knighton used to love her garden, but you can see she doesn't care about it any longer.'

Polly rang the bell. There was a pause and then the door was flung open by a shock-haired young man in torn jeans and equally mangled T-shirt, who said 'Yes?' in forbidding fashion. Without waiting for a reply, he yelled, 'Mum!' and disappeared, leaving the door wide open.

'Yes?' A middle-aged woman with a shock of dyed ginger hair, also wearing ripped jeans and worn T-shirt, appeared in the doorway. Mother and son? What was going on here?

There was a burst of pop music from above and a shock-headed young woman, dressed ditto, descended the stairs and disappeared into the back quarters without even glancing their way.

'Yes?' said the older woman again. And then added, 'Wait a mo. It's that Polly lady, innit? I'm Mavis, looking after Lady Knighton temporary like, with my kids to help.'

Polly produced a social smile. 'You're local, Mavis?'

'From the town. But there was this problem, see, about the rent, and our MP said we could help him out here for a few months when her ladyship's last housekeeper had to go home to look after her daughter that was sick, like. It's better than the last place with its leaking roof, I can tell you, though it's a bit out of the way for the kids. Now, is she expecting you?'

'Lady Knighton? She asked me to call, yes.'

'Well, don't stay too long. She tires easily and she's due for her next lot of pills.' Mavis gestured for them to go through to the sitting room at the back of the house, which might have overlooked the garden if the blinds hadn't been drawn down over the windows.

Lady Knighton was lying back in a big armchair with a rug over her knees. She had indeed become something of an invalid. She'd lost weight, and her hair was thinning. She might have been dozing but when they entered, she pulled herself upright and smiled.

'I expected you yesterday, Polly. Or was it the day before? Now, what was it about? I've been getting so forgetful lately. Oh yes. The raffle tickets; they're on the side table. You won't let me down, will you? I've been fretting that the coffee morning is on Saturday, and you hadn't come for the tickets.'

Polly bent to kiss the old woman's cheek. 'I was held up. You know how it is. But I'm here now. Do you remember my friend, Mrs Abbot? You met her some time ago, before Julian and I moved into the Hall.'

'Now, I may be forgetting all sort of things, but I remember Mrs Abbot. You run some kind of agency in London, don't you? And your husband paints, quite successfully. You've brought your little boy to see me? The very picture of his great-grandfather, Florian, isn't he? He looks at you, and you have to wonder what he's thinking. Now sit you down and tell me what's happening in the outside world.'

Polly obeyed. 'You heard about the break-in at the Hall, and that one of the security guards is missing?'

'Yes, yes. Someone let the raiders in, and killed the guard. Tck, tck. What is the world coming to?'

Polly decided not to argue about who had died, but went on. 'The work on the top floor at the Hall is nearly finished, but we're still waiting for the windows for the stables. There was a fire there, but it was put out and—'

'Oh dear. Tell me no more of death and disaster. Isn't there enough of that every time I turn the telly on?'

'Well, everything else seems to be chugging along nicely. Kylie's coping better than I thought she would at the toddlers' group, and the pub's started doing lunches in a side room.'

'Ah, what hopes we had for the future for you and Julian. Such a pity. They tell me you'll be out before Christmas.'

Polly said through her teeth, 'We're not planning to move, Lady Knighton. Julian's attending yet another planning meeting this afternoon in town, and Mrs Abbot is going to find an experienced nanny to look after us all.'

The old woman fretted. 'Oh dear, oh dear. That'll be another expense, and goodness knows how much Mona's wedding is going to cost. Marcus talks of hundreds of guests and opening up the old chapel, which dear Mr Colston thinks must be there somewhere but has got lost in the mists of time.'

Mr Colston strikes again! So he's been visiting Lady Knighton? With or without Marcus and Mona?

Polly persisted. 'Oh, the chapel. Well, I'll believe it when the experts confirm its existence. Marcus and Mona would like to get married at the Hall but we don't have a licence for that.'

Lady Knighton said, 'Well, well. No doubt Marcus will have his way. He's very forceful, isn't he, and it's nice to see Mona looking so happy. But what is poor Mr Colston to do? He's devoted himself entirely to this new history of the Hall that he's writing, but what will become of it, and of him, when you leave? I do worry about you all, you know.'

Polly held on to her patience. 'We've no plans to leave.'

Lady Knighton wasn't listening. 'They tell me you're going to divorce Julian. Such a shame; I had the highest hopes of him.'

Polly said, 'What? We're not planning to divorce! Why on earth should we?' And then she clicked. 'Oh, you've heard that silly rumour about Julian and Rosemary?'

'I'm told she's very pretty, and Julian's just like his grandfather, open to an invitation.'

'That's a lie!' Polly's voice rose, but she took hold of herself. 'Julian didn't. Rosemary didn't. When we heard there was talk, she left. Full stop.'

Lady Knighton shook her head. 'My dear, you can't draw the wool over everyone's eyes. He may have taken care to meet her in private in her caravan, but meet her he did, and you the last to know about it.'

Polly's colour rose. 'Lady Knighton, I know my husband through and through, and it isn't the first time he's been targeted by other women and his reaction has always been the same. He wonders what on earth they see in him. Also, I have an acute sense of smell and if Rosemary had gone anywhere near my husband, I would have known about it. She uses a particular shampoo and I can always tell when she's been in a room, never mind in bed with my husband. He himself smells of the herbs in the spring in the park, and I can assure you, I have never smelled that on her.'

Lady Knighton was becoming agitated. 'Oh dear, oh dear? That sounds . . . but I heard about it on the best authority.'

Polly was about to combust, so Bea decided it was time to intervene. She said, 'Lady Knighton, forgive me, but may I ask where you got this rumour from? Rosemary has had a difficult life which has left her with no desire for dalliance.'

Lady Knighton looked as if she were going to cry. 'Please don't shout! I heard it on the best authority. Marcus said . . . and dear Ian actually saw them together.'

Bea and Polly arrived at the same conclusion together. 'The major?'

'Yes, yes. Major Ian. He's been so good, keeping me informed of what goes on now that I can't get out and about as I did. He brings Mr Colston to visit me sometimes, and arranges for Marcus to drop in now and then. I don't know what I'd do without him.'

Bea held on to her temper with a firm hand. 'I'm so glad you have lots of visitors. Has the major been discussing a possible future working for Marcus instead of Julian?'

'Yes, indeed,' said Lady Knighton. 'Marcus couldn't do better when he takes over. He hasn't the time to worry about rents and repairs.'

'Perhaps,' said Bea, feeling a little guilty about being so devious, 'Ian's planning to bring his own people in to manage the farm shop and restaurant?'

'Naturally,' said Lady Knighton. 'He says Julian's put local people in place who really don't know how to maximize the assets. Prices will have to rise, of course, and that no-good Imran will have to go. The whole business needs to become more professional.'

Polly was so angry that she couldn't sit still any longer, but heaved herself forward in an effort to get out of the low chair she'd been sitting in, saying, 'I really think that—'

Bea cut across her. 'I hear the major's wedding has been deferred yet again? What's wrong with the woman?'

Lady Knighton shook her head. 'These modern women. She simply doesn't understand that a man must be head of the household and control the finances. She's built up quite a nice little business for herself and should be delighted to turn it over to a man who knows how to take it to the next level. If she lets him slip through her fingers, she'll be left on the shelf. And she's no youngster now. If she doesn't shape up soon, he'll be looking around for something younger, mark my words.'

There was a 'whoosh' and a 'ping'.

Pip had somehow escaped from his buggy and managed to get to the window where he released the blind so that it shot up, allowing a blast of wintry sun to fill the room.

Lady Knighton put up her hand to shield her eyes. 'Oh!'

Bea noted that the lawn outside hadn't been cut for a while, and that a branch had broken off a tree and fallen on to a bed of roses which were themselves in need of attention.

Polly was still trying to get up out of her chair, so Bea scooped Pip up and tucked him back into his buggy, ensuring that he was neatly fastened in and giving him his toy giraffe to nurse. She said, 'Apologies, Lady Knighton. Shall I pull the blind down again?'

'No, no. Leave it be. It's good to see the sun now and then. If only that new boy would cut the lawn. He and his sister are supposed to be helping their mother, Mavis, look after the house and garden, but he says it's been raining too much, and . . .'

There was a confusion of noise in the hall, and Lady Knighton suddenly looked smaller . . . even frightened? 'Oh dear! That's Nick. What does he want this time?'

The door burst open and a beefy young man pushed into the room past Mavis.

Was this Nick? The leader of the youthful gang?

'Out of my way! Gran, I need another card! This one's maxed out.' And then, seeing Polly and Bea, he stopped short, frowning. 'What the devil? Why, it's pretty Polly from the Hall who doesn't know how to make a cup of tea. What are you doing here?' He switched his eyes to Bea, decided she was an older woman of no account, and dismissed her from his mind.

Bea helped Polly to her feet, saying, 'Nice to meet you, Nick. I'm an old friend of Lady Polly's. Your grandmother asked us to collect some raffle tickets to sell.'

He was a big lad with big muscles, big mouth, and fair hair shaved at the sides. Bad tempered, bad skin . . . fond of the weed? Or worse?

Polly said, in a voice which refused to wobble, 'Yes, Nick. We've met, several times. Also, at the darts match last week.'

His eyes darkened. He remembered exactly what happened at the darts match, both the defeat of their team and the incident of his mates' theft of the smartphone. 'So what are you really doing here, bothering Gran?'

No manners and no patience. No wonder he'd lost his driving licence.

Polly said, 'Dear Lady Knighton, we have the car with us. We wondered if you'd like to come for a drive and perhaps a bite to eat somewhere?'

'Oh, dear. Yes, that would be very—'

'No, she wouldn't!' Nick cut in. 'Gran, I need to talk to you, in private.'

'But Nick, dear. I told you the other day, you've had my one and only bank card and I don't—'

'It's maxed out. So, write me a cheque and make it for cash.' He whirled on Polly. 'And don't you interfere with what's none of your business, Pretty Polly, right?'

FIFTEEN

Monday noon

Bea considered the odds and didn't like them much. Nick had a short fuse and was dangerously near flashpoint. If he tried to manhandle Polly . . . or even push her over . . .!

Could Polly use her pepper spray in front of Lady Knighton? No, she couldn't. Retreat was their only option.

Bea picked the pile of raffle tickets up off the table, saying, 'Well, another day . . . Come on, Polly.'

Bea trundled Pip out into the hall with Polly at her heels. Nick slammed the sitting-room door shut behind them.

Mavis wasn't going to cross Nick, either. She led the way to the front door, saying, 'It's high time for her pills, anyway. They keep her nice and quiet so she doesn't worry about things all the time.'

Bea said, 'Have you told his father what's going on?'

A shake of the head. 'He warned me that Lady K's gone a bit doolally. I make sure she takes her pills and then she's no trouble. Nick's all right really. He lets my kids hang around with him which gets them out of my hair.'

Bea said, 'Your children have both left school? Do they have jobs yet?'

'Not yet. They're waiting for the right job to turn up.'

Polly and Bea pushed Pip out of the hall into the sunshine and the front door closed behind them with a decisive snap.

Pip had fallen asleep.

Polly was breathing hard. She said, 'One of these days . . . I know I ought not to let him get to me . . .'

A somewhat battered SUV had been parked askew on the gravel. Was this the SUV the lads had taken into the park on their treasure hunt? No one was sitting in it. Nick was driving again? Without a licence?

Or did Mavis' son have a licence? Was he one of the group who'd invaded the park the other night?

Bea peered into the back of the car. Yes, the metal detectors were there. She got out her phone and took a couple of pictures of the car and its distinctive tyres. Then she collected Pip, fastened him into his car seat and put the folded buggy into the boot.

Meanwhile, Polly manoeuvred herself into the front passenger seat and sought for a tissue in her handbag to blow her nose. She was still upset. 'Bea, that horrible boy! I hate to see Lady Knighton being bullied like that, and going to pieces. And what are these pills they've put her on? She wasn't taking anything when I knew her. She seems almost afraid of Nick, and if the bank card she's given him is maxed out – and don't tell me that his own cards aren't maxed out – then can she really afford to go on giving him money? If he gets her to write out a cheque for him payable to cash, then how long will it be before he's gone through everything she's got? Suppose we tell her bank that her grandson is milking her account?'

'Without any authority from the family, they wouldn't take any notice. Why should they? Now, Julian said Nick's father and mother returned home last night and are going back to London sometime today. I agree that they ought to be told what's going on, but they're not going to welcome the news with shouts of joy or even with an open mind. Would they accept the information from you? Because, as they see it, you and Julian are their opponents in this game they're playing of who runs this part of the county? No, they'll say that any complaint you make must be politically motivated.'

'I don't care what they say.' And that was a lie, but a brave one. 'It's the right thing to do.'

Bea reflected that people like Polly sometimes lacked common sense and acted without thinking things through.

Polly shifted around on her seat, reclaiming the raffle tickets she'd been asked to deal with. She rolled her eyes. 'Would you know, these are for a coffee morning held last month, not this.'

'Give them here,' said Bea. 'What charity is it for, and whose phone number is that on the tickets? The treasurer of the organization? Yes. Is she a member of our MP's campaign team? Whether she is or not, she'll be someone he trusts and who has enough clout to be listened to if she asks him to look into something for her.'

Bea tried the number and reached a woman who sounded as if she'd been dealing with morons all morning and was going to do someone an injury if they complained about anything, ever again.

'Apologies,' said Bea, trying to sound more upper class than usual. 'I hate to bother you but, well, there's been a little misunderstanding. I was asked to collect some raffle tickets from Lady Knighton for your charity, but while I was there, her grandson arrived in something of a state, complaining she'd given him a debit card which was maxed out and asking her for cash. I was about to give her a cheque but then I thought that if he'd maxed out her account then the charity might not get the money.'

'What nonsense is this?' Then an indrawn breath. The woman knew enough of Nick to take the matter seriously. 'I'm sure there's nothing to worry about . . .'

But she didn't sound that sure of herself now, did she?

'. . . but if you will give me your name and a number where you can be reached?'

Bea gave her name and London office number, and rang off. She said, 'There, now. Hopefully that woman is going to make some enquiries. She won't want a regular source of income drying up because Nick's being greedy. Remind me to send the charity a cheque. It's a good cause.'

Polly said, 'You were *brilliant*! You told the truth, and nothing but the truth!'

'Whether it's enough for the MP to wake up to the damage Nick is doing to Lady Knighton, I don't know. It will be a few days, I suppose, before we hear anything.'

Bea started the car, and drove off. 'Polly, did you notice the grass hadn't been cut at the back or the front of the house, and that the rain had brought down a branch of a tree in the back garden and it had been left there to rot?'

'So?'

'Lady Knighton didn't mow the lawns herself in the old days, did she? So what's happened to her gardener? Someone's been living over the garage. Was that where her gardener lived? Was he the adult who was driving Nick and Co around when the lads went treasure hunting?'

Polly caught on. 'You think her gardener might have been the man who ended up dead in the amusement park? But if so, what's happened to Pete, and why is everyone keeping quiet about it?'

'Nick and Co are amateurs, too young to think clearly. I think they panicked when their driver died and switched identities on the spur of the moment, hoping their man would be mistaken for Pete . . . which is what happened. They were then left with Pete on their hands, alive or dead, or perhaps badly wounded. They couldn't bring themselves to kill in cold blood so took him away with them so that he couldn't identify them to the police. And where would be a better place to hide him but in the quarters previously occupied by the dead gardener?'

'But Lady Knighton must know . . . Oh, but she doesn't know anything, does she? What about Mavis?'

'Mavis knows, and probably her children do, too. I'm beginning to wonder if those two youngsters might be part of the group which Nick is leading into trouble. Mavis said he let them hang around with him. They look old enough to have driving licences.'

'So what do we do now?'

'We go back to base and see what's been happening there.'

All was not quiet back at the ranch. Workmen were unloading unwieldy packages in the stable yard, and there seemed more lorries around than usual. Bruno was nowhere to be seen outside the estate office, so Julian and Piers must still be out somewhere.

Polly clapped her hands. 'Oh, the windows have arrived! Come and see. Oh, Bea, we've been waiting for this for so long. It's going to make so much difference. I can't wait for us to get our own place.'

Bea manoeuvred a sleepy Pip out of his car seat and into the buggy, and followed Polly into the stables. On one side of the courtyard was the burned-out box, and on the other . . . Oh, yes. The family's new quarters were going to be quite something.

All was hustle and bustle as one after the other the windows were being fitted, changing what had been a building site into an elegant house.

Polly was over the moon. 'You see? We can live on the ground floor and leave the bedrooms to be finished later. The courtyard can be turned into a safe place for the children to play.' She stopped and put her hands to her back. 'Oh!' And then relaxed. 'It's nothing. Take no notice.'

Bea told herself there was no cause to panic. Pregnant women often had contractions for a couple of months before they gave birth. But . . . 'You must sit down and rest. Come on, you can admire your windows later.'

Somewhat reluctantly, Polly followed as Bea pushed the buggy back to the estate office, from which came sounds of strife.

Polly hastened her pace. 'Oh, dear. Is that the two babysitters? I thought I'd told Saturday night's girl not to come back. The other must be one of Jenny's protegees. I don't think either would be right for us. Too young by half.'

The estate office was now a battleground, as the two would-be babysitters went nose to nose. Mrs Maggs's relative had her hands on her hips in fighting mode, and the one they'd dubbed the sleeping beauty was definitely awake and standing her ground. Who was supposed to be interviewed that afternoon and who was most likely to get the job?

Polly said, 'Can I pretend I haven't seen them? I really don't feel up to this.'

'Don't worry,' said Bea, having spotted a neat grey figure putting the kettle on in the kitchen. 'Let Nanny handle it.'

Nanny was a woman you'd overlook in a crowd, but she'd be the one to administer first aid in the event of an accident. Fiftyish, with indeterminate colouring and that air of quiet authority to be found in all the best nannies. This was someone who could sing a lullaby, see that the toddler ate his greens and would know precisely when any particular child should begin toilet training.

Nanny acknowledged Bea's presence with a nod of recognition. She was not committing herself to the job until she'd seen what it entailed.

The sleeping beauty turned on Polly. 'I was here first!'

Mrs Maggs's young relative was a buxom lass who was bursting out of her clothes. Her hair was red, and so was her face. 'I've got more right to be here than . . .'

Polly raised her hands in dismay. 'That's enough. There's

clearly been a misunderstanding. I didn't expect to see either of you today, and . . .'

Bea unbuckled Pip from his buggy. He woke with a start and struggled to get out and on to his feet. She let him hold on to her till he'd got his balance.

Nanny brought a cup of tea and plateful of biscuits out of the kitchen and put it beside the big chair which Polly had sunk into.

'My aunt told me . . .' the buxom one began.

'Your aunt is an old goat who . . .' the sleeping beauty took over.

Nanny put a cushion at Polly's back and a stool under her feet.

Polly said, 'Thank you,' and let out a long, long sigh.

Pip got his balance and set off on one of his voyages of exploration. He bumped into a grey dress, toppled, and clutched the fabric. He looked up. And up.

Nanny studied the boy who might well be the focus of her life for the next ten years or so, and he studied her.

Bea was accustomed to seeing Nanny move in and create order out of chaos, and she'd also seen her walk away from situations in which she did not feel she could be of service. Bea understood that this was a make or break moment.

Nanny nodded. Pip smiled and reached up his arms. 'Down!' he said. She didn't argue, but picked him up, sniffed and took him to the table to change his nappy.

Polly said, 'Thank God.' And to the two warring girls she added, 'It was kind of you to come, but you see, Mrs Abbot has found me a trained nanny who will look after me and Pip. I am grateful for your offers of help, and I know where to find you if I need you in future.'

'Oh. What? Who?' And then another: 'Oh.'

Exit the warring girls.

Nanny cleaned Pip up and set him down on the floor again. Holding one of her fingers, he detoured to fetch his giraffe and then looked up at Nanny. He smiled widely. She smiled back.

Polly said, 'Welcome to the Hall, Nanny. We must discuss terms and where you're to live and so on. I know we're in a bit of a mess at the moment, but things should get better.'

'We'll be all right,' said Nanny. 'Mrs Abbot has given me an idea of what to expect. When I arrived, your housekeeper showed me the new house you're building in the stables, and a little flat upstairs in the Hall, which will suit me very well. I have my own car outside and Mrs Maggs says she'll arrange for me to have a room in the pub in the village for a week or so, until everything's settled and I can move in for good. Meanwhile, Lady Polly, you should take the opportunity to rest while Philip and I get acquainted.'

For a wonder, Polly stretched herself out, closed her eyes, and fell asleep.

Bea and Nanny looked at one another and each conveyed a message of concern about Polly.

Pip squealed, 'Down!'

Bea said, 'He means "Up".'

Nanny lifted him high, saying, 'Up!' and then lowered him to the floor, saying, 'Down!'

Pip laughed and raised his arms for a repeat. Nanny obliged, several times. Did he get the idea? 'Hungry, Philip?'

'Ssss,' said Pip. He led the way to the kitchen, pulling on Nanny's skirt so that she might follow him.

Bea stretched herself out in her chair, closed her eyes, sighed and also fell asleep. Nanny was in charge. Pip and she were going to get on like a house on fire and there was nothing Bea needed to do for a little while.

She woke with a start when Julian returned – without Piers – bringing a blast of chilly air in with him. Julian was on the phone, saying, 'No, Jock. That's perfectly all right. Thank you for letting me know. Keep me informed of anything else that may happen.'

He bent over Polly, who was struggling awake, and kissed her. 'My favourite sleeping beauty. I see you've been having a nice quiet time.' He saluted Nanny, who was feeding Pip's face at the table in the window. 'And you must be the guardian angel sent by Bea to look after us all.'

Nanny smiled. 'Yes, Sir Julian. If that is how you see it.'

Bea said, 'Where's Piers? He did set out with you, didn't he?'

'I left him in town. The camera wasn't ready so he stayed on to collect it and will get a taxi back. Is it going to rain again? It's getting dark outside already.'

He sat down beside Polly. 'Listen, my love. Things are moving. Jock says that someone from the council has been snooping around asking questions about fire precautions at the stables and wanting to know what the guards' routine may be. He also wanted to know when the guards go out on their rounds, and how long they reckon each one takes. They've never been interested before and so far as I know they've no right to ask those questions now. I'm hoping that means somebody is making plans to come in tonight.

'Another thing. While I was at the town hall, our Lord High Everything rang through to speak to me, issuing a most pressing invitation for you and I to a small party at his house this evening from six to eight. I explained that we had guests, and he said to bring them, too. He even said he could probably rustle up a babysitter for Pip. He said this was a great opportunity for me to meet some of the local movers and shakers. No excuses allowed. I conclude that the invitation to us is to make sure we're well out of the way when the gang make their move tonight.'

Bea was startled. 'But Lord High Everything doesn't know what's going on, does he?'

'No, of course not. It's a coincidence. Must be. But perhaps his son suggested it would be a good chance to bury the hatchet?'

Polly blinked herself awake. 'Either way, I'm not going anywhere. They might try to attack us in here . . . or at the stables again? Or even, set alight to the Hall?'

'No, I don't think they'd do that,' said Julian. 'Yes, the lads are escalating from shoplifting and vandalism. Yes, a man was killed because of their trespassing in the park, but that was not done in cold blood. They're fixated on the idea of digging for gold. This invitation is probably just in case, a diversion to make sure we don't get in their way. I've arranged for an extra guard to go on duty tonight and Piers is collecting the video camera to record it if they do try anything. We've set a trap and I think they've fallen for it.'

Polly protested. 'I'm in no state for partying. And you don't really want to go, do you?'

'No, of course not. I accepted the invitation for the four of us with delight. It was about time, I said, that we set aside the trivial disputes that had been troubling the village. I said I looked forward to it.' He grinned. 'Am I not becoming the most efficient liar?'

Polly blew him a kiss. 'You and Bea are a lot better at it than I am.'

Julian continued, 'I rang Mrs Maggs and asked her if she could possibly rustle up some food for us this evening, and she said she was planning to sleep in the housekeeper's room tonight as, if those bad lads were going to come looking for trouble, she'd set about them with the old poker that she'd found and laid by, just in case.'

Polly giggled. 'We'll have to stop her doing any actual harm.'

'Supper at half past six. Then . . . It's Nanny, isn't it? I'm sorry we haven't been properly introduced, but—'

Nanny kindly forgave him. 'You have a lot on your plate, Sir Julian. Now, I'll stay with you for a few days on trial, to see how we get on. I understand that some naughty boys think they might like to pay the Hall a visit and do some damage, and that you've been invited somewhere to make sure they are not disturbed at whatever they want to do. You will accept your friend's invitation or not as you please, but in my opinion Lady Polly should not be subjected to any stress or there'll be trouble before nightfall. If you wish to go out and about to deal with the bad lads well and good, but Lady Polly and Philip and I will stay here with the doors locked and the police on speed dial.'

Julian smiled. 'Yes, Nanny. You man the barricades and we'll catch them trespassing and hand them over to the police.' His smile faded. He put his hand on Polly's shoulder. 'Polly? You're not having contractions already, are you?'

Polly grimaced. 'A couple. As Nanny says, I'd better keep quiet or the baby might decide to come early.'

Julian and Bea did the maths and didn't like the total. It was too early for the baby to come. Babies this premature were usually viable but needed a longish stay in hospital followed by many months of careful nursing.

Pip transferred his attention to his father's jeans. 'Down! Up! Down!'

Julian picked him up, and gave him a cuddle. The boy hid his face against his father's neck, the toy giraffe dangling from his hand . . . and let it drop . . . only to be held by a string attached to the strap of his trousers. Nanny knew how to attach favourite toys to their owners.

Someone drove into the yard and Bruno barked a short welcome. Bea opened the door to find Piers paying off a taxi. He said, 'I've got it. Awkward shape. Can you help me carry it inside? It looks like rain, again.'

They were no sooner safely inside than another car drove up, and Bruno barked another warning. By the sharpness of this bark, Bruno didn't like whoever this was. Neither did Bea, nor anyone else in the room.

'The major!' Julian said. 'I suspect he's been told to make sure we vacate the Hall tonight between six and eight?'

The major burst in, beaming. 'Hello, there! Getting dark early, what? You're all in here? Yes, of course. Visitors, too. All ready to go? I gather Lady Polly's been upsetting old Lady Knighton, but that's easily done nowadays, they say. She should really be in a home but I suppose that wouldn't be cost effective unless they see sense and let me put the house on the market to cover the cost of her nursing home.'

He clapped his hands. 'So, shall we all go in my car? We mustn't be late. His lordship likes to start promptly, good food and drink flowing, and I gather your cousin Mona and her fiancé are honouring us with their presence tonight, too. Also Mr Colston. Quite a little gathering of the A-list. What, no glad rags? You don't want to let the side down, do you?'

Julian said, 'I'm afraid you'll have to make our apologies. Lady Polly is on bed rest.'

'What? Oh, nonsense! Liven her up, what? It will do her good to get out and about and socialize with the right people. A change from nattering with the nobodies in the village pub, what? You can't just turn his invitation down. So much hangs on your taking advantage of this breakthrough that—'

'My wife's health comes first. Please convey our apologies.'

Bea said, 'We are flattered to be asked, but you must understand, if Lady Polly has to be whipped into hospital then—'

'Oh.' The penny dropped. 'I see. Well, in that case . . . I'll have to tell him . . . he won't be pleased.' The major wasn't pleased, either. He chewed his lip, and fidgeted. He wasn't looking forward to telling his master that his mission to fetch Julian and Polly had failed.

'Thank you for coming,' said Julian. 'It was good of you, especially on such a dark night.'

'Yes. Well, I suppose if you have a medical emergency, he'll understand. And, if you're keeping watch here, you won't be going anywhere else tonight, will you? I'll have to tell him, I did warn him that . . . I'll be off, then. See you in the morning, bright and early. I note the windows have arrived for the stables. How you're going to pay for them, I do not know. Perhaps you'll reconsider letting the renovated building out for holidaymakers, right?'

He left, closing the door with care behind him.

Before they could recover, Mrs Maggs knocked on the door, saying, 'I'm serving supper in the kitchen at half past six, but I heard from one of the workmen that Lady Polly might not be quite up to it and was lying down, so she can have her supper where she is.'

Mrs Maggs took a breath and went on. 'I understand you're employing a professional nanny to look after Lady Polly for a while, but you should be warned that Old Jenny is on her way up after supper to make sure all is well.'

Nanny was equal to the occasion. 'Thank you, Mrs Maggs, that will do nicely, and I look forward to meeting your friend and exchanging notes on the babies we've looked after.'

Monday, after supper

Julian ate at Polly's side but the rest of them dined in the kitchen. No one took second helpings, and everyone jumped when a door banged, or when Bruno whined for attention. He was restless, though there was no apparent cause for alarm.

All was quiet. The phones were quiet. Nothing was happening.

Back at the estate office, Bea and Piers found Jenny installed in a corner, winding wool and apparently having arranged a truce with Nanny, who treated her as an honoured guest.

Nanny was quite clear about what was going to happen. 'Lady Polly shouldn't attempt the stairs. We'll consult the doctor tomorrow. They may decide to take her in for complete bedrest but we may be able to look after her here.'

Julian gave a sleepy Pip a cuddle until Nanny took the boy off him, saying, 'We'll all sleep down here tonight, then? Now, I see there's a nice comfortable cradle here for Philip, sound asleep, bless him.'

'Yes, Nanny,' said Julian, recognizing the voice of authority.

Polly said, 'Don't all look so serious. If I have to stay in bed till the baby has grown a bit more, then so be it. It will be worth it. I'll be all right with Nanny and Jenny to look after me. Julian, you and Piers go out and catch baddies.'

Julian said, 'Polly, I love you. We'll keep in touch by phone.' Off he went with Piers, taking the video camera and sound equipment with them.

Bea seethed to find that she was being excluded from the fun and games the men were planning. She told herself Julian was making sensible arrangements to deal with the problem. The security guards were all out on duty and if needed Imran could be summoned to help. What's more, Rosemary was floating around somewhere on her bike.

What could possibly go wrong?

SIXTEEN

Monday evening

Eight o'clock. Bea tried to settle to a book, and failed. She switched on the telly with the sound turned low, but was frowned at by Nanny and Jenny, who were in low-voiced converse about babies they had known. She couldn't make head nor tail of what was on the screen, anyway, so she switched it off again. She tried a crossword puzzle.

Nine o'clock.

Not a sound was to be heard. Jenny distributed soothing drinks all round. Bea accepted one but was then too tense to drink it. Polly was settled on the settee for the night. She and Pip slept. Jenny dozed. Nanny played a game of solitaire, and then nodded off.

Bea wanted to pace the room but couldn't in case she woke anyone up.

The guards sent a text through every quarter of an hour to say all was well.

Nine thirty. Nothing to report. Nothing was going to happen tonight, was it?

Bea wanted to scream. She knew, she just knew that . . .

Her phone rang. A hoarse voice. Was that Jock, one of the guards? 'They've blimming firebombed the guards' caravan! Where's the blimming extinguisher! Sir Julian, sir!' A pause. Then to himself, the man said, 'Wait! I've rung the wrong number.' The man rang off.

What! Bea shot upright in her chair. The sleepers didn't wake.

Bea opened the door and took a step outside in order to ring Julian.

The lights in the yard came on. She blinked in the sudden fierce light. Of course, they were activated by movement at night, weren't they?

She tried ringing Julian. Engaged. She sent him a text, in case the guard hadn't got through. *Action stations! Was anyone inside the guards' caravan? Had everyone got out safely?*

She rang the police and fire brigade. The guards would have reported the fire, wouldn't they? But just in case . . .

She got through. Reported what had happened to the police and fire brigade. Clicked the phone off. Clicked it back on. Julian might be free by now? No. Still engaged.

She paced up and down the yard. Tell Polly? No. Don't wake her. She needs her sleep and what can she do at the moment?

A text whizzed in from Jock. Firemen and police will be here in fifteen. All safely out. All quiet.

Bea closed her eyes and prayed. *Dear Lord, it's a distraction! Julian's going to rush down there, taking everyone away from the real target!*

A car drove into the yard behind her. She turned to see two figures get out, leaving the engine running. They were in dark clothes, wearing masks! Bea lifted her phone to take a photo but as she did so they rushed at her. Knocked her flying. She fell awkwardly. Felt her phone spin out of her hand.

Darkness . . .

Dazed, she tried to rise. Failed. The night was dark. She'd been knocked out? Why? She put her hand to her head. She hurt there and in a couple of other places. Lights out. Nothing moved.

She tried to force herself to her feet. The lights had gone out which meant there'd been no movement in the yard for a while. Which meant the intruders had gone.

If she could move, the lights would come on again. She moved one arm. And then tried to stand. Didn't make it.

But then did. The lights came on. The yard was empty.

The estate office door behind her gaped open.

Bea staggered to the door, knowing what she'd see if she looked inside . . . and yes, there it was. An empty cradle. And three women, deeply asleep.

They'd taken Pip!

Oh, Lord above! How could they!

Refusing to give in to an aching head, she winced back into

the yard, searching for and eventually finding her phone. Cracked but still working? Voicemail to Rosemary.

'Mayday! Mayday! Rosemary, the lads have taken Pip!'

Another text. To Julian. Pip's been kidnapped. I called Rosemary.

Polly slept on. So did Jenny. Nanny stirred but slept again.

A lightweight motorbike spun into the yard with Rosemary driving. She was dressed in leathers and a helmet. 'A car nearly ran me down on the way in. Was that them? Do you know where they'll go?'

Bea said, 'No idea. Can you activate the tracer you put in the toy giraffe? With luck, Pip's got it with him.'

Julian rang, shouting over the phone. 'Bea, what's happened . . .?'

Bea shouted back. 'We're on it. Rosemary and I.'

Rosemary pounded the delivery bag on the back of her bike, flattening it. 'Sit on the pannier.'

Bea hoisted up her skirt and slung a leg over.

Rosemary had those 'commas' in her ears so she could drive and talk at the same time. She fiddled with a bit of kit strapped to the handlebars. 'Yes, Julian. I've got the trace on the giraffe. Going towards the village.'

They were off! Bea was not comfortable. No. In fact, sitting like it was downright excruciating. At her age! Ridiculous! She hung on to Rosemary's slender figure with one arm while trying to alert Julian on the phone with her free hand.

'Two people came in a car. Dark clothes, hoods, and masks. Moved like youngsters. I tried to take a photo. They knocked me out. We've got a trace on Pip's toy and are following! You got the news that the guards' caravan's been fired? Police and firemen on their way?'

Rosemary made the turn round the corner of the house and Bea nearly fell off. The bike couldn't go very fast. The car they'd driven was not in sight. Was that headlights leaving the park? Was that them?

Bea closed her eyes. Found that was worse. Opened them. Screamed a bit, which didn't help.

She wished for a set of leathers and a proper cushioned seat . . .

unlike this torture chamber affair. She was going to slide off if she wasn't careful. Pray, Bea! Pray!

Dear Lord! Heaven, help us! Keep Pip safe! Oh, my . . ..!

She was jogged over a bump. She was not going to be able to hang on much longer.

Rosemary took the turn on to the main road and then switched into another road leading off to the right. And stopped.

'I've lost the signal. Any idea where they're heading?'

Bea looked wildly around. She knew this part of the world, didn't she? Ah, now she knew where they'd taken Pip. 'Straight on. The dower house. Where Lady Knighton lives.'

Rosemary said, 'Ah. Yes. The signal's back. Hold on!'

The ride resumed. Nothing could be worse than this. Well, Bea supposed that being thrown off at speed might be.

Julian was going frantic. 'Bea, Rosemary, where are you? Have you got Pip? Is Polly with you?'

It was Bea who replied. 'Hang on. We're nearly there, Julian. Polly's all right. She and the others are asleep. Perhaps you can get someone to stand guard over them? And tell the police. The dower house. Lady Knighton. A new housekeeper and her two children live there and are in cahoots with Nick. That's where they've taken Pip.'

'What! They'd never dare!'

'They have.'

They were passed at speed by a car going in the opposite direction, which made Rosemary swerve.

'Idiot!' said Rosemary.

They slid to a halt in the road outside the dower house, which looked dead. No lights were on at the front, anyway. The doors of the coach house had been left open. Had they been like that when Bea was here earlier? No, they hadn't. Or had they? Couldn't remember.

Bea said, 'Do you think that the car which passed us . . .?'

'Was one of the kidnappers, taking Pip up to join the others? No. The trace is clear. The giraffe is inside the house.'

Bea got off the back of the bike, groaning. And wobbled. She was so sore, she couldn't even begin to think how much it hurt.

Julian was still on her phone. 'Bea, what's happening? I've

told the police that Pip's been kidnapped but I'm not sure they believed me. I'm going mad here!'

Bea replied. 'We're outside the dower house, just about to go in. The giraffe's here. We'll know in a minute if Pip's still attached. Keep your phone on.'

Rosemary said, 'Back in five.' She disappeared. One minute she was a shadow standing next to Bea, the next she'd gone.

Julian said, 'If they've harmed Pip . . .!'

Bea said, 'It's a bluff. They're young, they think they're immortal and that this is just a game with no consequences. They think Nick is wonderful, and if he suggested it would be a lark to kidnap Pip for a few hours as a distraction, they'd laugh like mad and do it. They wouldn't hurt him.' She hoped that was true.

A gnat sang past her ear. Bother. If anyone was ever going to get bitten, it would be her, wouldn't it? 'They didn't hurt Polly. She was asleep when they took Pip, and remained so. But, Julian . . . how did they know it would be easy to lift the child?'

Julian let out a long, long breath. 'Someone who knew all the ins and outs of the Hall told them exactly where to find him. And where to look for gold here.'

'So Nick and Co did eventually turn up to dig for victory?'

'They did. I'm holding on, but . . . if Pip's been hurt! Or Polly! I don't know what to do.'

'Sit tight. The police are coming!'

Julian said, 'Yes, I tell myself that. No one would hurt Pip, would they? And Polly . . . but you say she's all right? I know, I've already asked you . . . Of course you're right. We've got to keep our heads. We're in the wood below the spring. We filmed them arriving in their SUV followed by another vehicle that I've seen before. They turned their headlights on the bluff and put the metal detectors to work. It's as light as day up there.

'The metal detectors started to whine right over that large boulder that sits on top of the spring, and that's what they're working on. The police did get the message about the caravan being set on fire and are on their way there. I'm trying to get them to look for Pip instead, but they're short-staffed and . . . I told them about what's happening up here and all they can say is that we should step back and let them deal with it. They don't want us trying to tackle the lads ourselves. Of course we can't risk another death, but . . . if they've got Pip up there with them . . .?'

'They haven't. I think he's here. So who's at the site with you?'

'Piers is here, in charge of the camera and sound equipment. Hal has come up from the village to help us. I've sent Henry and Bruno to guard Polly. Francine rang to say Imran's gone to help Jock deal with the fire at the guards' caravan, and making sure they report it as arson. The guards' usual time-table has been disrupted, of course, but they've called in the two who aren't supposed to be on duty tonight. The police can't seem to tell me where they'll go first. They're ten miles away and . . . will they go to the dower house, the caravan or here?'

Bea slapped at a gnat on her neck. 'My money's on Rosemary finding Pip and mopping up at this end.'

He said, 'Hang about. There's another car turned in at the west gate. Someone's come to join them. Another youngster by the look of it.'

'It may be one of the housekeeper's children from the dower house. He or she was belting away from here in a car as we arrived.'

'I can't tell if they've got Pip with them or not.'

Bea said, 'Wait, Julian. Rosemary's reconnoitring. If she says Pip's here, you can relax . . .'

Rosemary reappeared at Bea's side. 'Coach house empty, no cars inside. Stairs up to first floor. Door at top of stairs is locked, no light within, but I heard someone stir inside. No sign of Pip, or of Pete. They must be in the main house. There's lights on in the kitchen, telly on and two people talking. Also, lights and telly on in the room at the back.'

Bea worked it out. 'Two people talking in the kitchen mean Mavis and one of her children. Presumably the other drove the car away to join those on site as we arrived. What we don't know is, did they take Pip with them?'

Rosemary removed her helmet and fluffed out her pretty blonde curls. She looked about fifteen years old. 'Let's go and ask.' She rang the front doorbell. They waited.

Rosemary said, 'If they've hurt that child . . . !'

'They won't.' Bea crossed the fingers of both hands.

A young man opened the door. Tousled hair, black jeans and black top. Hooded jumper. Not particularly well endowed with brains but well muscled. Amused by their intrusion. Secure in the belief that, like his master, he was untouchable.

So it was the girl who drove off just now? Taking Pip with her to join the others at the spring?

Bea said, 'We've come to collect the child.'

'What child? Ain't no child here.'

From somewhere in the depths of the house came the well-known refrain, 'Up! Down!' And laughter. Lady Knighton amusing Pip? He wasn't afraid of her. He'd seen her only that morning.

Bea said, 'We've been told Pete's here, too. Is he well enough to see us yet?'

The man said a rude word and tried to close the door, but Rosemary was too quick for him. She was under his arm and into the hall before he could get moving. His legs went from under him, and he fell on his back against the wall. Rosemary shot off up the stairs.

Bea opened doors, looking for Pip. Dining room. Understairs cupboard. Cloakroom. No sign of him. She made for the back room in which she'd seen Lady Knighton earlier, only to be prevented by Mavis, who came storming out of the kitchen to confront Bea.

'What you think you're doing here? What've you done to my Gerry? I'll have the police on you, that I will! Gerry, you all right?'

Gerry staggered to his feet and put his hands up in what he clearly thought was boxing mode. 'She hit me!'

Bea said, 'No, I didn't. And anyway, you hit me first. Remember? Knocked me out and left me on the ground back at the Hall.'

'I never! What's it to you, anyway?'

Mavis folded her arms at Bea. 'You said you'd come to fetch the child. Well, it's been arranged with his mother that he's staying the night. So you can apologize to my son and take yourselves off.'

What's Rosemary doing? Looking for Pete upstairs?

Bea played for time. 'Your son or daughter collected him without asking his mother's permission, and I've been sent to get him back.'

Mavis didn't budge. 'Pretty Polly was asleep when she should have been looking after her child. We should call Child Protection Services on her.'

Bea said, 'Now there's a thought. Who else is not being properly looked after? I'm going to ask social services to look into your care of Lady Knighton.'

Mavis moved not an inch. 'I signed up to look after her, poor thing, because she's no longer capable of looking after herself and needs her pills taking regular. Her son's paying me well and she's no trouble, though I admit I'm not happy about her signing cheques for Nick and I've told him that, too.'

'And the old gardener?' said Bea, hoping against hope that she was right, and that Pete was being kept somewhere in the house. Or the coach house?

Mavis said, 'Nick says the old man's gone down with something catching, and has to have his meals up in the coach house, which I said I was not prepared to do but if my son or daughter can take the tray up themselves and fetch it down again later that's reasonable.'

Bea said, 'If he's too sick to get down the stairs, he should be in hospital. You're saying you haven't seen him since you arrived?'

'That I haven't. I'm not a nurse and I have to take care of myself, what with my diabetes and all. And I'll thank you to go away and leave us in peace.'

Rosemary flew down the stairs, shaking her head at Bea. 'All clear.'

Bea said, 'Pete's upstairs in the coach house.'

Gerry turned on Rosemary. 'I don't know who you're looking for, and you're not taking the child, so out you go! Out, both of you! Or else . . .'

'Or else what?' said Rosemary, at her most innocent.

'I'll throw you out for starters!'

'You can try.' Rosemary let him approach her, executed some sort of complicated sidestep, caught his flailing arm . . . and somehow he was on the ground, with one arm behind his back, screaming.

Mavis also screamed.

Rosemary said, 'Shut up and listen. It's over. Right? I'm immobilizing your son so he doesn't do anything silly, and you can sit down quietly or get locked into the cupboard under the stairs if you prefer. We're calling the cops to report you for kidnapping Philip Marston-Lang.'

Mavis screamed again, but not so loudly. 'I never . . . You can't touch us! The boss will have you for assault and . . . what are you doing to my boy?'

'Tying his thumbs together behind his back. Then tying the laces of his beaten-up old trainers together. Now, will you be quiet or go into the cupboard?'

A door at the back of the house opened.

'Up! Down!' Pip toddled into the hall, holding on to Lady Knighton's dress with one hand. He saw Bea, let go of the older woman and made it safely across the floor to his rescuers with a big smile on his face. He collapsed on the floor at Bea's feet, yawning mightily. It was way past his bedtime, poor little mite. Bea was amused to see that Pip's toy giraffe was still attached to his person.

Lady Knighton said, 'Oh, does he have to go back so soon? I thought he was to stay overnight. And what's with Gerry?'

Rosemary said, 'We're here to take Pip back to his mother. She didn't know you wanted to see him.'

Lady Knighton shook her head. 'Did I ask to see him? I don't remember that. It's all so confusing. Mavis, is it time for my night-time pill?'

The housekeeper said, 'Yes, Lady Knighton, you did ask if you could have him to stay, remember? There seems to have been a misunderstanding. Now, our visitors are just about to leave, so I'll bring you your pill and take you up to bed in a minute.'

'But what is Gerry doing on the floor, all tied up like that?'

Mavis said, 'It's a game we've been playing.' She turned on

Rosemary. 'You've got the boy back. Now get out and leave us in peace.'

Rosemary almost smiled. 'I need the keys to the coach house, please.'

'Suck yourself!'

Bea said, 'I expect Gerry's got them. And that he's been taking food up to their "guest".' She picked Pip up. He put his arms around her neck and let his head rest against hers. His toy giraffe flopped around his knees on the end of a piece of string. He trusted her. He yawned mightily and fell asleep.

Rosemary delved into Gerry's pockets and held up a bunch of keys. 'I'll check upstairs in the coach house before we go.'

Mavis said, 'I'll have the law on you!' She took a run at Rosemary, who picked her up – what muscles that slender frame concealed – and pushed the woman into the cupboard under the stairs, sliding the latch into place after her.

'I'll check on Pete,' said Rosemary, and departed to explore who might be in the coach house.

Mavis started banging at the cupboard door, shouting to be let out.

'What's happening? I don't understand . . .!' Lady Knighton fell back against the wall, afraid of she knew not what.

Bea tried to reassure her. 'It's all right. Help is coming.' With some difficulty as she was holding Pip, she also managed to speak into her own phone. 'Julian, we have Pip.'

'Thank God!'

'Lady Knighton's away with the fairies. She's innocent of any involvement in the kidnapping. She was told Pip was to stay the night with her. Her son is employing a housekeeper to look after her, whom I suggest needs to be checked out by social services. The housekeeper has two young adult children, a boy and a girl. I think it was they who attacked me and kidnapped Pip. The girl sped off in their car as we arrived at the dower house and I suspect has joined the rest of the crew at the spring.'

Julian said, 'Yes, she's here, working with the others in an attempt to move that boulder. What's happened to the housekeeper and her son?'

'Mother and son have been restrained and we're just about to ring the police to see how soon they can get here. By the way, the housekeeper maintains that Lady Knighton's old gardener and handyman has gone down with something catching and has to have his meals taken up to him in the rooms above the coach house.

'I suspect that it was their gardener who drove the lads on their treasure-seeking foray into the amusement park, that it was he who clashed with Pete and was killed. And it must be Pete who's taken his place above the garage here . . . whether as willing guest or not, I do not know. Rosemary's just gone to check.'

Mavis continued to thump the door, screaming, 'Let me out! You've no right to lock me up!'

Each time, Lady Knighton whimpered.

Bea said, 'It's all right, Lady Knighton. They'll be gone soon.'

Gerry was grunting with the effort of trying to free himself, but Bea told herself that Rosemary had done a good job on him, which proved to be the case.

Rosemary slid back into the hall. 'It's Pete all right. Upstairs, locked room above the garage in the dark. He took a nasty whack to the head. Running a temperature. I'm phoning for an ambulance as well as the police.' And did so.

Bea spoke into her phone. 'Did you hear that, Julian? Rosemary will have to wait here to explain what's happened to the police and to look after Lady Knighton, so can you send someone to collect me and Pip? He needs to be in his own bed.'

Julian sounded shaken. 'He really is all right? Yes, I can send someone . . . Francine, probably. Or Imran, if he's finished with the police at the caravan.'

Bea ached all over. Were they finished here? She opened the door to the outside world and breathed the night air.

'Up! Down!' murmured Pip, in his sleep.

Rosemary joined Bea on the doorstep. 'I'll have to stay till the police get here.'

Lady Knighton appeared, carrying a handbag and trying to put a heavy coat on. 'I don't understand what's happening. I don't want to be left here. Have you got a taxi coming? Perhaps you could drop me at a hotel somewhere. Or, are we going into town? Shall I pack a bag? I haven't been out at night for ages.'

SEVENTEEN

Monday night

Rosemary tried to lead Lady Knighton back inside. 'No, no. It's your bedtime remember, Lady Knighton. Things have been a bit strange recently, haven't they? Let's go into the back room and ring your son to tell him what's been happening. No doubt he'll be wanting to come back here to look after you.'

Lady Knighton was bewildered, but understood the voice of authority that Rosemary could summon up at will. 'Yes, but . . . I don't want to disturb him. Surely we can wait till morning to ring him? He's such a very important man, and he's told Nick to look after me, and he's moved Mavis and her children in, which is very thoughtful of him, though they are terribly noisy and the pills she gives me do seem to make me rather confused—'

'Nasty things have been happening,' said Rosemary. 'He'll want to know that you're safe.'

Bea stepped out into the night air as a well-used estate car roared into sight, turned into the driveway and braked sharply. Francine was in the driving seat. 'Mrs Abbot, you all right?'

'I'm fine. I'll get into the back of the car with Pip, and fill you in as we go along.' She then added, 'Do you know of someone who can come and look after Lady Knighton as of now? Rosemary's staying on to deal with the police and get Pete to hospital, but that poor lady needs—'

'One of Jenny's tribe, yes? Let me think.'

Francine drove fast – a little too fast for Bea's comfort – while making calls on a hands-free phone.

Bea concentrated on keeping Pip level and stopping him from being thrown about as Francine spoke to first one person and then another. Bea wondered if she were going to be sick. How embarrassing!

Bea closed her eyes and wondered if the girl had had police car training. Bea had understood it was mandatory for those who liked car chases . . . which Bea didn't.

Pip slept heavily. That was something to be thankful for.

Francine slapped the wheel. 'Got her. Retired nurse. We use her at the practice for emergencies; she's got her own transport and will report to Rosemary within half an hour to look after Lady Knighton.'

'Wonderful,' said Bea, 'I'll text Rosemary to expect her.' Which she did.

Imran's competent fiancée threw the car around another corner, saying, 'What a night, eh? Imran's at the guards' caravan. The fire's out, and he's sorting out a new roster for the security staff. The police still haven't arrived.'

Another call came through. Julian, this time.

'Francine, what's happening?'

'Sir Julian? Got the boy, and found Pete. We've left Rosemary in charge and I've got a retired nurse going over from the village to look after Lady Knighton. I rang for police and an ambulance. No sign of either yet. Have the bad lads found the gold?'

'You're bringing Pip and Bea back? Thank God for that. The treasure-seekers are getting excited about the signal the metal detectors are giving them. I think they've located my grandfather's watch and chain, that I shoved into a cleft at the side of the spring. They're still trying to shift that rock, more fools them. Don't try to come in by the western gate, Francine, or they'll hear you and there's too many for us to tackle before the police get here. Stop a little way along the main road by the trees. I'll come down to meet you and take Pip off your hands.'

Francine threw the car round the corner, and parked a little way along beside the drystone wall. She sprang out of the car, and helped Bea inch her way out of her seat, still holding Pip.

A watery moon had risen but there wasn't much they could see as the ancient trees thereabouts shut out the light.

Julian appeared out of the shadows to clamber over the wall and jump down into the road. He took a sleeping Pip off Bea, and checked he was all in one piece. He said, 'Thank you, Bea. Thank you, Francine. Can you two take him to the estate office now? He'll be safe there with his mother, and with Henry and Bruno to guard them.'

'Nonsense,' said Bea. 'I want to see the end of this.'

'So do I,' said Francine.

Julian hesitated. There came a shout and some laughter from above, and Julian swung himself and Pip back over the wall and set off back up the slope at the double. Francine scrambled over, followed by Bea, who was not enjoying all this physical activity but determined not to miss anything. And her tights had been laddered, anyway.

There was hardly a glimmer of light to be seen under the trees as they wound their way up the slope. The ground was soggy. It had rained a lot recently, hadn't it? Bea hadn't thought there would be much of a rise here but her leg muscles were soon telling her that it was so.

She could hear shouting. The bad lads, enjoying themselves? Secure in the knowledge Julian couldn't touch them with his son safely tucked away at the dower house.

They came to the end of the trees and could see the bluff where the spring rose in the meadow. There were now three cars there, with their headlights on the spot where the group was working. Bea counted the figures heaving at the boulder. How many were there? Four or five?

Gradually she made out that there were a number of people standing in the trees beside her. Beside Julian was the scarcely-to-be seen figures of Hal and Big-Teddy-with-the-bad-teeth. They were both filming the action on their smartphones. Piers was behind the video camera, mounted on a tripod.

Also now there was Francine, videoing everything on her smartphone.

Hal said, in a low voice, 'Oh, my. Mr Colston's right, there is some gold hidden here.'

Julian said, 'Maybe. Now we've got Pip back, we could withdraw till the police get here.' He hesitated, then said in a stronger voice, 'I'm concerned that the boys don't know what they're playing with. I must try to warn them.'

Bea was counting the trespassers. One, two, three, four . . . or was it five people there? Too many for Julian to tackle, even with Hal and Teddy at his back. Piers wouldn't be much help.

Julian stepped out of the trees, still holding Pip, and raised his voice. 'All of you! Stop! You're trespassing and what you're doing is dangerous! I have my son here and the police are on their way. I warn you, tampering with a water source is dangerous! Please leave, now! For your own sakes!'

'Pull the other one!' Laughter. Drunken laughter. A lad standing on top of the boulder was joined by another, using the branches of a small tree to help himself up. A slip of a girl joined them, laughing. Mavis' daughter?

The tree shivered as the lads laboured away, grunting, prising the boulder out of its base.

Julian turned back into the trees. 'If they manage to shift that boulder, it'll come down the hill at us. Move! Piers, you too! To the wall!'

'They won't shift that. Will they?'

Julian said, 'There's water built up behind that boulder. Move! Sharpish! Leave the camera! Let's get out of here!'

'No way I'm leaving it!' Piers moved, sharpish. As did the others. Francine helped Bea along. Big Teddy carried the tripod for Piers, and helped him set it up again. They reached the drystone wall. Piers re-aligned the camera and . . .

'It's moving!' The two lads on the top tried to jump back, but the boulder, eased away from its bed, was wrenching itself from the earth, carrying the tree with it . . . and the two lads . . . and the girl . . .

They screamed, but not as loudly as the two men standing below, who saw a great boulder tower over them, and slowly, slowly grind its way out of its bed.

They couldn't run as fast as the boulder was moving . . .

Turning over and over, slowly, slowly, gathering speed and weight . . .

The tree threw its roots up to the heavens and then its branches . . .

Screams cut short. Bodies tossed this way and that.

There was a powerful surge of water, unstoppable, powerful, gouging a path down the hillside, reaching the trees where Julian had been sheltering, uprooting the first, throwing it against its neighbours, crashing through everything.

The water smashed aside anything in its way . . . earth was

churned and thrown up . . . bodies appeared for a moment and then were lost, one arm raised, then gone, dragged underneath . . .

And the noise! Thunder.

Screams cut short!

Bea clapped her hands over her ears.

The noise lessened. The flood swept on and on down the hill. It pooled when it reached the drystone wall around the park. Rising and rising, forming a pool. The moon reflected in the water.

Spluttering noises.

'Help!' A weak cry.

Something glittered, carried along by the uprooted tree in the water, catching on something unseen, spinning off to one side, coming to rest beside Julian, holding his son in his arms.

Someone's head-torch shone on it. A misshaped bundle, sodden with water. A glint of something within? Gold? Really gold?

The bundle looked like an old leather satchel, torn apart by the water, revealing a tangle of gold watch and chain caught in the leather strap . . . and something else inside, gleaming in the moonlight.

Julian leaned forward and rescued the bundle. The tree, freed from its burden, turned over in the water and was swept down the hill, disappearing into the darkness.

Someone breathed, 'Oh my God! It's the buried treasure!'

The noise of the water subsided gradually. The flood became a stream. The stream diminished, no longer a threat.

The headlights of the cars still lit the scene, but where there had been a boulder embedded in the hillside, there was now a deep, dark cavern out of which the water rose. Gently.

The waters subsided, leaving four bodies strewn along the course of the stream. How many were dead? Ah, one of them was trying to lift his head, choking, his mouth full of mud.

One on his back, neck awry. Dead.

One man with broken legs? Moaning?

Yet another body, sinking under the water in the pool that had formed by the drystone wall.

Julian said, 'We have to get them out, if we can do so without endangering ourselves. Francine, call for more ambulances. Some may still be alive.'

Hal and Teddy splashed into the water which was hardly deep

enough now to cover their shoes. A police siren broke the exhausted silence which had fallen on the group.

Julian said, 'The major is still alive. I wonder why . . .'

Monday night, continued

More police were summoned. Statements were taken from the survivors. The video camera and recording machine were handed over.

Five bodies were taken from the water. The major and Clement, the MP's youngest son, were taken to hospital and, despite broken bones, seemed likely to survive.

Three others: Nick, the magnate's son Boris, and the housekeeper's daughter, were put in an unmarked van and removed to the mortuary.

Phone calls drew various people from their beds. There was shock. And tears. And rage. And threats.

Polly, Nanny and Old Jenny slept on. Pip was returned to his cradle, none the worse for his outing.

Rosemary directed operations at the dower house where the retired nurse, summoned by Francine, took charge of Lady Knighton.

Pete was removed to hospital and put on a drip. Mavis and her son Gerry landed up in the police nick on charges of kidnapping Pip and assaulting Bea.

Mrs Maggs and her team produced tea, sandwiches and comfort to the seemingly never-ending stream of people who trickled through her kitchen.

Julian laid a misshapen gold cross on to the table. Removed from the Hall at a time of terror, buried for years, long forgotten, it had been bent out of shape but retained its sheen. True gold. After restoration, it would be returned to the chapel from which it had come.

Tuesday morning

It was not easy for the police to sort out what had happened and why and Julian and Bea found themselves having to explain it all to them the next morning at the station.

Julian said, 'I find it difficult to understand the nature of the man who is responsible for so much damage. Lady Knighton's sanity is compromised, Tyra is told her husband – my security guard, Pete – is dead, while he has in fact been badly injured and a gardener living locally met an untimely end. Three youngsters, barely out of school, are no more, and considerable damage has been done to property and reputations. And for what?'

He turned to Bea. 'You seem to understand what drives this man. Tell them.'

Bea said, 'The man we are talking about seems, on the surface, to be beyond reproach. He is secure in his position in society, engaged to a local woman. Each time he moved from one job to another, he gathered more useful contacts and glowing references. His experience in life fitted him well to advise someone new to the business of an estate. Here was a man who'd commanded troops in the army. He'd won medals, he'd been important. He had connections with the local movers and shakers. He felt he was one of them in a way which he thought Sir Julian would never be. He felt he was invincible, untouchable.

'Rosemary has been researching his background and found nothing to his discredit except that he had moved on from job to job every few years and no one seemed to know why. She didn't ask the right questions. The problem for the major was that his occupation as a soldier had gone and whether knowingly or not, he looked for a substitute among the youngsters he came into contact with.

'He didn't set out to lead them astray, but I think you'll find if you question his past employers again, that sooner or later there'd be some problem with the youngsters with whom he came into contact. They looked for his approval and became reckless in sport or driving, or indulging in some dangerous activity. But he'd done nothing illegal, and he'd be referred on to another employer with glowing references. And so he ended up working for Sir Julian, whom he mistook for a soft touch.

'The worst that could be said of the major as an estate manager was that he ran the business to his own advantage, which clashed with Sir Julian wanting to run it in such a way as to improve the lives of those for whom he felt responsible. The major was genuinely taken aback to find Julian objected to his estate manager taking backhanders, which he considered part of his job.

'Moving here, he came into contact with a group of youngsters who had an equal sense of entitlement, who had far too much time on their hands and no respect for others. It was a perfect match. He became their role model and they were his troops. I'm not saying he knowingly led them into a life of petty crime, but his attitude encouraged them to think they needn't observe the rules that govern other people.

'At the darts match, the lads stole a visitor's smartphone and thought it hilarious that a local lad should be charged with theft instead of them. They expected the local police to back them up, which they did. Only the quick thinking of some local people averted a miscarriage of justice.'

The female police officer asked, 'Are you implying that he was grooming the young men . . . that he was a paedophile?'

'No,' said Bea. 'I don't think he's highly sexed in either direction. And the boys exhibited no signs that he'd tried to groom them in that way. No, it was simpler than that. He liked power and they needed a role model. How exciting he must have seemed to them! When he encouraged them to trespass in the park, they saw no cause to fear retribution, for was he not in charge here?

'They vandalized the farm shop and restaurant and discovered that the police were not going to do anything. Perhaps they'd have gone on to some other activity, perhaps the major would have worked out the remainder of his contract and gone on to another job without causing any real problems, but Mr Colston, Sir Julian's father-in-law, gave a public talk about there being buried treasure at the Hall. This sparked off what we might call "Gold Fever". And that's when both the major and the local youths saw a chance at fame and glory. The youngsters bought metal detectors and started poking around locally, protected – as they thought – by the major's position.'

The police officer said, 'But the youngsters needed transport, didn't they? And they hadn't a driver's licence between them.'

'Which is why they co-opted Jan, who was Lady Knighton's gardener. He could drive. The lads knew him because they were in and out of the dower house all the time. And there they found two more recruits, the housekeeper's son and daughter, who were also at a loose end and ripe for mischief. After the youngsters had finished in the churchyard, they thought what fun it would be to drive up into the park with the metal detectors, to see what they could find.

'And that's what they did. Only, they got their timing wrong and Pete spotted them at it. Now Pete wasn't a fool; he and the other guards had been talking about when and where the lads might strike and Pete was able to alert the others so that they'd come to his rescue. That night Henry and Hal were nearest and started out to support Pete. Unfortunately before they could arrive, Pete had been spotted, a tussle had ensued and the wrong man died. Not Pete. He was injured in the fight, yes, but not killed outright.

'I don't know who struck the fatal blow. Perhaps the police can discover who did it. Was it one of the lads? They hadn't set out to kill, remember. They were out on a jolly, hoping to turn up some treasure, but they were equally happy to cock a snook at the authorities. It might have been an accident.'

Julian said, 'I do wonder if it was the major who killed the gardener? He was the only one there trained to kill. His reactions to being discovered would have been instantaneous, and he had the coolness necessary to clear the site immediately after the death.'

An indrawn breath. A concentration on the facts.

Bea said, 'The major will have to be questioned about his part in these events. I don't honestly know if it was he who took a swipe at Pete and killed Jan instead. But I do think that the boys, left to themselves, would have fled the scene, perhaps even rung the police. Instead, some cool head put Pete's tag on Jan and made his face unrecognizable. And then made sure they left in good order . . . taking Pete with them in their car.'

'Why take Pete away?'

'Because he could have identified them. The major tried to make us believe the dead body was that of Pete, didn't he? Unfortunately for them, Pete's dog followed as they left the scene. When the boys realized that, they took a lane to the south instead of returning the way they'd come, beat the dog, threw it into a ditch and drove off. That was clever of them, as it put us off the track for a while. We did find Beauty; she is being cared for in the village and will be able to go back to Pete if he survives. The boys got away with it because the major was in a position to mislead the police and cast doubts on Sir Julian's belief that the wrong man had died.

'The major was pleased with himself. His troops had done him proud. Pete had been neutralized. They couldn't kill him in cold blood but when his condition worsened, they didn't take him to a doctor but left him to take his chances. Perhaps they told him he'd go down for murdering Jan if he didn't keep quiet, and promised they'd get him away to London when they could. One of them took Pete's phone and got Tyra to keep quiet by saying Pete was arranging to meet up with her elsewhere.

'When the lads discovered that Beauty had survived, the major feared the dog might attack him in turn. So he encouraged the boys to set fire to the stables where Beauty lay. Fortunately no great harm was done and the dog and her puppies are doing well.'

'Who drove the SUV to the stables?'

Bea said, 'I think it was most likely to be Gerry, the housekeeper's son. Or Nick, of course. He wouldn't care about not having a licence. As far as the major was concerned, the lads could now set about their treasure hunting again. Rumours circulated about the spring hiding some gold. Jenny's stories of healing water added to the excitement.

'I don't think the lads had any real understanding of what they were doing. It was all so mindlessly simple to them. To make a distraction, you set a fire in the guards' caravan. You took a toddler as a hostage. The result: tears all round.'

Three families lost a child.

The MP and his wife, his lordship and the housekeeper had to identify their dead children. All three refused to accept that it was their own lack of parenting which had brought them to this state.

The bereaved families wanted to sue Julian at first for the death of their children, but when shown the 'No Trespassers' notice and having the evidence from the cameras played back to them, they all agreed to accept the coroner's verdict of accidental death. The remaining youngsters stated that it was the major who'd killed Jan by mistake, and who'd encouraged them to hunt for the treasure. The police believed them and acted accordingly.

Some months later, the MP announced his wife was suffering from cancer and he would reluctantly have to resign his seat to take care of her. He put the family seat on the market and took her and his surviving son – who'd narrowly avoided a custodial sentence – to live abroad. He did not abandon his mother completely, but since it was clear she could no longer look after herself, he turned the dower house into a very upmarket retirement home for Lady Knighton, with a suitable couple to run it.

His friend, the all-powerful businessman, divorced his current wife and remarried a younger woman who might give him a replacement for his son. He never returned to the area.

The major lost one of his legs; the other did eventually mend but was never much good afterwards. He was charged with conspiracy and manslaughter and a dozen other matters and went from hospital to prison.

Marcus and Mona reluctantly agreed that it would be best to hold their wedding celebrations elsewhere, though Marcus said he'd still like to talk about restarting model trains in the amusement park at some time.

Polly's contractions subsided but Nanny and Jenny agreed to make her take more rest till her baby was due.

Pip managed another five words. 'Mum-mum' and 'Da-da' were very acceptable. Unfortunately he'd also picked up a word beginning with the letter 'F' from the workmen and used it frequently. Nanny and Old Jenny, forming a formidable alliance against all comers, said that if everyone ignored it, Pip would soon forget about it. Bea was not so sure about that, as Pip seemed to have worked out that every time he used it, adults reacted.

Rosemary's next job was very hush-hush and out of the country, but she left her mobile home in the local caravan park and promised to return for a holiday some time.

Francine slid into place at Julian's side as his new office manager and Imran managed the farm shop and the restaurant with such success that Julian had to re-apply for an extension to the car park. This time he got it.

Pete survived, swearing vengeance on all and sundry but

happily reunited with his wife and new baby; and also with Beauty and her pups.

Henry, Hal and Teddy cleared away the ruins of the guards' caravan and found a replacement at the salvage yard in town. Julian gave them so much work to do in the village that there was some talk of their buying a newer – if not new – lorry.

Two specialists arrived to look at the room which everyone was now beginning to call 'the old chapel', and said that yes, it really was so, but it was not to be touched till experts could be called in to undertake the removal of the centuries of paint and wallpaper.

Bea returned to London, promising to visit the Hall often. Piers departed to the States to fulfil his obligations there, saying he'd return soon to see what happened to the chapel.

Slowly, daily life resumed with the power base for the area shifting slightly towards the Hall.

Piers painted a charming picture of the Marston-Lang family with their children around them. It had pride of place in the entrance hall and everyone smiled and nodded when they saw it.

He also painted another, very different picture which hung in the National Portrait Gallery. Bea stood in front of it one spring morning, thinking that Piers had painted Julian looking older than he was now. His eyes were a brilliant blue, challenging the viewer and following them around.

The portrait showed a man who'd seen the dark side of life but had had the courage to take difficult decisions and the strength to carry them out.

Bea murmured to herself, 'A man for all seasons.'

Piers put his arm around her shoulders. 'So he is. And so are you . . . a woman for all seasons, I mean. It's the best thing I've done and I think I'm ready to paint you now. You're such a busy woman. Can you find time to sit for me?'